The Key of Damascus

....
By The Silver Fox

PublishAmerica
Baltimore

© 2005 by The Silver Fox.
All rights reserved. No part of this book may be reproduced, stored in a retrieval system or transmitted in any form or by any means without the prior written permission of the publishers, except by a reviewer who may quote brief passages in a review to be printed in a newspaper, magazine or journal.

First printing

At the specific preference of the author, PublishAmerica allowed this work to remain exactly as the author intended, verbatim, without editorial input.

ISBN: 1-4241-1281-8
PUBLISHED BY PUBLISHAMERICA, LLLP
www.publishamerica.com
Baltimore

Printed in the United States of America

July 4, 2012

To Brian + Jenna Harper

This book is dedicated to my wife Noreen who was indispensable during my writings and illness.

I hope you will find this book interesting and not too boring.

From your longtime friends

Noreen & Ed Albuletos

Feliz Dilder xot

Chapter 1

In the early morning of December 1999, two men walked along an ancient street of Jerusalem or as the Israelis call it "Yerushalayim" pronounced as Herushaleim. The sun was not yet visible, and the air was crisp. The sky was already gray from the faint light in the East.

One of them was clad in a Franciscan monk's garb with his hood over his head; the other wore a long white priestly robe. The one in white was tall and lanky. Strands of gray hair stuck out from under a straw hat with a large brim. He had it tipped slightly forward from habit to keep the bright light out of his eyes even thought the sun's rays had not yet reached them.

"So what do you want my son?"

The monk kept his head slightly bowed. "Before I answer; you must promise me that what I tell you will be kept under the seal of confession." The voice was barely audible. Since his head was bowed, anyone walking by would assume that the monk's eyes were directed at his feet. Nothing could have been further from the truth.

If observed closely, one would have noticed the rapid eye movements of the cleric. The pupils were shifting from side to side without stopping to look to the front. He depended on his companion to make the choice of the route and warn him of any obstacles in their path. Every once in a while he would turn himself on his heels and check to make sure that they were not being followed.

His constant restlessness gave an impression of a hunted animal. His eyes continually searched the cross streets and alleyways of the ancient city. From time to time he shot a fleeting look at the man beside him. The motion was so quick that the old priest was not even aware that he was being observed. During the last few months the monk had developed the ability to judge and "read" a person after one glance. His skill was honed to such a sharp edge that he was rarely wrong. He always reached the same conclusion that he would have if he had studied the subject in detail for a long time.

The strange events that he was about to reveal had unfolded in such a short period of time, or it seemed short to him even though they began five months ago. Since then he acquired a sixth sense to recognize danger immediately. Time was not a commodity he could squander or leisurely spend. His very life depended on it and he was getting more frightened with every step they took.

Even though the priest had an uneasy feeling that his companion was studying him he could not catch the monk in the act. The cleric's eyes shifted so quickly that the man dressed in white couldn't turn his head fast enough to make eye contact.

Both figures were somber and talked in low voices. A closer examination would have revealed that the monk's lips were curled in a slight smirk as though he was musing about some secret joke that he alone understood. His amusement came at the expense of his companion; whose appearance gave the impression of being a large toadstool, with the wide brimmed hat and the lanky body clad in a white pristine robe.

The tall man's face was dry and brown, it had seen many years in this harsh and unforgiving land. The deep lines etched into his skin covered his forehead. The tops of his cheeks resembled the lines found in the brown sandstone around this part of the world. The lower part of his face was hidden by whiskers almost as white as the ones protruding from the hat with a few dark strands still visible. The beard fluttered slightly in the breeze as he walked giving an impression that he was a prophet in this holy land. His arms folded in front of him and tucked inside his wide sleeves close to his body added to the "stem" appearance of a toadstool.

There was no expression on the priest's face until the monk uttered the last fateful words "…under the seal of confession."

The priest stopped abruptly so that the brown clad man ended up a few steps ahead of him before he realized that his companion was no longer beside him. The monk stopped suddenly. He was stricken with terror of finding himself alone because people tended to disappear around him in a blink of an eye since that dreadful day. Later they would turn up dead.

Turning around he saw the brown face of the priest a few feet behind him turn gray with anger. The white silhouette was frozen with his mouth wide open as though it was yelling, but no sound was heard. The tanned face of the priest was so brown that even anger didn't turn it completely white.

The monk couldn't make out whether his companion's twisted face was from being surprised by the request or if he was having some kind of a stroke. Before the Franciscan could ask the priest if he was all right the old man closed his jaw and began walking towards him.

As the priest got closer the monk turned his head away from him. He didn't want to make eye contact yet so that the priest whom he knew as his professor from the past would recognize him.

As they fell into step again the only noise that came out of the lanky man was a barely audible growl. He was clearing his throat.

They walked several blocks and turned a number of corners before the priest calmed down enough to get control of his voice. "Why should a Franciscan brother insist on such a pledge? He should know better."

The man in brown uttered softly, "What I have to say must have the protection of the seal of the confessional. I'm not a monk but am wearing these Franciscan robes for safety, besides it's a practical disguise, which keeps me comfortable in this cool air. This robe also helps me avoid harassment from local authorities. They are paranoid and think that everyone is a terrorist or an Arab spy. On the other hand the Arabs think that everyone not of their race is a Jewish spy. There is no end to the mistrust of these people. Besides, the hood over my head keeps my face from prying eyes. There are so many monks, priests and religious types around here that I blend into the crowds like a sheep in a flock."

The imposter felt quite proud of himself. He thought that these details added a little poetic flair in view of the location. It was the second time that he had surprised the priest, which made him stop again and stare at the man in the long brown robe. This time the priest hesitated for a moment, so that the other did not get caught off guard, as he had been the first time.

The *Franciscan* could feel the priest's steely gray eyes penetrate through the robe, his body and right into his soul. Suddenly a cold chill went up and down his spine thinking that he might be recognized before he was ready to reveal himself. He fidgeted and felt uncomfortable under this scrutiny. He mumbled under his hood, "Let's move on."

The priest moved closer to the man beside him, glanced around the vicinity. The street was empty except for some cat meowing in a doorway. Then leaning his head towards his companion whispered, "First of all both the Israelis and the Palestinians have reasons to fear each other, but I won't take up any of your precious time to go into details. The paranoia as you call it is very real and not imaginary, but I'm sure that is not why you called and asked to see me. Also your request for me to pledge that this conversation be kept under the seal of the confessional in the middle of the street is most unusual if not ludicrous, I must say."

The *Franciscan* made up his mind that he might as well reveal his identity now. If not, the priest may concentrate his attention in trying to identify him rather than listening to what he had to say.

He pulled his hood back enough so that the priest could make out his features.

The tall man was visibly shaken. "Brad Scott! My God! I haven't seen you since you graduated from the academy. What's this all about? I remember that we had to force you to go to confession when you were a student and now you freely seek it in the middle of the street? You said that you weren't a monk and I believe you, because that's the last thing I would have expected of you.

"You were too arrogant and too much of a rabble-rouser to join any orders. Compassion and humility wasn't part of your vocabulary."

During this outburst the man in white didn't comment on the impersonation.

The *monk* was more interested in making sure that they were alone and heard only part of the reproach. His mind was centered on his preoccupation with the danger that he perceived was all around them. Suddenly he turned his head and thought he saw some shadowy figures lurking in one of the side streets, but further scrutiny revealed it was the shadows of some statues protruding from a small square.

"So what is it that you really want? Are you in some kind of trouble? What's this nonsense about a confession? All you have to do is ask me and you know that I will keep whatever it is between the two of us."

The *monk* continued to probe the side streets and only stopped when something unusual caught his eyes. He didn't see anything. Suddenly he heard the unearthly shriek of some bird. He looked up and saw only a large shadow on the wall of one of the churches. Looking around he could not locate the source and when he looked back the shadow was gone.

He turned to the Jesuit. "Did you hear anything?"

"No." The old man looked around.

The *monk* was sure that he saw and heard the shriek but did not press it. "Ok. I haven't much time so I'll get to the point. I'm in mortal danger."

The Jesuit smiled and shook his head. "You always over dramatized everything. You should have become an actor. Did you?"

The man in the brown robe was getting angry. "I respected you as a teacher and that's why I came to you, but don't make light of my predicament. Nothing is, what it seems anymore."

The *Franciscan* began talking, as though to himself. "You know that we find ourselves in today's chaos because of the past few decades. This century has been a bizarre period. The world went through some terrible conflicts with the last world war being the worst in human history. Yet mankind has learned very little from it as the nations continue to bicker and find new and more efficient ways of killing each other. After the Second World War people seemed to have taken a turn for the better, but it didn't last long. Then came the sixties with love, free love, beatniks the beginnings of almost universal use of all types of hallucinogenic and other hard drugs as well as the rise of offbeat religious cults.

"It seems that people always seek instant solutions to their plight whether real or imagined. Even devil worshipping is becoming common. One is being told that this practice is an alternative and a benign religion to the fulfillment of human needs how little they know. Still others regress back into bizarre cults and organizations reviving the old pagan practices such as Wicca and Druid customs."

"You've become quite a philosopher. I remember that your only interest in the past lied in making money. Very well, I'll hear your confession if you come into a church with me."

"No!" The reply was so loud that both men were startled and jerked away from each other. The *monk* felt as though the voice came from another party altogether. After composing himself the robed man continued, "There is no need of a church, but we could go off to one of the quieter streets or a park where I could relate my story undisturbed as we walk."

Unknown to the priest, the man clad in the brown robe, his hands also tucked in his sleeves carried a heavy object. It was wrapped in a piece of rawhide that he was constantly tossing from hand to hand.

Finally the old Jesuit conceded. "All right, but don't look for an easy way out of whatever mess you have found yourself in, and don't think that I'll roll over and get you out as I did when you were a student. I used to think that there was something special about you and figured if I helped you there might still be some hope of salvaging the good side, but alas it was only a dream and I finally gave up. By now you must have learned that we Jesuits are a tough bunch."

The persistent criticism annoyed the younger man. "It doesn't matter whether you will give me absolution or not. My only interest is that you keep this conversation in confidence between us and no one else."

"Ok. I agree. Let's drop the subject. Let's turn down here onto that street." The priest pointed towards what looked like an alley with his prayer book that he carried in his hand. "There are fewer people in this neighborhood this time of the morning. Most of them are devout Armenian Christians and are at their masses."

They turned down the narrow lane. Long shadows covered both sides giving the impression it was evening instead of the beginning of the day. They walked in silence, each with his thoughts. The *monk's* head was deep inside his hood and before he realized, they had stepped into a deserted square where the rays of the sun pierced his eyes like arrows as he emerged from the murky darkness of the alleyway. He was forced to squint several times to enable him to adjust his pupils to the bright light.

Opening them he saw the priest pulling his right hand from the inside of his sleeve holding a stole. He kissed the little embroidered cross on one end and put the narrow strip of silk around his neck so that both ends hung on his shoulders and chest going all the way down the length of his robe. He made the sign of the cross as they walked and began to whisper something that was unintelligible.

There were a few minutes of silence, then he whispered, "After knowing me all this time you still don't trust me and since it's so important to you I'll hear your story under the seal of confession now."

The *monk* tried to organize his thoughts.

It was the heavy object in his hands that distracted him from his concentration. He could also feel the burning heat radiating through the wrapping even though miraculously it was not affecting the rawhide. He was also preoccupied with his goal of passing it on to the priest at the end of his 'confession,' which kept him from paying attention to what his companion was saying. The piece was getting heavier and felt hotter as time passed. Brad yearned to get rid of this thing that had caused him so much pain and forget the nightmare that had almost killed him.

The *monk* skipped over the part of the ritual that starts with, "Bless me father for I have sinned…" and immediately began at what he perceived to be the beginning of his dilemma. His voice was low, barely audible. He talked to the priest as though he was a son talking to his father about his troubles. Brad had a premonition that at the end of this conversation he would finally be relieved of his burden. "I..I.. don't know where to begin. When I left the academy I joined an international firm and worked my way up the ladder where I have become an executive in the Middle Eastern, European and African affairs consisting of investments and sales of subsidiaries.

"Everything went well just as I had planned until I got myself in this mess. This was not of my choosing nor did it happen suddenly, but rather slowly and a number of coincidences. If I were superstitious I would say some force played with me twisting and turning my actions until I found myself where I am now. When I finish you will understand why I can't continue nor am I equipped to carry on with this responsibility thrust upon me.

"I'm in my thirties now, still single and make more money than I need. I have a very good life, or so I thought until now. Traveling to many corners of the world staying in the best hotels, eating the best foods and drinking the finest of wines. At the risk of sounding immodest I must also tell you that I'm considered to be charming by women, or perhaps it's only because I can spend money without having any concern."

The priest remarked, "I remember humility was not your strong point."

The monk caught the sarcasm, but pretended he didn't and continued, "I don't know why, but a year ago, I decided to make a personal pilgrimage to this part of the world and especially Israel, to see why people make such a fuss about this land. Now I wish I never did.

"I had been here on business, but never spend any time on taking in the sights or trying to enjoy what it had to offer. There are many other historical lands that are just as interesting, but now I understand why I was steered to this direction.

"You remember me. I never was much interested in religion and my parents were Catholics only when it served their purposes. As I got older it seemed that the stories told in church were archaic and insulted my intellect. I felt that they should be told to children rather than grown intelligent adults."

The Jesuit asked in a dry tone. "So what are you trying to tell me? Are you trying to get back on the good side of God, the Church, or just bring your accounts up to date?"

"None of the above. My reason for seeking you out is selfish. I know that you have an acute sense of fairness in your judgments and are a staunch defender of the church. You've also have an open mind and do not spout the normal fire and brimstone rhetoric."

The man in brown continued his tale, "Instead of signing up with some standard tour to visit Israel and be brainwashed by some paid evangelist, I decided to make the trip on my own. Figuring that a person with my travel experience should have no problem finding the mode of transportation and the type of guide that I wanted to show me around the country as well as places that I would pick myself."

Suddenly the Franciscan stopped talking. This time he was sure he heard a grinding sound. Looking around he saw no one.

The priest also glanced from side to side. "What's the matter? You're nervous. Why?"

"It's nothing. I guess I'm just jumpy."

Just at that moment Brad lifted his head and saw a large stone teetering on a tower above them and was sure he could see some figures beside it with their shoulders pressed against it, but didn't have time to have a good look as the stone tilted and began its plunge towards the pavement. He pushed the priest hard with his left shoulder so that the old man fell and rolled over on the hard cobblestones in the square. The *monk* lost his balance and ended up beside him.

THE SILVER FOX

The priest looked at Brad shocked. "What the .."

Before the other could answer the block of sandstone came crashing just a few feet away as they lay on the ground. It was lucky that none of the large fragments landed on them, but they were showered by scores of small pieces that stung their hands as they covered their heads. The object wrapped in the animal's hide fell out on the pavement.

When the noise subsided both men slowly lifted their heads from the ground and glanced around. As they looked up towards the spot from where the stone fell they noticed two large birds circling high above as though surveying their handiwork. One of them began diving towards them. The shape was one of a triangle like the airplanes that kids make out of paper. The people coming out of their doorways shouting and pointing towards the sky must have confused and frightened it. Suddenly it became apparent that it had a visible body, neck, and head. Then with wings flapping began to climb into the sky.

The priest looked horrified. He was more alarmed at the actions of the bird than the stone that almost killed them. "What was that? I have never seen such large birds especially in a city this is ridiculous. They look like ravens, but they're too big. Lucky you noticed the falling stone and acted as quickly as you did, if not both of us would be have been flattened under that much weight and those birds must have figured that we were their breakfast."

The *monk* did not comment. He stood up first and stretched his arms to see if he had sustained any injuries. There was blood dripping from his hands where the chips hit him, but no serious wounds. Then he extended his right arm and grasped the priest's stretched out hand. "This was no accident. I saw a couple of silhouettes putting their shoulder to that block on the old rampart."

"What do you mean? Somebody is trying to kill us?"

"I'm not sure about you, but I know that they're trying to get rid of me."

The Jesuit noticed the bundle tied in rawhide lying a few feet away. "What's that? Is it yours? I didn't bring anything with me except my missal in my hand." He looked around to see if someone else might have been close by and dropped it, but they were alone, except for some people in their doorways some ten yards from them.

The *monk* quickly picked up the package and shoved back it in his sleeves. He didn't even bother to dust himself or to clean the bundle before he began to walk again keeping an eye on the priest to make sure he was beside him. "I.. it's mine."

The *monk* looked around until he saw a vaulted walkway. "Let's go in there. Perhaps we can avoid further 'accidents' and we will also be out of sight of those damned birds. Once we're inside we can take one of the side passages and exit a long ways from here."

As they entered the darkened passageway the younger man returned to his story as though nothing had happened to disturb their original schedule.

"I..I.. guess the whole thing started on July 8 of this year. I remember it was a Thursday because I had to finish a previous assignment before I could leave my office in the middle of the week. I arrived in Tel Aviv and checked into the Dan Tel Aviv Hotel on Hayarkon Street and went about finding myself such a guide. I talked to a number of cabbies who I thought would be the prime candidates, but didn't find anyone to my liking.

"Then sitting on the Patio cafe of the hotel I told the waiter of my predicament. He said his nephew Nachman was studying archaeology at the University of Jerusalem and was very familiar with the country's many historical digs.

"He said that the nephew was off for the summer and lived in Tel Aviv. When he brought my tab there was also another piece of paper. Unfolding it I saw a name and address. I settled my account and left. Taking another look at the paper and turning it over I noticed that there was a telephone number scribbled on the back, that I had missed when I picked it up from the table.

"Since it was too late to go anywhere that afternoon, I decided to phone and make an appointment for the next day. Returning to my room I rang the number and was in luck. A male voice answered. It sounded young, like a teenager. I asked if Nachman was there. He answered that it was he. I told him of my need for a guide, and my wish to visit some of the ancient out of the way places. I told him about my encounter with the waiter at the café in the hotel who had given me his name.

"We agreed to meet the next day at ten o'clock at the entrance of the Jaffa Market on Allenby Street in the Yemenite quarter. After making the arrangements I went to the Sabra Coffee Shop in the hotel and had my supper, then retired to my room. Turning on the TV I watched a news program in English for a while. At the end of the broadcast I turned the lights off and tried to sleep without much success.

"Switching them back on I searched through the drawer of my night table to find some reading material. I found a Bible that looked like it was written in Hebrew. I flipped through the pages, and then half way through I noticed that the second half of the book was written in English, so I started to read. Reading for a couple of hours made me drowsy, so I turned the light off and went into a troubled sleep."

The priest interrupted. His voice was curt. "You don't have to give me a blow by blow account of your stay in Israel."

The *monk* shot back. "I'm trying to prove to you that this mess that I find myself in began so subtly that I wasn't even aware that I was being manipulated by unseen forces."

"You said that you weren't religious. Did you go out as many younger people today looking for some offbeat cult that you believe took control of you?" Asked the priest.

"Everything in due course. You must allow me to tell it in my own way and at my pace."

Chapter II

"On Friday I got up and after a shower and shave I cleaned my teeth, and set out for my meeting."

The priest walked slowly in quiet contemplation. After a while he heard what sounded like a roar, "Am I boring you?"

Even though the old man's attention to the *monk's* tale had been interrupted by his own thoughts, he had heard the gist of it. He turned to his companion. "You don't have to shout. It's not the most interesting story, but I heard what you said."

The *monk* took up where he had left off. "Finding the entrance of the market as arranged I saw a little coffee shop nearby from where I could observe the street. Being early I found a table outside and ordered a coffee, I told the waiter that I would wait until my companion arrived before ordering breakfast.

"As I was sipping my coffee and glancing through my newspaper I noticed two men sitting a few tables away studying me. At first I thought that it was my imagination and that my eyes met one of them in the moment as he looked in my direction, but later as I peeked over my paper I could see that each of them stared at me at different intervals, but with the same intensity. Just as I had made up my mind to confront them I saw a young man who looked barely older than a boy appear around the corner of the street.

"He stopped and began looking around searching the vicinity. He was close enough, so that I could have waved at him, but not being sure that he was the one, I got up and walked over. My path took me towards the two men. As they saw me heading towards them they took off.

"My movements must have registered on the young man, because he began pushing his way through in my direction. I lost sight of him momentarily, but all of a sudden there he was with an outstretched hand. 'Good morning Mr. Scott, I'm Nachman.'

" 'Call me Brad. Let's go over to that table in the corner. I arrived a little early so I picked out a spot as inconspicuous as possible for us under the circumstances. You can see my Herald Tribune propped up on my coffee cup. I figured the paper would be as good as a reserve sign.' "

The *monk* shifted as they walked. "I looked around for the two characters, but they were nowhere in sight. Nachman turned his head several times as though he was also looking for someone."

" 'Are you looking for somebody Mr. Scott?'

" 'No. I thought that I saw a couple of men giving me the eye.'

" 'You're not in trouble with the police or the Palestinians are you?'

" 'Why should I be? I just arrived in Israel and am strictly here as a tourist. What would the police or the Palestinians want with me?'

"The waiter showed up again as we sat down. 'This is on my tab, I told Nachman. 'Go ahead and order our breakfasts since you're familiar with the menus here.'

"Nachman picked up a folded frayed paper off the table. 'Do you want some ham and eggs?'

" 'Yes'

"Imagine my surprise, because I knew that the Jews did not eat pork. I guess my face gave me away, because Nachman said right away, 'Most of our coffee shops and restaurants have an international cuisine. This is due to the large number of tourists that come to make their pilgrimages so one can order whatever pleases him.'

THE KEY OF DAMASCUS

"The waiter spoke a little German. Knowing the language I could make myself understand, at least to order the coffee, but had difficulty getting other items across to him.

"The young man in white put another coffee on the table for Nachman and went off inside. There was no greater contrast than the blue sky above and the shadowy opening to the narrow street at the entrance to the market.

"The shops were already open and the people in the street were beginning to filter in from the wide boulevard although the rush hour had not yet started. Only later did I realize at peak time how many people pack into these places.

"Out of the corner of my eye I could also see that Nachman was studying me. After a quick check of my surroundings I turned back to the table. As I picked up my coffee to my surprise he suddenly asked, 'You speak German?' "

The *monk* stumbled. "Caught off guard I sputtered, 'Y..e..s, my ancestors were German many generations ago, so I learned the language in school when I decided to go into international business. Afterwards it was polished during my travels and a stint in Germany with my company.'

" 'So what is it you're searching for? How long can you stay in Israel? And what can I do for you?'

" 'I've decided to take my vacation in this region and figured I would start with Israel. I want to see some of the ancient ruins and monuments, but not the conventional way through a tourist agency.'

"Nachman looked puzzled. 'Why not? After all they're professionals and their only goal is to satisfy their client's needs and curiosities'

" 'I decided to hire someone who knows more than the superficial or canned history of these places. It would give me a better chance to get more detailed information that can be provided by a tour guide. I also want to make sure that the person I deal with would have as much time as I need to spend with me explaining thoroughly my questions without affecting some preset schedule. I figured if I could get a list of a number of sites with a short history of each, I could pick out the ones that I would like to see. I haven't much time and want to make the most of it.' "

The *monk* cleared his throat. "Nachman opened his notebook, 'Are you an archaeologist interested in historical places or does your interest lie only in Christian holy sites? By the way are you a Christian?'

" 'Well sort of, I was brought up as a Roman Catholic, but my parents never really pushed religion at home. They went to church only on feast days. So you might say I'm a part time Catholic.'

"My companion smiled at some personal secret joke, 'There are many like you in all religions'

"I figured it was an opportune time to turn the tables on him. 'Are you a devoted Jew?'

" 'I..I.. do believe in God, but every now and then I have doubts. My uncle told you I'm an archaeologist working on my PhD, and sometimes science and religion mix like water and oil.'

" 'I thought that all Jews were very religious. It never ceases to amaze me, this continual argument between science and faith. I would think that if God exists, he must have a laugh at this conventional wisdom. If he doesn't, then it makes no difference. It seems like an eternal seesaw between the believers and the non believers.'

"Nachman looked a bit surprised. 'You're a bit of a philosopher. That is an unusual combination in a businessman.'

" 'Why? Are all the businessmen suppose to be blockheads who can only understand their activity without having any other interests in matters of creation, life and death?'

" 'I didn't mean to insult you. Please forgive me.'

" 'Never mind. One thing that a successful businessman needs is a thick skin if he is to survive. In your case when the waiter who gave me your name, told me that you were working on your doctorate, I expected an older man. When I saw you on the corner I thought that you were still an undergraduate.'

" 'Many think that when they first meet me, but I'm older than I look.'

"A few moments passed as we sipped our coffee. 'I'm not an archaeologist, but I'm interested in history and this region is full of it. I plan to see Israel during this trip and next year visit one of the Arab countries. I'm nuts about ancient civilizations.'

"Nachman pushed his cup away from his notebook. Scanning his notes he asked, 'If you're so interested in history why didn't you go into that field rather than business?'

" 'What! And take on a profession where one barely makes enough to survive as some teacher or professor?'

"Nachman lifted his eyes from his book and stared at me. 'There are other reasons for living besides making huge amounts of money.'

" 'I have no arguments with this train of thought, but that life style is not for me. I figure I can satisfy my curiosity and fulfill my fondness for history doing what I do.'

"Nachman lowered his eyes back to his notebook. 'You told me what you wanted in general, but what is it that you want from me specifically? Do you want me to be just a personal tour guide or do you want me also to perform other chores?'

" 'I guess a combination. Of course I don't intend to sit on my butt and let you do all the work. I would envision it more like a partnership. We would each contribute whatever we can to make this trip a success other than I will pay for all the expenses and reach an agreement on your fee before we leave.'

" 'When I was told that you were in archaeology I figured you were the perfect candidate for the job. If you could supply me with a list of places, we could discuss it and perhaps I may find the sites that will fit my needs in the short time I have available.'

'I would like to have a summary of the history of these digs and they must be off the ordinary tourist's itinerary. I'm also interested in knowing their locations as well as the time involved to get there, visit, and get back. Please bring a map with you. I have only three weeks starting next Monday. I figure that preparations for the expedition and the day or so that I need before I catch a flight back home would take up a week. That would leave two weeks for the actual journey.'"

The *monk* stumbled again. The uneven large stone slabs in the street were dangerous if one did not pay attention. Regaining his composure he continued, " Nachman made some more notes. 'Since you haven't put any restrictions on which type of sights you want to see, I'm sure I can come up with some very interesting digs for you. Even though you don't want to see the mainstream ones, we could still visit a few of them. Some will be on the way to our planned destinations.'

" 'Very well, but I don't want to waste too much of my precious time on these trivialities.'

"Nachman's face-hardened and turned red at my remark. 'My opinion is that all archaeology should be valued in context and relation to history, which leaves no place for trivialities.'

" 'I didn't mean to upset you or insult your country, but I want you to be aware of exactly what I want, so that there is no misunderstanding.'

"We dropped the subject and spent the rest of the time talking about supplies, transportation and other mundane arrangements for the trip.

"Nachman looked at his watch, "I know someone who has a four wheel drive pickup truck, but he'll only rent it to you if I drive it. I can get a better rate from him than a commercial leasing company. Unfortunately I can't get in touch with him now, it's too early in the day. Normally I can reach him very early in the morning or when he gets home late at night. Are you interested?'

" 'Sure. As long, as the price is reasonable and the truck will not break down. Get hold of your friend and see if he can meet with us tomorrow.'

"Nachman closed his notebook. 'I'll have the suggested list with me as well as a schedule so that we don't waste any time visiting places that you're not interested in seeing. In the meantime, why don't you take in some local color? Even though you don't like the tourist traps. It could be fun and the guides are very professional. I went on some of the short trips and the tour guide knew almost as much about a sight as I did.'

" 'Maybe I will.' I lied. I really didn't want to go with a group who constantly asked petty questions. I do have the rest of the day and have nothing better to do.

"We said our good-byes and went our own ways. We agreed to meet at the hotel in the lobby the next day. I walked through the market, but the noise and the hawkers peddling their wares gave me a headache, so I left and wandered the streets away from the bazaar.

"I went to the Hamedina Square along Dizengo and Ben Yehuda to browse in the shops and boutiques, which catered to the tourist trade.

"These people sure know how to conduct business and provide the tourists with everything they want or don't want. When they are finished with the poor gullible buyer, the mark goes away confused, but happy with his lot.

"The reflections of multi colored lights created by replicas of ancient Christian relics, as well as Jewish and Muslim souvenirs created impressive rainbows.

"I didn't realize that there was so much brass employed in decorative items. It was the main metal in the displays with some bronze and clothing. I was amazed at the abundance of gold jewelry with curious settings.

"As I gazed in some of the windows I saw reflections of passersby. I was studying a large brass plate when I saw out of the corner of my eye the reflection of two men looking at me from the edge of the sidewalk. I thought that they might have been the same two from the restaurant, but when I turned to confront them they were gone."

The priest interjected in jest. "So the paranoia of this land began to haunt you too?"

The *monk* didn't break his stride. "I had no intention of taking a local tour, but as I walked I thought it would be interesting to check and see what tours were available and their costs. By now it was almost noon. The heat was becoming unbearable. Since the shops were going to close for mid-day, I decided to catch a cab back to my hotel and grab some lunch at the Sabra Coffee Shop. I figured an afternoon nap would do me some good.

"I went looking for a cab and saw one half a block away. As I made my way to it I saw two figures get into it. I was sure it was the two guys that were tailing me. The cab made a one eighty and sped away from me.

"I walked further and found another taxi. I hailed it and returned to my hotel.

"I did as I planned and woke up around four o'clock in the afternoon. Pulling the curtains open I looked out to see the sun still high in the sky, but it did not seem as bright as it had been before.

"I took a shower and went downstairs. By the time I entered the lobby it was almost six o'clock in the evening. The place was nearly empty. I wandered around. It was quiet so I went into the Lobby Lounge and ordered a cold beer settling down for the evening. I was in no rush, so I could dine at my leisure; besides the restaurants didn't really start serving until nine o'clock and I had made my reservations in the La Regence Grillroom.

"As I sat there I noticed a man across the lounge at the bar with an Arabic headdress sipping on some kind of a green liquid from a glass with several leaves sticking out of the top. I didn't pay much attention to him. Yet I had the uncomfortable feeling that he was watching me. Every time I looked in his direction I saw him staring at me, then he would quickly look away as soon as he saw my eyes directed towards him. His persistent attention made me feel uneasy. I figured that he was probably a fag and I didn't want to give him a reason to come and join me."

The priest looked puzzled, "Not being American, I don't understand this word fag."

Caught off guard by the question the *monk* said, "H.o.m.o.sexual."

Reorienting himself he continued his story.

"I was concentrating on my drink when I noticed the man was still staring at me. Since the bar was on the other side of the room some distance away I could not make out whether he was an Arab or not. I'm surprised how many of the ethnic groups around here wear the Arabic headgear and are not necessarily Arabs. Not wanting to attract his attention I took out a pamphlet out of my pocket, which I had picked up earlier from the lobby and began reading it, when I noticed a shadow on my table. Looking up I found the man standing before me.

" 'Good evening.' His accent was heavy and distinctly Middle Eastern. I didn't reply to his greeting. I wanted to spend a quiet evening alone and hoped that he would get offended and leave me, but he didn't.

"I couldn't make out his nationality, but as he stood across the table I could see that his skin looked dark even in the shadows of the café.

" 'May I join you?' Before I could answer he was sitting in a chair opposite me.

" 'It has been some time since I have been in a city, I'm an amateur archaeologist and dabble in some small unimportant digs. All the significant ones are allocated to large universities, which are mostly foreign and people like me are not allowed to invade these inner sanctums.'

" 'So why are you telling this to me. I'm not an archaeologist. Are you an Israeli?'

" 'It depends on your interpretation, I'm an Arab, but live in Israel and am a citizen of this country.'

" 'So, you're a citizen, but do not consider yourself an Israeli?'

" 'I'm foremost a Palestinian and citizen of Israel second.'

" 'So how do you get along with the present government and the Jewish state?'

" 'We have an uneasy peace between us. I don't bother them and most of the time they leave me alone.'

"We sat there, each sipping our drinks, then he asked. 'And you, what brings you here? Business or pleasure?'

" 'Pleasure', I told him curtly hoping that if I gave him the impression that I wasn't interested in continuing this conversation he would go away, but he made no move to leave.

"His eyes glittered. 'What type of pleasure are you looking for?'

"I was feeling ill at ease, I was sure he was a fag. I told him that I'm on vacation and planned to visit some of the more remote excavations.

"His eyes lit up as though he caught me with my hand in the cookie jar. 'I thought that you're not an archaeologist?'

" 'I'm not but I like to find out how our ancestors lived.'

" 'So. You're an Israeli? Are you a Jew?'

"I taunted him. 'No. I meant humankind. Aren't we all from the same family?'

"He took another sip of the green liquid from his glass. 'Y..e..s of course.'

"I made it clear to him that I hated crowds and small talk. I thought that he would get the message and would leave, but he still didn't move.

"During our conversation I noticed that the man kept fidgeting in his seat. His eyes continually shifted around in their sockets as though he couldn't control them. He looked like a hunted animal about to be caught. He didn't seem to pay attention to what I was saying. I had heard that the people of the Middle East were polite, but he was not one of them. He irritated me and lacked the basic courtesy to even pretend that he was interested in what I had to say. After all I didn't ask him to join me and he would have done both of us a favor if he had just left. Yet when I stopped talking he asked me some questions directly relating to what I had said. Imagine my surprise! He was aware of everything I told him!

"He asked, 'Do you have someone to show you around?' I thought Oh! Oh! Here comes his offer to accompany me, but instead he said, "If you don't, I know of someone who is very capable. His name is Nachman.

"I wondered what was going on. This is the second time that someone recommended the young man. 'What does this Nachman have that you are willing to risk your reputation by recommending him to a stranger? Do you know him well?'

" 'Not personally, but I heard of him. You see, even amateurs like me keep track of the good ones. In addition the man is honest. This is a rare virtue these days.

" 'If one makes a discovery and is an amateur without accreditation such as I, then it's impossible to get any recognition.

There are many so-called scientists that would steal your last drop of water in the desert if they had the chance. Not so with Nachman, he will make sure that everyone involved will get the credit they deserve.'

"I lied. 'Give me his name and address, and I'll see. If the one I'm in the process of hiring does not work out, perhaps I will contact him.'

"I wanted to test him and also find out later how this man who seemed to be so shifty knew the man that I hired. I felt uneasy and thought that perhaps I may have to find someone else.

"I handed him a piece of paper and a pen. He jotted down the same address and telephone number that I already had. 'Whoever you have or will hire tell him that you want to visit an old dig at Munhata. It is not large, but very interesting. It goes back to pre Bronze Age.'

" 'Why? Anything in particular?'

" 'I don't want to spoil it for you. If you're interested in old civilizations, then you know that most of the fun is the mystery. Like a beautiful woman, once you get to know her, then she is just another woman, but ah! The pleasure of the game.'

"By this time we had a couple more drinks and talked more about some of the old civilizations of the area. He seemed very well informed. His annoying glances around the room continued. His general behavior and the combination of his seemingly inattentiveness kept frustrating me.

"He finally stood up. 'I must leave, but don't forget Munhata.' He added. 'I wrote the name of the old dig on the back next to Nachman's address so that you won't forget.'

"He handed the paper back to me. Before I could say anything further or ask his name he bowed slightly touched his lips and chest said, 'Salem Alekum,' and turning around walked briskly towards the entrance.

"As he left and slightly staggered towards the door, he kept glancing behind him as though he expected someone to follow him. Perhaps it was just his obsession with this land, the type of business in which he was involved and was afraid of the authorities. I was not sure and didn't really care.

"I thought about him as he walked away from me and couldn't really picture this man digging in some dusty ruin to find something, only for the sake of its historical value. In fact I couldn't see him digging for any reason. His mannerism reminded me of someone shrewd, more like some of the hawkers I had seen at the market than an amateur archaeologist. Even though forbidden by law in all countries, I know that there is money in the sale of artifacts to private collectors. I finished my drink and checking my watch I noticed that it was eight thirty and time for dinner.

"It's strange how one reacts to sight, I hadn't felt the pangs of hunger until I checked my watch and realized it was eight thirty. I motioned to the bartender who sent over a waiter. After settling my account, I looked at the piece of paper with Nachman's address and then noticed the large letters, Munhata. I folded the note and put it in my pocket wondering what this amateur archaeologist was selling.

"Why did he mention the name twice and why did he write it so large on the paper? After all I wasn't blind, nor did I wear glasses. After an excellent shish kabob of lamb and goat meat with a bottle of wine I went to my room for the night. I figured that tomorrow I better be in good shape. I anticipated a long and wearisome day."

Chapter III

The old priest stopped for a moment to get his bearings. The *monk* kept on walking. He was too absorbed in his own thoughts that he didn't notice the absence of his companion. Suddenly he felt alone. Turning around he saw the Jesuit some five feet behind him. He stood there motionless waiting until the man in white caught up with him. Then he resumed his tale as though there was no interruption. "On Saturday I met Nachman and the truck owner in the lobby as arranged.

" 'Brad meet, Eli Wulf. He likes to be called Eli.'

" 'How do you do.' I shook hands with him and we went into the Patio cafe for breakfast. We ordered some coffee and rolls and began our negotiations.

"We came to an agreement on the rate and I promised Eli that only Nachman would be the driver. The owner told us that he had bought the truck from an American who was working in Israel with the government, and who had imported the vehicle for personal use when he came on a three-year contract. When he left he sold the vehicle. Eli was a soil specialist who worked at the Technion Institute. The truck was in immaculate shape. At the last moment I could see he was uncertain whether he should let us have the vehicle, because he kept repeating, 'Make sure you return it in the same condition'

"I tried to ease his mind. 'I have excellent insurance. It covers all contingencies.'

" 'I rather have it back in the shape that it's in now.'

"I assured him, that since Nachman would be the only one behind the wheel, he didn't have to worry. We agreed on two thousand US dollars for the two weeks. I promised him one thousand dollars when we took delivery of the truck. The balance would be paid when we returned it. He mumbled something to Nachman in Hebrew and then nodded.

" 'I have to take my tools and gear out of it. When do you want it?'

"I didn't reply. I was about to ask Nachman when Eli turned to him. Before he could repeat the question again, my guide responded, 'We'll need it tomorrow so that we can get all our gear on board and be prepared to leave early on Monday morning.'

"No one spoke for a few seconds. There was nothing else left to say. I agreed with my guide. 'It's Ok with me. I guess that's all. We'll meet here again on Sunday s..a...y...ten o'clock?'

"Eli turned quizzically to Nachman. 'Fine with me.'

"Nachman nodded his head. 'I'll be here.'

"Eli glanced at his watch. 'I must run now. Nachman do you want me to drop you off somewhere?'

" 'No, I have some other things to discuss with Brad. We need to talk about our supplies and the trip.'

"The man extended his hand to me, then to Nachman. 'Shalom.' Turning around a couple of times on his heels to get his bearings he spotted the exit and left the cafe. The three of us had stood by the table during the last few seconds of our conversation. After the owner of the truck left, the waiter seeing my new guide and I standing came over, 'Would you like your bill?'

"I wanted to go over some other logistics and negotiate our arrangements. 'Not yet, please bring us some more coffee.' Nachman and I sat down. I cleared a spot on in front of us. He brought out a binder with some paper and we began to talk about the trip.

" 'Before we get into the details, would you like to settle our fee arrangements first?' I asked.

" 'Y.e.s, we should get it out of the way." He was visibly nervous.

" 'My proposal is to give you a thousand US dollars for the two weeks. In addition if I'm completely satisfied I'm prepared to give you a five hundred dollar bonus after the whole thing is over. This bonus hinges on me being back in Tel Aviv on the specified date as long as I have seen everything that we have agreed on.'

"Nachman was surprised. 'Sounds fair to me. I think he figured it would take some haggling before we agreed on a price, but I didn't want to waste precious time to save a couple of bucks.' "

The priest interjected. "Not understanding fully the 'American' language, please tell me what are bucks."

The *monk* was taken aback by the question, "I'm sorry, I meant dollars. It's slang."

The man in brown was anxious to finish his tale.

"The quick resolution of our financial arrangements seemed to put him at ease and his tone became friendlier. I noticed that my guide had a familiar accent. 'Nachman you speak excellent English, I mean an American dialect. I found that most of the people that learn to speak English in school talk more like the Englishmen.'

" 'I was born in Chicago, then I decided to come to Israel and join the army. In fact my parents still live in New York.'

" I quipped. 'You didn't have to come here to join the army. You could have done it in the United States.'

" 'It's not the same, and it would be too complicated for me to explain it to you.'

" 'It's strange that we met. I'm from the Chicago area as well. I live in the suburbs. I don't know whether you heard of Palatine, it's north west of the city.'

" 'I know where it is.'

"This common bond brought us even closer together and established a trust. We needed this bond. For the next two weeks we would be alone in some of the worst parts of this land where we would rely on each other constantly. We hardly finished reminiscing about our neighborhoods when the waiter showed up with the coffee and cleaned off the table. He left us a fresh carafe. 'If you need me just raise your hand and I'll come.'

" 'Thank you.' I handed him my glass that was on the other side and we settled down to business. We spent a full two hours going over every detail of the trip.

"Suddenly the waiter showed up out of nowhere. 'It's almost lunchtime. Do you gentlemen plan to eat here? If you don't then I must apologize, but I need the table to prepare it for the mid noon meal.'

"Glancing at my watch I noticed it was eleven thirty. I looked at Nachman and since I didn't see any reaction from him I replied, 'Y..e..e..s I guess so.'

"The young man dressed in white motioned us to another spot. 'Why don't you move to a fresh table while I clean up this one? If you wish you can return afterwards. If not I'll serve you there.'

"We picked up our papers and followed the waiter.

" 'Before we start thinking about food, I would like to take a look at our travel plan,' I told Nachman. 'Let's see the list and places that you're recommending and how far apart they are.'

"I wanted to see if he had Munhata on it. The Arab had ignited my curiosity.

"While I read the list that he gave me, Nachman cut in. 'I drew up the plan going north from Tel Aviv, to make the best use of the time that you have. Of course there are as many interesting sites south of here, but that would mean back tracking. We may still have to, but it will be minimal.'

"I glanced at the itinerary. 'No, that's fine give me a few seconds to peruse it.'

"The first name on the list was Samaria the old capital of Israel dating back to 925-721 BCE, then Caesarea, afterwards Megiddo, Hatzor and Dan. 'Some of these places such as Caesarea, Megiddo and possibly Hatzor are well known. I saw them on some of the tours available through the local agencies.'

"Nachman assured me. 'You're right, but what I will show you no tourists have seen. You will have access to areas and finds that are inaccessible to the public. We must make sure that our timing is such that when we arrive the only people present are the diggers and the delegate from the appropriate institution that has been authorized to dig. Also these places are famous, so you will have something to share with your friends when you get home.'

" 'OK, I'll leave it up to you. By the way how come Munhata is not on the list?'

"He was sipping his coffee when I asked him the question. He coughed a couple of times. I didn't know whether it was nervousness or if he had choked on the drink. He cleared his throat. 'No one goes there anymore! There is nothing nearby, except some ruins dating back to the pre Bronze Age. I spent one summer at that dig. It's an interesting location for archaeologists, but would be dull for anyone else. We found many clay statuettes and vessels, but nothing else. There were also some rumors about some mysterious key, but nothing ever came of it.'

" 'What kind of key?' I asked him.

" 'I really don't know much about it, some kind of a Christian relic that was there during the Roman times. Anyway we found nothing and I never went back.'

" 'I would like to stop there, even if it's only for a few hours.' I didn't tell him the real reason, but something inside seemed to draw me there. I don't know whether it was the way the Arab blurted out the name or his subtle insistence that I should go there.

" Somehow the name, the Arab and an inner sense pulled me towards this dig. 'I would rather spend a day or so on that site, instead of some other place where the ground has already been trampled by thousands.'

" 'Let me see the list.' Nachman took the paper from my hands, and studied it for a moment. 'Lets follow our schedule and since Munhata is south of the Sea of Galilee it should not really interfere with our plan. Why don't we arrange to spend the night there? I don't think you'll want to stay at this place very long, because there is very little to see. We'll try to compress our trip so that we'll make time for this extra stop. If not we'll skip Hatzor or Dan.'

" 'It's a deal,' I agreed.

" 'Why do you want to go there?'

" 'I heard the name somewhere, and I'm interested at least to have a quick look.'

"He didn't pry. After we finished reviewing our list of supplies that he suggested, we itemized and priced it according to Nachman's best estimate. We agreed that we would meet the next day, take possession of the truck and go shopping. When I looked up, I saw the waiter making his way towards us. I could see that people were beginning to file in through the entrance into the restaurant for lunch.

"Arriving at our table the waiter laid down the menus. 'Do you want me to wait while you study the Carte De Jour or do you want me to come back?'

" 'How time flies when one is busy. Can we continue our discussion during lunch?' I asked Nachman.

" 'Sure.' Then he turned to the waiter, 'Please bring us a couple of beers while we decide.'

"The young man was back shortly, with the beers. 'May I recommend the fried sardines? They are excellent this time of the year.'

"Nachman didn't answer, so I picked up my menu. 'Thank you, we'd like to take another couple of minutes to see what other delicacies you have to offer.'

" 'As you wish.' He withdrew while we discussed the various choices and then he showed up in the distance with a bottle of mineral water in his hands. Nachman looked up. 'He must know you well that he already brings a bottle of water to our table without being asked.'

" 'I have been eating here off and on during the last few days and I guess he knows that I can't eat without water, even in the morning when I have my tea or coffee.'

"When the waiter arrived, we each gave him our order and he disappeared.

"We finished eating and agreed that Nachman would contact the owner of the truck, and arrange for us to meet at the hotel at nine o'clock on Sunday rather than ten if possible. We figured we could use the extra hour to load it before the heat of the day would make it impossible to work. At least for me as I'm not used to this infernal climate.

"'Is there anything else?' I queried Nachman.

"'No, I guess that's all for now.' He gathered his papers and left."

As they walked the *monk* kept glancing at the side streets. After a few seconds of silence he returned to his recounting of the strange events that led him to the priest.

"As usual I returned to my air-conditioned room and took a nap for a few hours.

"Later in the afternoon I got up and took a walk. By this time the air had cooled off and my wandering around the district was very comforting. I turned down one of the vaulted streets to gawk at the myriads of glittering objects on display. After a while I decided to sit down in one of the small cafes for some tea. I noticed that an especially tall man dressed in white came to serve me. He had a cold stare, and was overly courteous, which made me uneasy. 'It's a beautiful evening sir. Don't you agree?'

"'Yes it is. Please bring me some tea.'

"'Yes sir.' He disappeared behind some curtains.

"He brought me the tea, which tasted very sweet, but bitter at the same time. I didn't think much of it and sipped it leisurely, not realizing that the brew was drugged. I began to feel tired and closed my eyes for what I thought was a moment.

"I don't know how long I was under, but I could feel being half carried half dragged behind the curtains and into a dingy small room.

"In my stupor I could see two faces staring at me who would change into the heads of some prey birds that scared the hell out of me. Later I figured I was hallucinating from the drug.

"I heard one of them say softly, 'Relax Mr. Scott you have nothing to be afraid of. Its something that we put into your tea that make you relax. It's harmless. You'll be all right. You see we had to give you something because we knew that you would not accept our invitation willingly.'

"The other one had a glass in his hand and lifting my head poured come cold liquid down my throat. 'This will make you feel better. Sit up now.' He grabbed me and pulled me up on the bed.

"I sat up, but the room spun and the distortion of their faces didn't help. 'What is it that you want of me? I don't have much money on me take what you want and let me go. Also I'm not rich so kidnapping me for ransom is a waste of your time.'

" 'We're not after your money. We're after information.'

" 'What information?'

" 'We would like to know what you're doing in Israel and where is Nachman taking you?'

" 'Who are you people? The Mosad? No? Palestinians?'

" 'We're asking the questions Mr. Scott and have no time to answer yours.'

"One of the men took a menacing step towards me, but the other stopped him. 'My colleague has no patience so I would suggest that you answer our queries without delay.'

" 'I..I..'m here on a vacation and Nachman is going to be my private guide to visit some archeological digs. I have no interest in your disputes whatever side you represent. I'm tired let me sleep.'

" 'We'll be done soon and you can sleep all you want,' said the man in charge.

" 'Now tell us the locations where Nachman is taking you.'

" 'I don't know he has a list and nothing has been settled yet. We will finalize tomorrow.'

"As I began to drift into oblivion I heard one of the men say, 'Let's get rid of him. I guess that's all we're going to get out of him.' In my stupor I felt them picking me up and thought that these were the last moments of my life. Everything turned black and I passed out.

"I woke up in an alley with little memory of what had happened. It was like I had dreamt the whole thing. I recalled bits and pieces, but could not remember what the men looked like. I retraced what I thought were my steps in the vaulted street, but there was no such café anywhere. I gave up returned back to my hotel.

"Only some months and after other incidences I began to piece what happened to me that fateful night.

"As I approached my hotel I checked my wrist and saw that it was two o'clock in the morning on Saturday. I had lost six hours since I took the first sip of that tea."

Chapter IV

The man in brown stopped talking for a moment. He thought that he heard the priest praying. He looked at his companion.

The other noticing it said, "Please continue."

"Sunday, Nachman phoned me around eight o'clock in the morning. 'I talked to the owner of the truck and he agreed. He will pick me up and we'll be at the hotel at nine.'

"I went outside and strolled back and forth on the sidewalk in front of the entrance to get some exercise. I also figured that it would be a good chance to see the truck and inspect it so that if there were any visible dents they would be readily noticeable. I felt that we could also conclude our business immediately giving Nachman and I more time for our preparations.

"It wasn't long before they showed up with the truck. I walked around the bright, shiny vehicle while Eli jumped out of the driver's seat. I gave him the thousand dollars in cash as agreed and he departed. Nachman was in the passengers seat with a briefcase beside him. He slid into the drivers seat moving the briefcase to the passenger side between us. 'Get in. If you're ready, let's get going.'

" 'All set.'

THE KEY OF DAMASCUS

"He looked at me rubbing the thumb and forefinger of his right hand together. 'I hope you have enough money with you.'

" 'I only have dollars. Do we need to find a bank or a foreign exchange bureau?'

" 'I know a banker who will give you an excellent exchange rate.'

"The way he said banker I got the idea that this wasn't going to be an official bank.

"We drove through some tortuous streets finally arriving at a classy looking house. Yet it blended well in its surroundings. It exuded opulence of the middle class family occupying it. A careful look revealed that the house was anything but normal; all the windows had ornamental iron bars on them and a heavy steel door with a little slot in the top. It was not so much a peephole, but rather like a small window with a sliding latch. Nachman rang the doorbell and after some time the slot slid open from the inside.

"My companion brought his head close to the opening so the person inside could see him clearly.

"The face inside was shadowy. Nachman greeted the silhouette. 'Shalom'. I heard a muffled reply from the other side. The slot closed and the door opened creaking on its hinges.

"We entered an elegant foyer. The man, short and stocky with a round brown greasy face said something unintelligible in Hebrew to my guide. From the tone of the words and the look on his face I could tell it was a question. Nachman said something to him, which satisfied the others curiosity. The man did not say anything else. He gave me the once over, and then said in English, 'Please come in.'

"He guided us through a courtyard into another room that had a desk, and some chairs. This time Nachman spoke in English. 'We're going on a two week trip and need some money. All this gentleman has is US dollars. He needs to exchange some of them into Shekels.'

"The man turned to me. 'How much do you want?'

"I did some quick calculations in my head. 'I figure I need to change about a thousand US dollars for the supplies and another thousand for expenses during the trip.'

" 'No problem.' he turned to Nachman. 'Please pour yourselves some tea, while I get the money.' The man turned around and walked out of the office.

"Nachman stood up and poured us some tea from a kettle sitting on a small electric plate in a corner. He turned to me holding a cup in his hand. 'Sugar? Lemon?'

" 'A couple of teaspoons of sugar. No lemon.'

"Just as Nachman sat down with his tea the man showed up with several wads of bills in his hands. He threw them on the desk. 'Are the dollars in cash, travelers checks or a personal check?'

" 'Personal check?' I was surprised. 'You mean you would take a personal check from me? Even at home one has a problem cashing a personal check. I'm amazed that you would offer to cash one for me here, but I have enough cash or travelers checks for this transaction.'

"He stared at me for a moment. 'It doesn't make any difference to me, but since you are a friend of Nachman's I will tell you a little secret. I can give you a better exchange on the personal check.'

" 'It works for me. How much more can I get for a personal check?'

" 'One per cent,' he replied.

" 'Very well, but aren't you taking a chance with it?'

" 'Nachman told me a few days ago that you might need cash so I did a little checking on you. We trust you like one of our own.' There was something unnerving the way he said it. I shifted in my seat.

"I wasn't going to argue with him lest he changed his mind. I took my checkbook out of my pocket. 'To whom should I make it out?'

"He gave me a number with Ltd. at the end of it, which I knew represented an offshore company in some tax free zone. I wrote three thousand dollars and after signing passed it on to him. He gave me the bundles. As I began putting them in my pocket he asked. 'Aren't you going to count them?'

" 'Since you trust my check and I trust Nachman I don't think that there is any reason why I should. Do you?'

"He gave me a wry smile and made a gesture with his hands indicating that we were done. We finished our tea and after some small talk stood up to leave. When we reached the door the man took my hand as though I had been a long time acquaintance and pressed it heartily. 'Shalom, and if I can be of any further service please just tell Nachman. He knows where to find me.' Then he closed the door behind us.

"We spent the rest of the day buying the necessities for the trip, which included two tents, food, containers for water, as well as a couple of cans of fuel, lanterns and other paraphernalia. I was amazed at Nachman's resourcefulness. Even though it was Sunday we were able to buy everything we needed from Arab or Jewish supply shops, which were open. The majority of the shops were closed on Saturday for the Jewish Sabbath, but reopened on Sundays.

"We loaded the provisions and still had plenty of time left. The sun was high in the sky. As we drove, after some trivial conversation Nachman added. 'Since you wanted to include another stop to our trip, perhaps you should check out of the hotel now and we might be able to reach our first site today. Even if it's late when we arrive, we'll have a head start early in the morning to visit the dig.'

" 'That's a good idea I'm anxious to get going. I'm getting bored sitting in the hotel and am not keen of trampling through the streets anymore.' "

The Jesuit looked at the *monk*. "That's a fine story, but I still don't see where any of this should interest me, and where it's leading, let alone be part of a confession."

"When I finish the story, you'll understand why I couldn't leave anything out. Perhaps at the end you can also figure out and enlighten me why this whole mess ended up in my lap, because when I think about it I'm still mystified. Let me continue, as time grows short. When I get done you can give me your opinion."

The object that the *monk* was holding inside the wide sleeves of his garb kept getting hotter and heavier. He began tossing it from one hand to the other to relieve the stinging pain from his palms, but the priest could not see the movements because of the drooping sleeves.

"Some of the facts I tell you about this whole affair may bore you, but I can't take a chance. You must be familiar with the whole chain of events. When I'm done you will also realize how all these strange coincidences tie in."

"I checked out of the hotel and we left Tel Aviv after filling our containers with water for the Samaria (Sebaste) dig. Nachman gave me a brief history lesson as we drove. He told me that Sebaste was the capital of the ancient kingdom of Israel between 925-721 BCE built by king Omri about 800 B.C.

"I only half listened to his lecture. The story was interesting enough, but I was anxious to get there. 'How far is it and how long do we have to drive before reaching it?'

" 'Not too far, about 44 km or 33 miles. We'll drive along the coast to Netanya and then eastwards towards Nablus. It lies a few miles north of Nablus. The city was destroyed by the Assyrians about 950 B.C. and rebuilt several times. Since tradition tells that John the Baptist had been buried there I thought perhaps it might be of some interest to you.'

" 'Yes, I wouldn't mind spending a short time there. The legend must attract thousands. The sites, and streets must be worn out by Christian pilgrims.'

" 'There is no doubt that the major sites have had many visitors over the centuries, but there are places where only archaeologists are allowed and I will show you a couple of these spots, but first you should see some of the sights that are on the visitors' tours.'

"We arrived at the dig as the sun began to set. I was amazed how quickly the day here turns into night. Nachman knew the place, and stopping within earshot of a bonfire crackling in the dusk, jumped out of the truck and walked over to a group of people huddled around it. Wanting to stretch my legs I followed him.

"Going closer, to the light of the fire I could see some men and women huddled near the flames for warmth. Someone recognized my companion and called out, 'Shalom' then the others muttered in unison the same greeting.

"Returning their gestures he asked. 'How are things progressing?'

One of the men stood up and came towards us. 'Not too bad we're making some headway, but slower than planned. Today being Sunday we only had some lectures. We didn't do anything at all yesterday. Are you here to help us?' Since most of the diggers were foreigners they had two days off from their physical toils. Saturday and Sunday.

" 'No, a friend and I are heading north and I thought we would stop here for the night.'

"The man pointed to a little knoll. 'There is a good spot over there. After you get organized come back, we have some interesting things to talk about.'

" 'I don't know whether I'll have time tonight, but I'll try.' Nachman turned and made his way towards the truck.

"As I came closer Nachman stopped. 'You knew the man that stood up?' I asked.

" 'Yes. He attends one of my classes. He is an undergraduate and is planning to major in archaeology.'

" 'Do you always speak English between yourselves?' I asked.

"Nachman looked surprised. 'I'm sure you noticed that they're not all Jews. They're from many countries and when there are foreigners present we always speak English between us. Don't you know that English is an international language?' He teased me.

"We hurried to set up camp, but the darkness came up suddenly so we had to prepare our meal in the light of the lanterns and the flickering coal oil stove.

"When we finished cleaning up after eating Nachman picked up a lantern, and headed towards his tent. 'We better hit the sack. We have a long day ahead of us tomorrow. Walking around in this heat will take a lot out of you. For one not used to these temperatures, you may want to take a break in the middle of the day. Many people here have a rest around noon and then take up their tasks again later when it's not so hot. It gets very sultry and uncomfortable in the middle of the day.'

" 'OK, I do feel a bit tired. What about you? Are you going to join the others at the bonfire?'

" 'No, I decided to visit with them in the morning.'

"We said our goodnights and retired. I could hear the muffled voices of the people sitting around the fire, which gave me a feeling of security and helped me drop off into a deep sleep."

Chapter V

They came to a step, which ran right across the narrow street. The priest had seen his companion stumble a couple of time before. "Watch out for that step coming up."

The *monk* was grateful because in his preoccupation he had missed seeing the obstacle.

"Monday I awoke to the noise of some awful bird cackling in one of the trees. Getting out of my tent I saw ruins of an ancient city all around me. There was a street and colonnades that didn't seem to go anywhere, but after thousands of years' one couldn't expect to see its destination. I didn't bother to walk the distance to find out, as the street was not fully excavated. From my vantage point I could see that what had been uncovered at the far side looked like a palatial building facing the end of the row of pillars.

"Turning around I saw other ruins in various stages of being exposed to human eyes after thousands of years under the stony dry soil of the land. I looked towards the spot where we had placed the stove the night before and saw Nachman busy with a pot. He was adding coffee to it and taking other bits and pieces out of a box for breakfast.

" 'Shalom.'

"He turned to me surprised. 'Shalom. You're beginning to talk like a native and we have only been on this trip for one day,' he kidded.

" 'The coffee smells good.' Walking over to the kettle I poured myself a cup. Looking back I didn't see Nachman drinking, 'I'm sorry I thought that you already had a cup.'

" 'No I haven't. I've been busy with the bread and trying to find the damn cheese.'

" 'Do you want me to pour you a cup?'

" 'Yeah. Thanks.'

"As we finished eating Nachman pointed to the surroundings. 'If you want to wander around feel free until I clean up and then I'll take you to where my colleagues are digging. I come here from time to time. We feel that we have one of the more interesting spots. We have to penetrate and dig through the Roman era before we can reach the ancient Israeli time.'

"I stood up. 'I think I will. How long do you think it will take you before you're ready to go?'

" 'Oh, probably half an hour.'"

"I walked off towards where the excavation of the street had ended. I ran into an American expedition who had dug down some twenty feet in one spot, below the present ground level. They were bringing up pieces of pottery as well as other artifacts from the times of King Omri. I introduced myself and spoke to the professor in charge who explained the details of their find. Glancing at my watch I noticed that it had been almost an hour since I had left Nachman.

" 'It's been very interesting, but I'm sorry, I must return to my colleague. We're going to see another dig.'

" 'Who's your friend?' Asked the professor.

" 'Nachman from Tel Aviv.'

" 'I know Nachman well, give him my regards and if you have time drop by later.'

" 'Thanks, I'll tell him.'

"As I hurried back I was amazed how well known my guide was by the archeological community. Approaching our camp I saw that Nachman had everything packed in the truck.

" 'I'm sorry I'm late. I ran into some Americans. The man in charge said to give you his regards.'

" 'Thanks. I know some of them, but not real well except for professor Anderson who is in charge. Strange coincidence, last year he told me that he was going to do some digging this year in Africa. He's from the museum in Chicago. Did you tell him that you were from the same place?'

" 'No! The subject never came up.'

"He stood up after putting the last tin cup into a bag. 'Now let's go see what my associates are doing. We can leave the tents set up just in case we decide to stay here for one more night. If we decide to leave we'll take them down when we get back.'

"He gestured with his head towards a young man sitting on a rock nearby. 'I hired him to watch our stuff while we're wandering around. We have no way of locking everything up in the truck.'

"He went over to the young fellow said something in Hebrew and pointed towards the end of the old Roman street.

"He came back and we headed down the ancient walkway. 'It seems that everyone here is from Chicago. I'm amazed that anyone is left back home.' I jested.

"Nachman laughed. 'Sometimes it does seem like everyone is here digging at one place or another.'

"We walked in silence between the colonnades. I admired the various statues and other reminders of bygone eras, when I heard Nachman's voice through my reveries. I looked at him, and saw that he was pointing in the distance. 'There it is towards that little depression. Be careful, there are many small test holes around and you might twist your ankle in one of them.'

"Nachman exchanged greetings with a young woman as we arrived. 'This is Sarah. She is a graduate student at the university of Jerusalem and is working on her doctorate as well. She is second in command. The only reason that she is number two is that she doesn't have her doctorate, but soon she'll be a big boss.'

"She came towards me with her extended hand. 'I'm pleased to meet you. Don't let Nachman tease you like he does me. I'm used to

THE KEY OF DAMASCUS

his practical jokes, but if I thought that he was serious I would lop his head off.' She made a circular motion with her knife that she carried, which she used for some delicate digging and scraping.

"He jumped away from her as though he was afraid that she really meant what she said. Then putting his arm in front of him as though to protect himself he chuckled. 'She's a tough one, and acts just like my sister, but I like her anyway.'

"Then he got serious. 'Have you found anything of interest?'

" 'The usual pottery and some coins from the times of Caligula.'

" 'Let's go see them, Mr. Scott here is from Chicago and is interested in archaeology.'

"She turned to me and put her hand before her eyes to deflect the early morning sun. 'Are you an archaeologist Mr. Scott?'

" 'No. Just a history buff and call me Brad. I feel uncomfortable and old when people start calling me Mr.'

"As we walked closer to the dig Nachman kept turning around surveying the area. 'I don't see professor Javinsky. Is he hiding in one of the holes?'

" 'No. He went off to Jerusalem a couple of days ago. We found an artifact that he wanted to take to the lab. He said he wanted to be there when they authenticate its age.'

" 'What was it so important that he left the dig for a couple of days unattended to make this trip?'

" 'What do you mean unattended?' Shot back Sarah. 'He left me in charge so you see I have been number one the last few days.'

"Then she answered Nachman's question as an afterthought. 'It was a clay tablet with some writing, which seemed to refer to some type of Key.'

"We walked over to a makeshift tent, inside there was a table, where several young people were numbering and cataloging the bits and pieces strewn all across it. Nachman took me to the other end of the table, and picked up a coin. He turned to me with the object between his fingers. 'Brad, come here look at this coin.' He handed me a gold like coin that was mostly green with age. 'Can you make out Caligula's head on this side?'

THE SILVER FOX

" 'Yes, very interesting! Just think people have handled this coin some two thousand years ago and no one has touched it again until now. It stood up very well over time for a bronze piece.' "

The priest said, "There are many artifacts from the times of the Roman occupation in Israel. They are quite common and with very little intrinsic value. A friend of mine has found many such coins and gave me one as a souvenir."

The man in brown ignored the interruption. "At that moment a fellow ran into the tent out of breath, shouting, 'Nachman! Sarah! We found something beside a small wall that we were excavating. Come quickly.'

" We left the tent on the run, down a narrow path some twenty feet away. Approaching we saw that everyone had stopped digging and were standing in a semicircle around a partially excavated wall. As we came closer Nachman ordered the spectators. "Move over make room!" Clearing a path for us between them.

"My guide and Sarah jumped into the hole while I stayed with the crowd around the edge. I didn't have a good view, but both of them seemed to take a painfully long time to dig around the edges of a buried object. I ran out of patience watching them *play* with some brushes and trowels. I asked the fellow standing beside me who had brought the news to us. 'What is it? Something of value?'

" 'Yes, but it's the mystery that is keeping us all on edge.'

"It reminded me of the words the Arab had spoken in the lounge. '.........then you know that most of the fun is the mystery.'

"I was amazed that these people did not know what they found.

" 'What mystery. I asked. Don't you know what you have found?'

" 'Yes. It's just an ordinary urn, but still sealed. Can you imagine what might be inside it?'

" 'No. Something of value hidden by its owners during the destruction of the city I presume.'

" 'For sure, because it was hidden under a stone in the floor near the kitchen wall. When the stone in the floor was lifted the urn became visible under the wall. The ancients used to conceal valuables and money in such places. There were no banks in those days so everyone with any means had a hiding place somewhere in their residence. That's why when the building collapsed it did not crush it. Then fine sand had filled the cavity over the millennia.' He sounded proud of his knowledge and was more than happy to share it with me.

"We stood there for what seemed like hours, but I'm sure it was no longer than fifteen minutes when Nachman turned around holding the object about fifteen inches long and six inches at the widest part. He was handling it as though it was a precious egg that would disintegrate in his hands at any moment. He came to the edge and called to the young man standing beside me. 'Jacob take the urn so I can climb out. Be careful.'

"The fellow took the urn with great care and held it in the same way that Nachman had. As he held it in front of him, he rotated the jug slightly trying to see all around it. Sarah came out first with my guide on her heels.

"As soon as Nachman was out of the hole, he turned to Jacob. His eyes fixed on the vessel. 'Bring me the urn.'

"Then he turned to me. 'Did you ever see anything so beautiful in your life.'

" 'No.' I lied. The object intrigued me, but the urn did not look any different than any other, except that I could see some decorations in between the dirt that still clung to its sides.

"The group headed at once towards the tent with Nachman leading the parade. Arriving he began to issue orders. 'Bring some rags here I don't want this vessel to crack before I open it. Also prepare a bath to wash the soil from it.'

"People were scurrying around like ants carrying out his commands. I went over and took a closer look at the urn. It was no big deal it was an ordinary clay urn, of not a very good quality. Of course I'm no expert, but it seemed to me as if it was made by some second grade potter. There were two drawings on each side of the bulging part of the urn. The pictures were parts of two separate fishes. The rest were of the images were obscured by the dirt. I surmised that the urn had probably been the property of some fisherman many years ago. As I studied the designs, Nachman came over and looked at the same spot.

" 'The urn was probably owned by some Christian. They used to decorate their things with fishes in those days.'

" 'I thought that it might have been the property of a fisherman who was proud of his trade.' I commented.

" 'I doubt it, but when we clean it up, we'll be sure. Then we can see what the rest of it looks like. This is a great find. I know that we have our schedule to keep, but do you think we could stay here a day or so until I open the urn?' Asked Nachman.

" 'No problem, I'm just as anxious to see what's inside as you are.'

"Once the urn was cleaned up the pictures of the two fishes appeared clearly. The vessel fired out of red clay did not have any signs of ever having been glazed. 'There is no question that this object is of the first century A.D. and its owner was a Christian,' said Nachman with authority.

" 'How do you know?' I asked.

"Looking at the underside of the vessel he pointed to the center. 'See the inscription in Greek on its bottom. It tells that it was made in 38 A.D. when Caligula was emperor.'

"Then he turned to me. 'We'll open it tomorrow. I have sent for some special chemicals that we need, for the preservation of whatever's inside.'

"Carefully I picked up the urn. 'What do you expect to find in there?'

" 'Probably a scroll of some type. People in those days always stored their writings in jars. When sealed they were protected from decay and insects. I also sent word to professor Anderson at the American dig and asked him if he would like to be present for this momentous occasion.'

" 'What about gold, money or other precious objects? Perhaps the owners were trying to hide them from some invaders that would kill them and rob them of their wealth.'

" 'Brad, you are a true capitalist. Your first thoughts are of wealth, but I must disappoint you. The weight of the urn gives it away. If it was full of any kind of metal it would be a lot heavier than it is. Yet it it's heavier than it might be containing just a scroll.'

" 'Then what is it?'

" 'We'll find out tomorrow when we open it.'

"The mood was one of festivity. Sarah looked around, and seeing the people standing about began to usher everyone out of the tent. 'We'll not accomplish anything by standing here. Let's get back to work.'

"The crowd mumbled something unintelligible then a voice boomed above the rest. 'OK, but you must promise to let us all come here for the opening of the urn tomorrow.'

"She glanced at Nachman who slightly nodded his head that he agreed then she turned around towards the crowd. 'Very well, you can all come here to the tent rather than your assigned spots first thing in the morning.'

"Leaving Nachman in the tent I decided to do a little more exploration. That evening we joined the diggers in their camp around their bonfire speculating what might be in the clay urn. Nachman had been right, the sun the hot air and the dust did me in. I went over to him. 'I'm going back to our camp and go to bed. I'll see you in the morning. Shalom.'

"The group turned to me as I was walking away waving their arms. 'Shalom Brad'.

"When I got back I saw our guard sitting near the fire hypnotized by the flames. When he spotted me he jumped and came towards me. Figuring he didn't speak English I pointed towards my tent trying to make him understand that I was going to bed. To my surprise he made an affirmative gesture with his head and said, 'OK Mr. Scott, good night.'

"I waved at him and got into my tent."

"I had a restless night tossing, and turning, waking up, and falling again into a troubled dream where I saw the urn being opened. It seemed that it was I who was reaching inside it and touching something that felt slippery, wet and gooey. I tried to get my hand out, but like the story of the child with a handful of cookies I couldn't get my hand out of the jar. My fist had become larger than the neck of the urn and I didn't want to open my hand to let go of what I had in it. Yet I didn't know what was inside of my palm. Fear gripped me, and the harder I tried to get my hand out the tighter the neck got. I began feeling something pulling me into the urn. It was ridiculous, but my arm was up to its elbow and kept slipping into it further and further. I began screaming, but no voice came out of my throat. Then all of a sudden I heard someone call, 'Brad! Brad!' and when I awoke I saw Nachman with a lantern in his hand at the entrance of the tent."

Chapter VI

The priest asked, "Do you have these nightmares often?"

"I never did until I got involved in this mess, but please let me continue."

"Suddenly it was Tuesday morning. There was a gray tinge coming in through the flap of the tent. I jumped up. 'What's going on? What's the matter?'

"Nachman motioned towards the darkness. 'I made some coffee and left a couple of sandwiches for you. I couldn't sleep so I decided to get up and go over to the dig. You can go back to sleep. We have arranged the opening for seven o'clock if you're up to it.'

" 'What time is it?' I asked.

" 'Five thirty.'

" 'OK, I'll be there.' I promised and laid back down.

"I tossed and turned, but couldn't go back to sleep so I got up and after a quick wash wolfed down the sandwiches Nachman had left. I drank a couple of cups of coffee gazing into the fire of our camp stove. I could see the place where the bonfire had been laid and a few red coals still glimmering in the ashes. The young man that my companion had hired to watch our stuff was sitting to one side smoking a cigarette. 'If you want to go ahead, I'll clean up,' he said.

" 'Thanks, that's kind of you.' I looked at my watch and saw that it was already six thirty. The dig was not far away, but I didn't know whose watch Nachman would choose for the opening of the urn, and if mine was slow I could miss this historic event. One thing I was sure and that was that my companion would not waste a second of his precious time. He was so anxious that he couldn't sleep that night. Standing up I waved at the young man. 'I'll see you later.' and left for the dig.

"Arriving at the site, I went directly to the tent where some people were standing around. The place had an air of an exhibition.

"There were people, whom I had not seen the day before. They were standing in groups drinking coffee and talking in several languages.

"No one paid any attention to me as I made my way to the tent. When I arrived at the entrance a couple of men barred me from entering.

" 'Sorry, you can't go in. The announcement will be made in time, so you'll have to wait out here with the others. Help yourself to a cup of coffee.'

" 'I'm with Nachman and I was here yesterday with him. We made plans together.'

" 'Just a moment.' One of the guards disappeared inside the tent.

"A second or so later Nachman appeared from the inside. 'Sorry about the misunderstanding, but word got around the area and as you can see we're beginning to attract a crowd, so I had to take some security measures.'

" 'No sweat.' I followed him into the tent.

"I saw the clay urn sitting inside a makeshift holder, designed to keep the vessel upright. Some tools lay beside it.

" 'We're ready to go,' he said and sat down on a chair beside the table. My guide took one of the instruments that looked like a pointed knife and began pushing it into a seam that was evident on the neck between the urn and a plug.

"The top moved after a few minutes and Nachman carefully worked it out of the neck of the container. He pulled it out slowly revealing some type of material on the inside used to provide an additional seal.

"He laid the top to one side and asked Sarah. 'Pass me the penlight. I want to see inside it before I start to poke around. Also make sure that the solution is ready, because as soon as I remove the contents, I may have to drop them into it. We can't afford the material whatever it is to be exposed to the air for any length of time, otherwise it may simply disintegrate.'

"She passed him the penlight. 'Everything is ready.'

"Nachman shone the light inside the vessel and declared. 'It's full of something. Probably fine sand that has seeped into it with water over time. If so the contents may have decayed and may take a lot longer than I thought to retrieve them. If it's a scroll, then we may never be able to read what is written on it. I guess the seal was not as tight as it looked.'

"He turned the clay vessel upside down and some white grains from the inside began to pour out. Instantly a number of people began to clap.

" 'What's all the excitement about?' I asked one of the women standing beside me.

"For some reason the sand is dry. If it had hardened we might have had to cut the urn to reach the contents or soak it for a very long time before we loosened the sand to find out what it contained. Also the condition of the materials inside may disintegrate in the process, after all these centuries.'

"She was interrupted by Nachman's words. 'I was wrong the seal was tight. It's not sand, but salt!'

"When I looked at him I could still see his finger near his lips.

" 'The urn is full of salt to protect whatever it contains from humidity. Ingenious! The plug was so snug that no humidity breached it.'

"He had to shake the urn a few times, because something was holding the rest of the salt from coming out. Again taking the penlight he looked inside and let out a low whistle. 'Just as I thought there's some type of a scroll in it'

"He turned to Sarah. 'Pass me those tweezers.' Pointing to a long tool that looked more like a school compass than everyday tweezers. Then he carefully inserted the device in the urn and played with it until he had grasped the item inside. It seemed to take him hours to get hold of the material, but in reality only a few minutes. At last he pulled out a rolled up parchment tied in the center. Everyone's eyes were fixed on the scroll and when Nachman laid the roll on the table the small group stood there like the statues in the courtyard outside. The silence was deafening.

"It was Sarah, who broke the stillness. 'The parchment looks almost new, but it couldn't be, it's not possible. We all saw that the urn was sealed and it was in such a place all these centuries that it could not have been tampered after it was hidden.'

"Nachman turned and looked at one of the men. 'Where was the urn kept during the night?'

" 'Here in the tent, and I stayed with it all night. I never left it even for a moment. I can assure you that no one was near it since you left it last night.

"Nachman didn't answer, but to reassure himself he poked at the rolled up rawhide a couple of times with the tweezers to see if the document was really in as good a condition as it looked. Being satisfied, he picked it up and untied the thin strap holding it together. He unrolled it and since it was still partly dark in the tent, not raising his head from the table asked, 'Will someone pass me the lantern.'

"The piece of leather was only about twelve inches in length and six inches wide. It had some writing on it, which Nachman studied for a few seconds. 'Strange. It has been written in Hebrew, but it seems to be in an ancient dialect, perhaps Aramaic.'

" 'Let's see if I can decipher it, and make a simultaneous translation into English for my foreign friends here. Then after we make an announcement outside, we can send it off to Jerusalem.'

"He began reading the words of the scroll. '…The Key…has…been sent to…Damascus…for…safe…keeping. …The…Romans are…getting…closer and…we expect…to…be attacked…anytime. …Since we don't…figure that…we will…survive, we can't…afford to have…this Key…with its…powers…fall…into their…hands. Look…for a…fishmonger…named Mustaffa…in the…market, …when you…get to…Damascus, and…ask him…to…take you to…the Key.'

"The text sounded like a note written for someone that would be coming to look for some Key and the writer did not expect to be there to meet him. The message ended as abruptly as it began. We were all speechless. Professor Anderson a lanky gray haired man went over to the table and peered over Nachman's shoulder. 'What else does the message say?'

" 'Nothing, that's it, there isn't even a salutation or signature on it. I thought that it would be more difficult to translate, but it wasn't. There is no hidden meaning and it can't be translated in any other way.'

"The Professor leaned over to get a better look. 'The parchment looks in excellent condition let me see it. It must be some kind of a prank or game that someone is playing on you, Nachman.'

"The young archeologist handed the piece of hide to the professor who took it and rubbed it between his forefinger and thumb. 'It sure feels new. There is no way that this parchment is older than a year at the most. Salt or no salt.'

"Scrutinizing further he commented, 'It looks as though it was scribbled, rather than written. A scribe in ancient times took pride in his work and would be very meticulous about his craft rather than scribble something so carelessly. In those days writing was more of an art than just a means of communication. I…I…just don't know.' He rubbed it a couple more times between his fingers.

"I was close to the professor so I touched the leather by a corner and felt it between my fingers before he handed the parchment back to Nachman. I'm no expert, but the hide did feel soft and pliable. Almost like the leather shammy being sold at home to wipe the cars dry after washing them.

"Nachman taking it into his hands studied the writing again. 'You may be right professor, but also the reason for such bad handwriting could be that the person may have been in a hurry and did not have time to apply himself to the task.'

"We stood there for a moment until Sarah spoke up. 'Who, is going to make the announcement to the crowd outside, and what are we going say?'

" 'You can have that honor,' Nachman told her. 'Until we determine what's going on here. Tell them that there was a parchment inside the urn and that we have read the writing very quickly and made a hasty translation. Also say that it is an insignificant message left by a person unknown to his acquaintance about some Key from the times of Caligula. Tell them that we are sending it to Jerusalem to establish the age and authenticity of the piece. Now let's have it packed and get it out as soon as possible.'

"She went outside and made the announcement in several languages. We heard some disappointing sighs, but her calm voice settled the unrest and grumbling. Immediately the people started to disperse.

"As she re-entered the tent, the small group inside looked at her as though it expected some revelation. She looked at us a little surprised. 'Well it's done. They all seem to be satisfied and are leaving, but I thought I sensed a couple of reporters in the crowd and they may not buy our story. The two of them were like bloodhounds and I don't think that they're going to give up so easily. They probably smell a story whether this find is genuine or not.'

" 'We'll know for sure after we have it dated in Jerusalem,' declared Nachman. 'I'm interested to know their findings even though the parchment looks new, I'd swear that the urn had not been opened since it was buried there many centuries ago.'

"Sarah was right, a couple of men hung around. When Nachman and I came out of the tent they ran over and started asking questions. 'Did you find the Key as well? Does it say where the Key is now?'

"They were obstinate and I almost tripped over one of them. Nachman was annoyed. 'The answer is no to both questions.'

" 'We don't know what Key the scroll is referring to, and where it is now. If in fact this Key ever existed, or exists now. Please no more questions, we got work to do. If there are any new developments I'll announce them as they come up. Now, please go away.'

"As we began to walk away from them Nachman turned to me. 'We can leave now. There's nothing I can do here, anymore.'

" 'We looked in the direction where the two men stood and saw no one. It was strange. We should have seen them leave. There were no obstacles for some distance in the ancient court to obstruct our view. The two men vanished as quickly as they had shown up out of nowhere.'

"My guide asked some of the people around the dig if they knew the men after describing them, but no one could identify them nor had seen them arrive. They seemed to have materialized in the crowd. The people that we did ask told us that they did remember the two standing amongst them."

The priest observed. "Surely with all the people present someone would have remembered them."

"That's what I thought, but they swore they didn't."

The monk continued his tale in stride. "Nachman turned to me shrugged his shoulders and started toward our truck. 'Let's go.'

"We paid the guard and he took off. The young man had us loaded, but did not do a good job of it and our efforts to repack our stuff did not improve it very much. By the time we rearranged our things in the truck it was getting close to noon. The road was rough for about five kilometers before we reached a paved highway. The bumps in the road, jerking and vibrations of the vehicle caused our gear to bounce inside of the pickup box coming close to falling out. Nachman looked in his rear view mirror. 'Perhaps we should eat lunch here by the highway. When we get to Caesarea we can visit some of the ruins, have dinner, then pop by the dig tomorrow. The break will also give us a chance to repack our gear.'

" 'OK, by me.'

"After lunch we repacked some bits and pieces into the truck and took off for Caesarea. Pondering over the day's events I really thought that professor Anderson was right. 'Well I must hand it to you this was quite a show. I'm no expert, but I handled rawhide at home and that parchment felt as though it had just come out of a store.'

"I could see my companion's face redden around the ears. 'Do you really think that I orchestrated this find just for you?'

" 'Well it entered my mind. It would have been a nice touch, but somebody screwed up and used a new piece of rawhide.'

" 'I'll wager my reputation that the urn is as old as I said. Also since the vase was not opened from the time when it was buried, it stands to reason that the parchment is as old as the urn. I agree with you, it's excellent condition puzzles me, but sometimes-strange things happen here in the desert. Besides my reputation, I'll wager the bonus you promised me against five hundred dollars, that you'll be surprised when we hear the news from Jerusalem.'

" 'I'm a sporting fellow, but you haven't earned your bonus yet, so I would be betting against myself.'

" 'I can assure you I'll earn that bonus, but just in case I don't you can take it out of the fee we agreed.'

" 'Now that sounds more like it. I'll take that bet, but you'll have to agree to let me get a second opinion if the news from Jerusalem is in your favor.'

" 'It's a deal.' Nachman reached over and shook my hand to seal the bargain, but I could feel his uneasiness at my request about the second opinion. From there we drove in silence for about twenty minutes.

"When we got closer to Caesarea I could smell the Mediterranean. By going to Samaria originally, and then partly doubling back we covered more miles than if we would have gone directly from Tel Aviv. Caesarea is only about halfway between Tel Aviv and Haifa on the coast."

The Jesuit was bored, since he knew all the mileages and locations of these places better than the man telling the story, but he had promised to listen to the end so he kept quiet.

"Arriving at the site Nachman again found a group of diggers and went to talk to them. A short while later he returned. 'We'll stay here for the next couple of days. Even though I'm not involved in these digs, the crew here knows me well and will give us a tour of their project. Normally the discoveries of a dig are a jealously guarded secret by those in charge until they're published. The fear is that someone will steal the credit for the finds as well as take the impact out of the announcement if it gets out prematurely.'

" 'I don't believe it. I thought that academics were above such tactics.'

"Nachman threw me a side-glance. 'I guess people on the outside know little of what goes on in the world of academia. I have never been in business, but I would venture to say that avarice and competition in our field is just as keen and ruthless as any commercial enterprise.'

"I was surprised. 'It sure makes things look different, because I always held you guys as being above the normal greed and egotism that drives people in business.'

"We found a spot and set up our tents, but this time did not need the lanterns as we had plenty of sunshine left. 'Why are we camping when there are so many first class hotels around this place?'

" 'I thought you wanted adventure. You can stay in a hotel anytime. Anyway we will be close to the dig and you'll experience the inconveniences that some of the people who work in these places go through while they dig.'

" 'We have already had the experience in Samaria and I assume will have more until we finish this trip.'

" 'Do you want to go to a hotel?' Asked Nachman. 'It's your money.'

" 'No. I guess this is what I really want otherwise we'll end up fighting the tourist crowds in the hotels.'

"After dinner we took a walk around the ruined city with Nachman giving me a personal tour. Again my companion hired a young lad to look after things.

"Then when we returned to our camp he went over to his knapsack and pulled out a bottle of cognac. 'Would you like to have a night cap?'

" 'Wow! Gladly, because I'm beginning feel quite cool, and a bit of cognac is a welcome relief.'

"I was surprised, as I had been told that one never caries any alcohol when one goes out into the desert, and so I didn't even suggest to buy any before we left on the expedition. However Caesarea is far from being in the desert. Even the Samarian dig was not really in the wilderness. The plant life in this land is sparse in some places, but far from being a desert. There were always bushes some grass and a few scraggly trees, depending where we went.

"He cracked the seal and poured some of the cognac into our coffee from a bottle that he had kept in a little sack tied at the top. 'Having traveled Europe and especially France there are only a few ways to drink cognac and putting it into coffee is one of them. You know us Americans, when we drink; it's for the sake of drinking. We drink things out of plastic cups, plastic glasses, and plastic bottles. Everything seems to be in plastic. On the other hand the Europeans make a ceremony out of their drinking. The French need quality crystal to drink champagnes and cognacs. The Germans need Steins to drink their beer otherwise they say it doesn't taste the same. I don't know what the Italians or the Spanish do, but the Eastern Europeans and Russian's favorite refreshment is vodka out of anything that can hold it.'

"Nachman looked at his cup. 'I'm not a real connoisseur of wines or whiskies, but I always carry a little for such occasions as today, to celebrate an interesting find. A short drink will warm us up and will help us to sleep better tonight.'

"I changed the subject to my present concern. 'What about safety around here? You guys are always fighting with the Arabs. Also what about muggers near the cities and bandits in some of the more remote posts?'

" 'You didn't see it and I didn't tell you, but you should be aware that I have packed a couple of assault rifles and ammunition. When we go to the west bank or outside of the cities we're always armed. Some people walk around with hand guns on them all the time.'

"The cognac began to work on me. 'I'm glad you mentioned it. By the way if we have to fight our way out of something what do you do? Do you deputize me or something?'

THE KEY OF DAMASCUS

" 'If and when the time comes, which I hope it doesn't you won't have to worry about being deputized or anything else. You'll have no choice if you'll want to live.' He snapped.

"I realized that he didn't appreciate my sense of humor and that fighting or shooting someone around here was a serious matter. I thought that the best tactic right then was to lighten the atmosphere. 'I'm trying to figure out how I'm going to spend the extra five hundred dollars that I'll have at the end of this trip. Since I won't have to either pay you the bonus or the full amount of your fee I will have an additional five hundred dollars left from my budget.'

"The tension dissolved like a fog in the morning, Nachman was a good sport. 'As I told you previously don't count your chickens before they're hatched as they say in Chicago. Strange things happen in the desert and remember this is truly God's country. Many objects have been found under bizarre circumstances and in very unusual conditions which were never explained.'

'This time I was serious. 'Do you really believe that the parchment you found is as old as you make it out to be?'

" 'I truly don't know, but the condition of the urn, the place where it was hidden, the undisturbed soil and the hole packed by silt which must have taken water centuries to fill intrigues me.' He said.

" 'What about this Key?'

" 'I don't know. There are many legends in this land with some going back to the times of pre-written history. Some in time have been proven true and others have slipped into the twilight as folklore being told around bonfires at night for entertainment. I remember something about a Key from the early Christian days, but can't quite recall the story. Anyhow perhaps Jerusalem will shed some light on it.'

"While Caesarea has been developed into a tourist attraction with hotels, a golf course and public baths, there are still some pockets where the archaeologists are digging deeper and deeper to discover some of the secrets of its Phoenician past. The general public is kept away for safety reasons, unless accompanied by a guide.

"Nachman glanced at his watch. 'I'm going to hit the sack. If you want to stay up, please do.'

" 'No, I think I'll turn in as well.'

"We finished our coffee and retired for the night."

Chapter VII

The priest asked, "So this is where you first had some concrete proof of existence of this Key?"

"Yes. Or I guess the any tangible proof besides the legend according to Nachman."

The *monk* squirmed. "Wednesday and Thursday we spent with various diggers at their sights viewing fragments of pottery and other uncovered artifacts. Most of the items were of no intrinsic value, except to the scientists that studied them.

"To the archaeologists they were priceless. Once in a while they would uncover some jewelry or a weapon that had been decorated with precious stones, or gold. These items were immediately catalogued and locked up. It was these objects that thieves and international smugglers coveted and later sold on illegal markets to clandestine collectors.

"We were shown a Jewish dagger that had such decorations on its handle, plus a large Roman ring with some type of design and letters in Latin on it, which Nachman said had been used as a seal. We were also shown some jewelry, which I was told was Phoenician.

"Next morning as we stood beside the podium of Herodian construction Nachman gave me a few historical facts about the structure. "This pedestal is thought to have formed the substructure of the temple that housed a giant statue of Augustus. Herod built the edifice to honor Augustus who was his benefactor and at whose pleasure he ruled."

"I walked around the large platform to get a look at the other side, while listening to my guide's historical narrative following me as he talked.

"As I turned the corner I noticed a couple of men standing at its base. We wouldn't have paid any attention to the two figures, but as soon as we came into their view, they quickly disappeared around the structure and out of sight. This unexpected encounter and their immediate reaction to our presence startled us.

"Both Nachman and I saw their behavior, so he came closer to me and motioned with his head whispering, 'Let's turn around and go the other way and we'll meet them head on. I wonder what they're up to? Why did they take off as soon as they saw us?'

"We did what my friend suggested and ran into the two men who were expecting us to come from behind them. When we turned the corner they were standing so close that we almost stepped on them. One of the them turned towards us. 'F..a..n..c..y meeting you Mr. Nachman and you Mr. Scott. We didn't expect to see you here,' he lied.

"His stony face startled me it showed absolutely no emotions, when he spoke his lips didn't appear to move yet his words were clear and crisp. Suddenly the place and the four of us seemed to be standing in some surreal place as if the whole thing was an illusion. The man looked like one of the statues in the square.

"A normal person would have been jolted or shocked to suddenly find himself confronted by people that had materialized out of nowhere as we did, but not him.

"The other one also had his head turned looking behind him. As he turned around he had the same blank face and hypnotic eyes. They both stared at us. Somehow I felt that they knew that we would come to this place, and this meeting was not by chance. Yet how could they have known where we were going and when we would arrive, since we had told no one of our plans? We had decided to take in this site on the spur of the moment so that we ourselves didn't know it until we actually wandered into the area.

"The second one had a few seconds to compose himself before he turned around to face us and therefore the surprise had less of an impact on him.

"He followed the first man's lead. 'Good day Gentlemen. It's a beautiful day isn't it?' His voice was quiet and velvety, yet somehow sounded cold and frightening.

"It was we, who got caught off guard. He continued. 'You probably wonder what we're doing here. You see Nohmed and I are both writers for a small archaeological periodical. We are gathering material for our next story. This is delightful, we wondered if we would have a chance to talk to you again and here we are...... We thought that you would stay longer in Samaria after such an interesting find there.'

"He glared at Nachman. Just for a split second I thought that his eyes glowed like two red embers. Perhaps my sight was playing tricks on me in the sun. At the same time I thought I could feel a deep-rooted hate radiating from them, almost inhuman. Immediately this hatred engulfed me as though I was inside them and could feel this passion towards everything around us, but especially towards my companion and me.

"My partner also saw and felt it. I could see his expression twist into a repulsive grimace. His face twitched as he fought this overwhelming feeling of hate and fear. Nachman seemed to show fear or panic as he replied politely. 'T..h..e..r..e was nothing else I could do in Samaria, so my colleague and I decided to continue our trip.'

"The man's eyes did not move in their sockets yet he looked at me at the same time as he stared at Nachman who was talking to him. I don't know how to explain the phenomenon except that it's like some of the painted portraits that follow you around with their eyes without actually moving them. Scientists explain that the reason a portrait exhibits this unusual manifestation is that the picture is a two dimensional object. 'So you are also an archaeologist?' he asked of me.

"He never moved, but as he addressed his question to me I felt a shiver ran up and down my spine and suddenly I could feel the features of my face change. Somehow I had a feeling that my guide spotted in me what I observed in him.

"The feeling that I could experience what they felt was getting stronger as though I was being sucked into their bodies.

"It was confusing, I couldn't understand. This emotion of revulsion, which filled my whole body, was not directed to anything or anyone in particular, but rather at everything and everyone under God's creation. I was disoriented, and frozen in this hypnotic state.

"Then snapping back to reality. 'N..o.., just a tourist who had the good fortune to find an expert to give him a personal tour.'

"I don't know why I bothered to answer his question, because I felt that he already knew what it was before I gave it to him.

" 'Why don't the two of you join us for a drink later?' Asked the second man.

"While I tried to understand this sudden strange emotion of fear and revulsion in the pit of my stomach, I tried to find the right words, but nothing came out of my mouth. By this time Nachman had a chance to compose himself and came to my rescue. 'We'd like to say yes, but we're running behind schedule and still have much to do.'

"I finally found my voice. 'T..h..a..n..k..s for the invite, but perhaps some other time.'

"The man did not push. He turned to his buddy. 'Pity. It could have been very interesting.' They bowed slightly and turning on their heels walked off.

"As they got out of our sight Nachman whispered, 'I don't like it. I don't know why, but these two give me the creeps. I have been in the army, have seen some unexplained phenomenon in my life especially in the field of archaeology, but somehow.........'

"I felt foolish about my unease and experience so I did not comment about my state of mind. To this day I don't know whether Nachman had noticed it or not. Perhaps he did, and was trying to make me feel more comfortable by admitting his anxiety. A few minutes later they appeared again and passed bowing to us without uttering a word.

"As they moved by us one of the men accidentally brushed my hand with his arm. I felt genuine terror. I reacted as though my hand had touched a burning object and pulled it away quickly. 'This is ridiculous I think they're trying to psyche us out.' I murmured to Nachman as the two made their way towards the far side of the platform.

"We turned to give the men a last look, but again they were nowhere in sight just like in Samaria. We walked around the pedestal to see if they were on the other side, but there was no one there. The air was thick with apprehension.

"To reduce the tension Nachman kidded. 'I'll recommend those two to Mossad. They could use people who have a talent to appear and disappear at will.' We laughed nervously at the remark, but somehow I don't think that either one of us found it really funny.

"We took another day to relax in Caesarea, and spent the afternoon on the seashore, then visited a couple of bars until late in the evening.

"I glanced at my wrist. 'It's ten o'clock.

"Nachman took a quick look at his watch. 'I'm going to bed. Tomorrow will be another long day. What about you Brad?'

" 'I think I'll take a little walk by the seashore. It's a beautiful evening and it will give me a chance to clear my head from all the smoke and booze.'

"My guide turned and headed towards our camp. 'See you in the morning.

" 'Good night!' I shouted after him.

"The lights of the city became dimmer as I got further away from the street. When I reached the seashore I could see some of the stars. I looked towards the horizon of the Mediterranean Sea; the shining dots in the sky were breathtaking.

"As I stood by the shore I became aware that I wasn't alone. I felt that someone was watching me, but when I turned around to see who it was there was no one there. I began to walk, but couldn't get over the foreboding feeling that I was being followed.

"When I stopped and looked there was no one there but a peculiar noise like the whispering of many voices stayed with me. I felt cold all of a sudden and fear began to creep into my bones. It didn't make any sense. The beach was empty and the closest human activity was on the street a long way from where I stood. I called out, 'Who's there?'

"There was no answer. Then suddenly the murmurs stopped and I made out the swishing of feet in the water behind me. Turning around some ten feet away by the water's edge I saw a figure sauntering along the beach.

"I waited and finally made out the outline as one of the diggers that I had met earlier. It was the middle-aged woman who had told me that she came every year to join one project or another for the adventure. 'Good evening, Brad. Isn't it a lovely evening. I couldn't sleep so I thought I would take a walk.'

"My heart was pounding and even when I could see her clearly I was still stunned. She came closer. 'My, what in the world is the matter with you? You're shaking like a leaf. Are you sick?'

" 'N..o..o.. I don't know, but all of sudden I got the chills.'

" 'Perhaps you should go into our camp. We have a nurse there who could have a look at you. You could have a fever and that is nothing to fool around with in this climate.'

" 'N..o..o I'll be alright. Nachman and I hit a few bars and probably this is the result of our celebration.'

" 'Well, make sure that it isn't something serious.'

"We walked for a while and then went our own ways. For a moment I thought of taking the walk back to camp along the beach, but decided against it and headed towards the lit streets.

"The uneasy feeling persisted with me and when I crawled into my sleeping bag the smallest noise seemed to be amplified. I would hold my breath and my heart would start to pound again while I was trying to identify the source. Finally fatigue overcame me and I literally passed out.

Chapter VIII

"Friday early in the morning while it was still cool and comfortable we left for the ancient dig of Megiddo, which was next on our list.

" 'How far away is Megiddo?'

"Nachman did not answer my question. 'Where have you heard of Megiddo?'

" 'Everyone has heard of Megiddo. Even, part time Catholics like myself. Isn't it in the book of Revelation? It's where the ultimate battle is suppose to take place between the forces of light and darkness isn't it?' I was proud of myself to be able to identify the ancient name of the Christian word Armageddon.

" 'Yes. The teachings assure us that the forces of good are going to win, but before it's all over a third of the world's population will have been decimated,' explained Nachman.

" 'I don't know. Some of these teachings seem to be far out. I feel that a number of the texts are fabricated to frighten the believers so that they'll submit absolutely to God without question. The reason is always given that we would not and cannot understand the eternal goals of the Almighty.'

" 'I'm not trying to influence or change your beliefs. Whether the teachings are truthful or not is a question of individual faith,' remarked Nachman.

"We drove in silence for some time, which gave me a chance to enjoy the countryside. The landscape was picturesque, but picturing it two thousand years ago it must have been extremely difficult to scour a living out of this rugged land. Even with today's technology it's not the most productive land that I have seen. Lot's of stones in the fields, but there was some sparse barley waving in the slight breeze creating the illusion of water. I didn't see any irrigation equipment, but I felt that without it even this miserable crop could not survive.

"Since he hadn't answered me the first time I asked again. 'How far is Megiddo?'

" 'About nineteen miles or twenty six kilometers, but it will probably take us three quarters of an hour unless you want me to speed up. I thought that I would take my time to give you a chance to enjoy the countryside.'

" 'We're on schedule so there is no rush. I like the view. It's a great contrast to the type of farm land that I'm used to seeing.'

"We arrived in Megiddo about nine o'clock and began to search for a place to camp.

"Nachman pointed directly in front of us. 'There is a small knoll over there. It also has an old olive tree. A little breeze will be nice when it gets hot during the day and the tree will provide some shade. Even in the shade it's hard to get relief from the heat, but a puff of air once in a while helps.'

"I looked at the gnarled old tree. It wasn't much, but beggars can't be choosers. We were lucky to have the luxury of the shade regardless how sparse the branches. 'I'm all for comfort.'

"We drove up, stopped on the shady side of the tree and began to set up our little camp. It didn't take us long but soon the heat became quite unbearable. Nachman was right. When we finally sat down in the shade of the tree it was quite comfortable.

" 'It's going to be another scorcher. Do you fancy a big lunch or do we grab a sandwich?' He asked.

" 'I think that we can wait to cook until tonight when it cools off. I'm in favor of a sandwich.'

"My guide brought over the satchel with the bread, some cans of sardines and a few onions in it. We munched on the food. The bread was getting stale, but still tasted good. This was sort of a brunch since we had not eaten breakfast that morning. We washed the food down with water from our canteens.

"It was almost twelve o'clock so we were hungry regardless of the temperature. Many times when I had found myself somewhere in an arid climate, the only craving I had was for a drink, but this time it was different. I guess living outdoors and the work out one gets from being continually on the move makes one hungry regardless of the heat.

"Nachman stood up and surveyed the vicinity. 'Let's rest for a couple hours and then when it gets a little cooler we'll go and visit some of the digs and see if they have discovered anything interesting.'

" 'Do you know anyone digging here?'

" 'I usually find that I know someone at every dig. I have been as you say a few years in the business.'

"We brought our sleeping bags into the shade of the tree and after getting rid of some rocks so that the ground would be even I lied down and fell asleep.

"I was awakened by loud sounds of men arguing. I could not see them but could distinguish three separate voices. I got up and stood on my toes so that I could see over the box of the pickup truck, which still had some of our supplies in it. I saw three men talking but since it was late in the afternoon and the sun was in my eyes I couldn't make out any of them. I did recognize one of the voices. It was Nachman's, but didn't know which one, so I made my way towards them.

"As I got closer I began to make out the others even though I couldn't distinguish which voice belonged to which man. I finally got close enough to recognize Nachman. I couldn't place the other two, but when I got within a few feet I made out the two journalists.

"The two men had their backs to me as I approached them. They both turned and greeted me at the same time as though they had eyes in the back of their heads. 'Good afternoon Mr. Scott it's another beautiful day. We meet again.' They sounded comical. They looked like a duo on a stage, except I didn't feel any amusement. I thought that we were rid of them. Seeing them so suddenly again angered me.

"I could not hide my surprise and blurted out. 'Y..e..s it would seem so. Perhaps we could save a lot of expenses if we traveled together, because it looks as if we're visiting the same sights.'

"I could see Nachman's red face. He was just as irritated as I was with these two. I didn't know why, but just their presence bothered me. I wondered if they had arrived just ahead of us again, or shortly after we got there.

"One of the men looked at the surroundings. 'Interesting this spot. Do you know the story about this place in the Book of Revelation Mr. Scott?'

" 'Yes, I'm quite familiar with it. This place is mentioned not only in the Book of Revelation, but also by every great power of the ancient civilizations of this area. It was the Egyptians' first step to empire building and an important international road in those days. Being located in this particular spot it accumulated great wealth, which was coveted by every ruler in the area. For that the people suffered great wars and continual destructions over millennia.'

" 'You're well informed and quite a historian. Do you believe it? I mean the battle between the forces of light and darkness? If it could be construed that it would happen which side do you think would win such an encounter?' The man glared at me.

" 'I always root for the good guys.'

" 'Ah! But which ones are the good guys? In your cowboy movies they always wear white hats, and the guys with the black hats are bad because the producers say so. Is it that easy to distinguish them? Perhaps it's the other way around. The ones depicted as good guys are really the bad ones.'

" 'You're quite a scholar yourself for a reporter. I thought you guys stuck to the facts and stayed away from delving into areas of religion and spirituality. I don't recall your name.'

" 'I didn't tell you before, but no matter I'm glad to introduce myself. I'm called by many names but one of the most common is Lucis.'

" 'Doesn't it mean Light in Latin?'

"His eyes gleamed. 'How interesting that you know Latin, but of course you're right.'

"I didn't know what else to say so I turned to Nachman. 'That's a strange name for a person. I never heard it before. Is it typical to this region?'

"Before Nachman could utter anything the man interjected. 'It's an ancient name and does not pertain to any particular region.'

"He changed the subject. 'I'm sort of a student of conventional wisdom. One could say I've spent an eternity in the study of the human species and it never disappoints me.' There was a certain detachment in his voice as though he was talking about some aliens rather than us including him.

"I was annoyed at this reference. 'I'm surprised in the form of your sentence using the words human species like some animals in a laboratory.'

"I didn't like the individual so I thought if I said something to demonstrate it, then he and his partner would go away so I continued. 'Well this is where we disagree. I'm quite disappointed in my own species as you put it. Man's inhumanity to man over the millennia never ceases to amaze me. You would think that with all the achievements that we have made technologically, that we would have learned compassion and tolerance for one another. Yet we still think that some of us are better than others. It's ridiculous for rational beings to carry this baggage of bigotry.'

" 'You're quite a scholar of human nature yourself for a businessman. Don't you have to step on others to be successful and wipe out your competition regardless of the price?' His face seemed to glow at the pleasure that he derived from of this statement.

"I got angry. 'It would seem that business is always responsible for all the ills of this world. Some places it's even considered a dirty word or occupation. Yet the world can't live without it and everyone makes use of it to gain his or her own ends. No matter what walk of life you take, there are always people who crave for success regardless of the price, but it's not necessary. There is plenty out there for all of us. This applies to all walks of life.'

"He listened attentively so I continued, 'Even people who dedicate their lives to God sometimes fight between themselves to climb the ladder of success within their organizations, so don't load the baggage only on the business world. I find competition healthy up to a point and don't tell me about the media and the way you operate.'

"I didn't notice until I finished talking and really looked at the face of Lucis that he was gleaming with pleasure.

"He bowed slightly. 'Pardon me for being so insensitive. What could I have been thinking? Of course you are right.' He stared at me with a slight smile curling his lips. 'We should get together. We may have a lot in common and much to talk about.'

"I didn't want anything to do with him. 'Perhaps some other time.' I lied.

"I wanted to get away quickly so I took a stance that I did normally in business when I wanted to conclude the issue and leave immediately. 'I'm presently busy with plans of my own. Nachman and I must go now.' "

The priest stopped for a moment. He was surprised at the words that the *monk* had said to Lucis, there is plenty out there for all of us. That's not a common view of a businessman. The cleric saw his companion in a different light. Something was bothering him about the name of the journalist. "What was the name of that reporter again?"

"He said Lucis. I had never heard of anyone called by that name before. I thought that his parents must have felt he was an exceptional child to name him Light. Later to my chagrin I found out what it meant."

The priest looked puzzled, but remained silent.

The *monk* did not stop so the priest had to speed up his pace to catch up. The man in brown resumed his tale.

"At that point in time neither Nachman nor I gave it much

thought. When the name really hit us later we laughed it off. There are all kinds of nuts in this world who name their children after the most bizarre things. Imagine the arrogance of the parents who think that their child is the light. Perhaps it is in their lives, but the child carries the stigma of the name the rest of its life and is made a laughing stock by others.

"Except in this case the man was proud of his name.

"We left the two figures standing and went off to visit Nachman's colleagues. 'That was quite an exchange of views that you two had back there.' Observed Nachman.

"I was still aggravated. 'I can't stand them, yet they have a talent to draw me into a conversation and waste my time. I despise myself afterwards to have been lured into a discussion and steered in a direction that I had no intention of going.'

"We walked a few steps in silence, but the incident bothered me. 'Only after the whole thing is over and it's too late do I realize that I have walked into the trap. This makes me angrier at myself than them for being so stupid.'

"Nachman was absorbed in his own thoughts. 'You're right. That's exactly where I was going before you showed up. I think if you wouldn't have appeared at that moment, it would have been worse.'

" 'What do you mean?'

" 'They wanted to join us and their scheme might have succeeded, because regardless how I protested I felt I was loosing the argument. I didn't want them anywhere near, but the way they were manipulating the conversation I felt as though I had no choice. The reason for my shouting was that I was getting frustrated and couldn't do anything about it. I feel ashamed, because there was no good reason for me to loose my temper.'

"We walked over to a dig where one of the American Universities was excavating, and as we approached Nachman waved to a man with a wide brim hat. 'Shalom!'

"The man yelled back. 'Shalom!

"When we got closer my companion stretched out his hand to a gentleman in his late fifties. 'How are you my friend? How is your luck?'

" 'You know we always find something in this dig. Pottery is plentiful. With all the wars that this city or should I say these cities have seen. They were rebuilt each time on top of the old ruins. There is enough pottery to build a house of clay from the fragments. We also find quite a few arrowheads or an old bronze sword from time to time.' The gray haired man turned towards me with a quizzical look.

"Nachman noticing, turned to me. 'I'm sorry. I should have introduced my traveling companion. This is Brad Scott from Chicago. He's a businessman who is interested in history and archaeology. He decided to spend his vacation this year absorbing some of the character of Israel.'

" 'Brad. This is professor Jonathan Barber form Loyola-Marmount University.'

" 'How do you do.'

"The gray haired academic wiped his hand on the side of his pants. 'H..o..w.. are you. Excuse my hand, I have just been inspecting some of the finds.' He picked a fragment of a bowl in his left hand covered with dirt stretching out his right hand to me. 'You can see the condition of the find when we dig it up after many thousands of years.'

"I took his hand. 'Don't worry I'm sure that soiling one's hands is part of the price one has to pay in this profession. I'm glad to have the opportunity to meet Nachman's friends. The last few days have been very enlightening.'

"The professor peeked at me over his glasses. I could not make out whether it was further curiosity or if he was just trying to size me up.

" 'Nachman, come and see some of the items that we are preparing and you Mr. Scott come along. You'll have a chance to see objects that have not seen daylight for at least three thousand years.'

"We went into the tent where a number of bits and pieces of pottery all numbered were strewn on the table taking up about three quarters of the space. To my untrained eye they looked scattered helter skelter in no particular order, but on closer inspection I could see that they were all numbered in sequence. The last quarter of the table contained some metal objects encrusted in dirt. Inside the tent worked a couple of young women and one man. One of the women was drawing, the other was writing into a ledger while the young man was cleaning and scraping some of the jagged pieces.

" 'Nachman you go ahead and browse while I give this young fellow a quick course in archaeology 101.'

"He picked up a piece that was pointed at one end caked with dirt. 'Can you identify what this may have been in its days of glory?'

"I took a closer look. 'It seems as though it's some kind of a knife or sword, but it's hard to tell with all that hard dirt on it.'

" 'You're right this piece dates back at least three thousand five hundred years. We judge it from the layer in which we found it. There was a lot of soot and coal preserved from a disastrous fire and since this city is known for being attacked by invaders in the bronze age, there is no question that, its probably from one of those events.'

"I took the object from his hands and examined it turning it over from side to side. 'Very interesting. It's a wonder that people kept rebuilding the city if it was continually razed to the ground.'

"The professor muttered. 'The only answer that we can come up with is that the people kept coming back because of the location. It's on a trading crossroads in this area and I guess they figured it was worth the risk. You know what they say in the Real Estate business, Location, Location.' He jested

"We looked at a few other metal items and some pottery. Each time the professor gave me his version of what the article's history might have been.

"After a while Nachman joined us and we all went to the older man's tent for tea.

"Pouring the drink, the professor casually mentioned, 'There was a couple of strangers here earlier asking whether the two of you had arrived yet. Are they acquaintances or friends?'

"Nachman picking up his cup shook his head. 'We thought that they were following us. I think they try hard to give an impression that they're the ones that are following some plan, and we are following them.'

"The professor added some lemon to his tea. 'What do they want from you?'

"I listened while Nachman tried to explain. 'We don't know. They keep asking about a Key.'

"The old man added some sugar to his tea. 'News travel fast even between digs, I heard that you had found an urn with a message inside it referring to some kind of a Key. I also understand that the parchment was in a very unusual condition.'

" 'You're right news does travel fast, but there was nothing else on it except the reference to a Key. I sent the urn and the parchment to Jerusalem for analysis. We haven't received a reply yet.'

" 'Is this alluding to the legend of the Key of Damascus?'

"Nachman took a sip of his tea. 'It could be, but you know as well as I do that there is no foundation to this myth.'

"I added some lemon to my tea. 'What intrigues me is that for a nonexistent Key there seems to be a lot of interest. Those two guys claiming to be journalists appear just ahead of us wherever we go and keep asking about the Key.'

"The professor looked at me in a curious questioning way over the rim of his glasses. 'Perhaps they smell a story here. Can you imagine if somehow the legend became fact?'

"We drank our tea in silence for a few seconds contemplating what the professor had said, 'I don't know what Nachman's opinion is in this matter, but I have a feeling that those two guys are not looking for a story.'

"My companion put his cup on a crate that served as a table in front of him. 'I agree with you. They don't act like journalists.'

" 'Nachman here accuses me of being capitalistic, but if these guys think that this Key really exist can you imagine what they could get for it from a private collector on the black market?'

"The professor rubbed his chin. 'Of course an object such as this would be priceless both for a private collector or a museum. There are many unscrupulous people who pay a fortune for genuine archaeological treasures.'

"I put my cup down. 'I'm beginning to think that they are either agents for some international black market dealer or are dealers themselves. I don't think that they smell a story, but rather something tangible that they could peddle.'

"Nachman picked up his cup walked over to the kettle and poured himself some more tea. 'Then they must have a lot more faith in the legend than I ever had to even consider that there is some truth to it.'

"As we were finishing our drinks the professor lit up his pipe. 'I guess you fellows will find out sooner or later what these two guys want.'

"We thanked our host, shook hands and said our goodbyes.

"We walked back to our camp in silence.

"It was Nachman who broke our contemplation. 'I think that we better watch ourselves. Those two guys could be dangerous.'

"For the first time I revealed my feelings about the two journalists. 'I'm scared whenever I am close to them. Its foolish, but I can't explain it. I think that's the reason why I get so agitated when I see them. There is something about them that makes me uneasy. My opinion is that they would resort to whatever steps they felt were necessary to get their hands on this Key if it really exists. At the present for the life of me I can't figure out what they're trying to achieve by following us. We don't have this Key and they know it, otherwise I'm sure that they would have made an effort to get it. They must have obtained our itinerary somehow and to throw off suspicion they arrive each time a little earlier than we do just as you have said.'

"Even though I didn't ask a question Nachman seemed to answer what was on my mind. 'The only thing I can think of is that they really believe that the legend is fact, and we know more than we are telling, but it's preposterous.'

"We returned to our camp, broke out the provisions and opening a can of lamb stew warmed it up for dinner. Nachman brought out the last of the stale bread. Dipping into the stew helped to soften its crust and made it quite palatable.

" 'We better find some bread tomorrow,' he suggested.

" 'Why don't we buy some pieta bread? Wouldn't it keep better?'

"Nachman rubbed the piece of bread between his fingers. 'You're right, but being used to western bread I didn't think that you would eat it.'

" 'You would be surprised what I have eaten in my travels. To survive in my job you have to be adaptable, because you can't always find what you want.'

" 'I assume that you're quite successful in your profession, otherwise you couldn't afford this expedition.'

"We cleaned up our pots and dishes and made our preparations for the night. Most travelers in these parts sleep on a blanket under the clear sky. The tents and foam mattresses were a luxury in these circumstances. We said our goodnights and retired.

"I stretched out my mattress and unrolled my sleeping bag. When I lied down I felt some hard lumps under the mattress. Lifting it I found some stones that I had forgotten to clear underneath and threw them out of the tent.

"I crawled into it again and fell asleep immediately.

"I was very tired, but still couldn't find peace. I started dreaming, which turned into a nightmare. I began to dream that I was walking over a narrow suspension bridge. The walkway was very narrow, so that I had to put one foot exactly in line in front of the other. Under the bridge was a deep gorge filled with flames that created a draft and made the ropes that held the span together sway violently from side to side.

"I tried to keep my eyes fixed in front of me to the other end. I could hear a shrill laughter coming from behind me. Then I heard a voice a voice screaming. 'You can't escape me. I'm always where you are.'

"I stopped for a moment, looked back and saw two figures that continually changed from some hideous creatures to the two men that had been following us during this trip and back again to their original revolting forms.

"I was wet with sweat from fear and hurried to get to the other side. As I got near the end of my odyssey, I saw two figures in front of me waiting there. When I was near enough to make them out I saw the same two creatures with the same shapes that were behind me. I heard a shrill laughter and one of them thundered; 'I told you that I'm always with you wherever you go!'

"I was exhausted became dizzy and fell off the bridge, but before reaching the flames I awoke drenched in perspiration.

"I sat up in my tent for a while until I calmed down. It took me quite a while to fall asleep again. I couldn't get the nightmare out of my mind."

Chapter IX

"This key and the legend made you paranoid," commented the priest"

The *monk* barely broke his rhythm. "On Saturday, morning as usual Nachman came to my tent. He pulled the flap back. 'It's six o'clock. I'll make some coffee. Since we don't have any bread I'll find the biscuits and cheese. There isn't much of each, but it'll have to do.'

"I was very tired. 'I'll be out in a second."

"I closed my eyes, for a moment, and then I heard Nachman's voice at the entrance again. 'If you want to take advantage of the cool morning we better get moving. It's been half an hour since I called you the first time. It's going to get hot before we reach Munhata.'

"I glanced at my watch. 'I didn't realize that half an hour had passed. It felt as though I had closed my eyes just for a moment.'

"By the time I finished my sentence he was already on his way back to the bonfire. I heard his voice from a distance. 'I'll see you at breakfast such as it is. The coffee is ready.'

"Even though it was Saturday it did not seem to create any problem for Nachman. Being Jewish he should have adhered to the religious tradition and not work on the Sabbath.

"As I approached the fire, Nachman took out my tin cup and poured me a coffee. 'You know how much you want so get your own sugar. The whitener is in a satchel beside it.'

"I added the condiments to the coffee and took a couple large gulps of the hot brew. The drink cleared the cobwebs from my brain and I began to think more clearly. Curiosity got the better of me. 'How come you're driving today? It's the Sabbath. Aren't you're suppose to do nothing, especially something that would be considered as work?'

"For a moment I thought that I noticed some sign of regret on his face, but it soon disappeared. 'I told you I wasn't very religious. My opinion is that some things written in ancient times were created as instructions from necessity, but I don't think they apply in this day and age. People and especially slaves worked seven days a week so something had to be devised to give them some rest. Also time had to be set aside by decree for the worship of God.'

" 'Doesn't this teaching apply to these days? We're all slaves of something or other, our work our dedication to causes, or just plain greed trying to make a buck. These activities take up all our conscious time. We still don't have time to rest or pray to whatever God we believe.'

"Nachman was pragmatic in his reasoning. 'That's true, but today the decision rests with the individual. It's his personal responsibility and not forced on him by others so in my opinion the mandatory order is archaic.'

" 'I thought that everything written in the Bible was on God's instructions. If it's true then the law of God can't change, otherwise you say that God and his deeds are subject to modification. If so then he is not constant and therefore cannot be the eternal being that religions teach.'

"Nachman looked at me in astonishment. 'I didn't know that in addition to being a capitalist you're also student of theology.'

"I didn't reply to his sarcastic remark and dropped the subject.

"My companion picked up his biscuits and put some cheese in between them. 'We can get some fresh baked regular and pieta bread as well as cheese at Afula on the way to Munhata. We won't have to waste time waiting for the bread, it's baked early in the morning while its still cool outside.' "

The *monk* turned to the priest slightly. 'I don't know if you have heard of Munhata. It's not very well known today, but lies approximately nine miles or fourteen and a half kilometers south of Lake Tiberias or the Sea of Galilee as we call it today."

"I have heard someone mentioned Munhata once, but I can't remember who or when, my knowledge in archeology is limited. On the other hand you don't have to translate the name of Lake Tiberias, after all I am a Christian and a catholic priest or have you forgotten."

The *monk* ignored the sarcasm. "I guess I got myself so wrapped up in my story that I forgot to whom I was telling it."

"We stopped as planned and picked up our bread from a baker with an outside hearth in Afula and then found a small shop where we found some goat's cheese. We refilled our water containers for tea and bought a few bottles of drinking water.

"Surprised that Nachman bought some bottled water and finding a chance to get even with his previous sarcasm I asked, 'You told me that I could drink the regular water, so why did we buy this bottled water?'

"He ignored my quip. 'We probably can drink the water in our containers, but sometimes due to the difference in the mineral content in certain areas it affects the stomach. It may not bother me, but you being from the America may have a delicate stomach. We can't afford to take the risk of dysentery, which is very dangerous in these parts. If it's not stopped immediately the person can dehydrate and could die from before he reached a doctor or hospital.'

"The road snaked through the rough countryside. I wanted to know how much longer I would have to endure the pounding of the hard suspension of the truck. 'By the way I forgot to ask you how far is Munhata?'

"Nachman thought for a moment. 'I don't know exactly from here, but it's around 24 miles or 32 kilometers.'

"We arrived in Munhata with the sun still high in the sky in the early afternoon. The heat began to take its toll on us. Both of our shirts were wet from sweat even though the windows of the cab were open.

"When we originally picked up the truck I noticed that it had an air conditioner, but forgot about it. I had other things on my mind until I felt the sweat run freely from my brow as though someone was pouring water on my head. I could even feel the droplets forming before they came cascading down my forehead. 'Maybe we should turn on the air conditioner?' I suggested.

"Nachman did not reply and also did not make a move to turn on the switch. For a moment I though he didn't hear me. I was about to repeat my question when he pointed to an old crumbling wall. 'It's too late. We're here and in a few minutes we will be at the old dig. We can relax a few minutes and cool off in the shade before we unload our supplies. I don't like to use the air conditioner, because one can get a cold with the abrupt changes in temperature and I don't want anything to interfere with our plan if we want to meet our timetable in the short time that you have available.'

"He parked the truck on a level spot close to an old olive tree that was trying to survive in the sand a few feet away from a wall. We could see some shade protruding from the inner corner of the crumbling stones like short daggers.

"Nachman got out and looked around. 'There is no one here at the present. From time to time someone gets interested in this spot and comes to spend the summer here. There isn't much left, but one never knows. This place was inhabited by people well before the history of the Hebrews so the local universities have a limited interest.'

"I glanced at the corner of the old decaying structure. 'That spot over there looks good to me! I would think that it would be a good place for the fire later tonight. It will be protected from the wind on both sides.'

"He got out and began to unload the tents. 'You're beginning to learn. Why don't you stick around these parts? You might even get to like it. I could make an archaeologist out of you.'

" 'No, thanks, this isn't my game. I don't mind doing it for a week or two, but my idea of real camping is to travel around in a twenty foot motor home and park it where I have access to all services.'

" 'You Americans. You're like the rich of the last century. When they went on a safari, they took their silverware and china dishes with them.'

"I couldn't let him get away with that. 'What's wrong with a little comfort if you can afford it?'

" 'Nothing I guess, but one can also learn to like this mode of traveling. Comforts can be defined in many ways. Also when you lay down and look at the stars you come to the realization of how insignificant you are in the scheme of things.'

" 'Then why did we bring along the tents if we intended to sleep under the stars?'

" 'Sometimes you get a wind that stirs up sand and dust so its better to have some cover, but you could be just as comfortable outside as in the tent.'

"We pitched our tents in the corner of the crumbling wall and then went in the shade of the tree. We brought our sleeping bags and unrolling them stretched out to relax during the heat of the afternoon. I don't know how long we were there, because I felt tired and dozed off, which seemed like a few minutes.

"When I awoke Nachman was gone. I stood up and almost fell down. I had a cramp in one leg, but after a few steps it limbered up. I walked around the truck, then looked around, but could not see him.

"Beside the ruins the barren land stretched out as far as I could see. By this time the sun was low on the horizon and the shadows protruded from everything in sight like triangular sails or some grotesque creatures.

"I walked back to the place where I left our gear and then across the little compound to a spot where the wall had been breached, either by a long ago battle or diggers so that they could get the dirt out of the inside through a shorter route. Loose stones were strewn all around so that if one wasn't careful a false step could twist an ankle or worse.

"The ground by the wall seemed higher so I headed towards it. As

THE KEY OF DAMASCUS

I approached I could see a worn path. When I reached the pathway I saw Nachman at the far end stooping on his haunches talking to someone. It was difficult to make out if it was a man, or a woman, and since they were too far away I could not hear them.

"I was just about to call him when he turned towards me and seeing me waved his arm shouting, 'I'm coming! I'm coming!'

"I figured that he didn't want me to go to him; otherwise he would not have motioned that he was coming. I turned around and went back to our campsite.

"I was in the middle of unloading the rest of our supplies and gathering some of the large stones to form a circle for our fire when I heard a crunching sound behind the wall. As the figure crossed the path, I could only see the silhouette. The sun was in my eyes so I paused. I assumed it was Nachman. 'I unloaded the rest of the supplies and gathered some more stones to protect our fire from the wind.'

"There was no reply from the approaching figure, but I heard a voice come from another direction. 'I told you that by the time we'll be finished you'd be an old hand at camping and without a motor home.'

"I was on my hands and knees unrolling my sleeping bag that I had brought from beside the tree when I noticed two worn sandals facing me. Before I could see who owned them and whose feet they were I heard a voice from above. 'Good evening. You two seemed to be prepared for anything. You know how to travel in comfort.'

"The voice sounded familiar, but I couldn't remember where I had heard it and looked up into the face of the figure. He was holding his scarf covering it. He caught me by surprise. 'Y..e..s we've tried to be prepared.'

"At the same time I looked around for Nachman who came from behind the truck making a gesture with his hand to his head and lips shouting. 'Salem Alekum!'

"'Shalom!' Replied the man in Arab's garb. Since they greeted each other I figured that the man wasn't the one that Nachman had met at the other end of the excavation. I wondered whom it was that he had met and did not want me to know.

"Even though he was some distance away Nachman made a gesture with his arms inviting the visitor to sit down at the same time shouting, 'I recognize you anywhere Ben Jusef even from a distance!'

"The name sounded Arabic, hence the invitation in English. 'Please join us.' I wondered how he recognized our caller since the man was holding his scarf to his face that covered everything except his eyes.

" 'Thank you my friend,' replied the stranger.

"By this time the Arab had wandered closer to the fire and a spot where the rays of the sun were still reaching the ground. To my surprise as he moved his hand away from his face and the cloth fell away I recognized him from the bar some days ago. 'G.o.o.d e.v.e.n.i.n.g. I remember you from Dan Tel Aviv.'

"I was stunned to see the Arab at such a remote place where Nachman said there was nothing to find or excavate anymore, so it was curious that anyone would come here. Also in that fleeting moment I wondered to whom Nachman had spoken earlier if it wasn't the Arab.

"My thoughts were interrupted as the visitor came closer to me and stared into my face. 'Ye.s.s.s, y.e.s.s, I remember you. That was a pleasant evening we had in Tel Aviv and I see you took my advice and hired Nachman.'

"By this time my traveling companion had come closer. Overhearing our conversation. 'What's this I hear? Are the two of you conspiring?' He jested. 'I want to introduce…'

"I was still trying to rationalize the intruder's presence and was not completely coherent. 'I..I.. that is w..e..e..'

"The Arab responded. 'We met a few days ago in Tel Aviv and I recommended you to my friend here. I told him that you were the best in your field.'

"The young archeologist looked surprised and puzzled. 'Thank you for your faith in my abilities.'

"Nachman looked at me puzzled. I finally found my tongue. 'Yes this gentleman gave me your name, but I already had it from your uncle. I asked him to write it down because I didn't know whom he meant and whether you would be available since I hadn't talked to you yet. Also I wasn't aware that the person he was talking about would be you.'

"The Arab turned to me. 'Pardon my manners. I have not introduced myself to you properly. My name is Ben, Abou, Jusef.'

"Nachman reached for the kettle and poured some tea into three cups, and then stretching his arm towards Ben, Abou, Jusef gestured. 'Please have some tea.' The invitation sounded almost like an order.

" 'Thank you very much, you are too kind. Companionship and tea during these lonely nights is welcome. Allah be praised.'

"We sat down around the fire, which was beginning to flicker. The flames were getting smaller and smaller so Nachman stood up and brought some more wood from the back of the pick up truck. 'We'll have to buy some fuel tomorrow. Our supply is beginning to dwindle. We should have done it this morning when we stopped for bread, but I didn't think of it.' He threw a couple more pieces of a gnarled branch that we had brought with us and the flame rekindled.

"Ben Abou Jusef sipped his tea. 'So, you gentlemen are looking for the Key of Damascus?' He said in a matter of fact tone as though it was a fait accompli.

"I wondered what made him think that we were actually searching for some key. I was sure that either Nachman or I had not met him since my encounter in Tel Aviv. I was upset to think that my guide might have talked to him somewhere during our trip and had a personal agenda while I was funding this excursion.

" 'I don't know about any key. I came to Israel on a vacation as I told you in Tel Aviv and I'm following my plan.' I looked at my guide waiting for his version. After all if he had a hidden program, then perhaps we need to re-negotiate our agreement.

"There was a moment of silence. My traveling companion must have realized that I was staring at him. He looked up at me rather than the Arab. 'I don't know anything about searching for any key either.'

"His words were directed to me as much as Ben, Abou Jusef. 'I told you about the legend of such a Key, because you asked, but have no plans to go searching for it, even if it really exists.'

"The Arab smiled. 'My mistake. Since I found you gentlemen here I thought that you were looking for the Key.'

"Then he turned to Nachman. 'So your next stop is going to be the digs at Hatzor?'

"This time it was Nachman who was surprised and instantly turned to me as though expecting an explanation. I didn't say anything.

"Then turning to the Arab he said, 'Yes, it so happens that we are going to make that our next stop. How did you know?'

"Ben Abou Jusef didn't reply, but all of a sudden his face went somber and his eyes stared at the dancing tongues of flames. 'Good, because I have some business in Hatzor and I would like to return your hospitality.'

"Then he continued. 'Suppose I tell you gentlemen that the Key of Damascus really exists.'

"Nachman and I both choked on our drink. My guide was quicker to react while I was still coughing. 'I don't believe it. The legend has been around for many generations and no one to date has claimed to know the Key's whereabouts. Even if anyone does, the legend does not mention where this Key is suppose to be kept. You're saying that you know of its existence with certainty?'

"Silently we all took another sip of our tea.

"I taunted the Ben Abou Jusef. 'If you are so sure then you must know of its location and if you do I'm sure that a businessman such as yourself would have already made arrangements for its disposition.'

" 'You, my young friend still have a lot to learn. Perhaps after you hear what I have to say, you will understand that this object must be handled in the most delicate manner. You westerners especially, ridicule the ancient ways and thoughts, because your world is rich and has made great advances in technology. You feel that your materialistic society has nothing left to learn.'

"I got angry. Who in the hell was he to talk about greed? Most likely he was involved in looting ancient sights for profit. 'I don't want to insult you, but I don't think that materialism is only a disease of the west.'

"The Arab took another sip of his tea. 'Alas! That is quite true, but we do not replace Allah or make a religion of this vice. At least some of us speculate that mysteries still exist that are beyond our understanding, but you are so arrogant that you dismiss such things as the musings of ignorant and uneducated peoples.'

"Then quietly he went on. 'I apologize, let's not get into arguments over philosophical differences as I can see that you are getting angry.'

" 'You insult us. Call us arrogant and I should not get angry?'

"The Arab's voice became very soft. 'Forgive me again I shouldn't have said what I did. I got carried away. If you don't want to hear the story I will not bore you with it.'

" 'No. I'm interested, but I get irritated when I think that people try to insult my intelligence with folklore and tell me that it relates to actual events or time. Their attitude is always, you don't understand these mysteries because you are from the West. The Cliché sounds too much like the one our religious teachers preach. You can't question anything you don't understand that is written in the Bible because it's the word of God. I think people use these lines when they don't know the answers themselves.'

"The Arab turned with his cup towards Nachman who reached for the kettle to refill it. The young archeologist stayed out of this sparring between the Ben Abou Jusef and I.

"His cup full of tea the Arab turned to me. 'I will tell you a short version of what I know about the Key. Let's say it's my payment for your hospitality. Nachman will confirm that as we travel in the evenings we entertain ourselves by telling stories to each other. As you see there are no lights to read a book or electricity to watch TV. It gets pretty boring.'

"He began. 'It is said that Jesus Christ gave a Key to Simon/Peter and told him that it held the secret to the Gates of Heaven.'

"I interjected. 'Excuse me for interrupting, but it was suppose to be figuratively speaking and not a real key. Christianity teaches that it has to do with the forgiveness of sins and the Roman Catholics believe it is directly related to the confessional.'

"He paused for a moment until I finished and then continued ignoring my remarks. 'The legend states that there was a real Key, because the apostles were poor and uneducated men and continually needed not only parables, but also real objects to understand the rabbi's abstract teachings. There is a description of the Key. It refers to a heavy bronze object cut out in a strange shape, but nobody seems to remember the pattern of the lock.

" 'Further the legend expands that this is the same Key that God used to lock the Gates of Heaven after the fall of Adam and Eve. Even though the Key is made of bronze it shone brighter than gold, when it was in God's possession until the time of Christ. Originally it was as light as a feather and cool to the touch.

" 'The belief is that the Key would absorb and store the sins of everyone until it was time for judgment. As time passed and humanity's sins began to accumulate beginning with the original sin of Adam and Eve, the Key became darker and darker, it also got heavier and hotter.'

"I took a sip of tea. 'That is a most interesting tale for children around camp fires to keep them occupied.'

"Ben, Abou, Jusef glared at me and made what was to be a prophetic statement. 'Do not be so arrogant and cynical my young friend. If any of this is true you might have to come up with some pretty good answers when your turn comes.'

"Then he continued. 'According to the legend the Key was taken out of Jerusalem for safe keeping just before its destruction in 70 A.D...'

"The subject of this imaginary Key everywhere we went was beginning to get tedious. 'It's very interesting. Let's say there is some truth to what you say, why would anyone take this Key to a little town of Samaria in the middle of the desert where we found the parchment? The writings did make a direct reference to some type of key. The place is of no consequence and one would think that an artifact of this importance if it really existed would have been handled by very important people rather than a humble dwelling where the urn was found.'

THE KEY OF DAMASCUS

"Ben, Abou, Jusef made an indifferent gesture with his hand. 'It was actually destined for Damascus and finally reaching its destination stayed there for several hundred years. That is why the legend refers to it as The Key of Damascus.'

He continued. 'The rumors began to circulate within and outside the Christian community that this artifact was in the city, and that it had great powers. Everyone including the king with all the might at his disposal began to search for it. He offered large rewards for the Key. He also issued an edict that anyone knowing its whereabouts or possessing it and not informing the authorities or turning it in would be put to death in the most excruciating manner.'

" 'What about the Romans?' I asked.

" 'They didn't care, this region was so full of legends and stories that they ignored it completely.'

" 'Then why did the king of Syria want the Key?'

"Ben Abou Jusef never took his eyes away from the flickering flame. 'We don't know for sure, but it was surmised that he wanted to get his hands on it to gain the power that the Key had to destroy the Roman might.

" 'The situation became such that it was decided to move the Key to another place. This location was not recorded anywhere or at least no one has found it. During the move, the Christian Crusaders attacked the caravan and slaughtered everyone in it. There were men women and children, people of all beliefs, Jews, Muslims and Christians traveling with the caravan, but that did not stop the Europeans from killing them all. Some say it was the Templars, but since it's only a legend no one knows what the real truth is.'

" 'Even today does anyone know what the real truth is about anything?' I asked.

" 'That's a strange statement. It is written that Pontius Pilate said exactly the same words to Christ.' Observed Ben, Abou, Jusef.

" 'You seem to know a lot about Christianity for a Muslim.'

" 'Even though I had no formal education in this field I pride myself in my knowledge of the three religions. I have spent much time studying them as they are all intertwined in this region, and without knowing something about each one, a person would have great difficulty understanding what he finds.'

"I noticed that during all this time Nachman stayed silent and didn't comment or interrupt our guest.

"Ben, Abou, Jusef continued. 'It is said that during the first century the Key supposedly given by Christ to Peter was to open the Gates of Heaven and was accompanied by a book or a gate.'

" 'Isn't this story getting out of hand? I have never heard nor has it ever been revealed to anyone that such a Book existed. Nachman have you heard of anything about it?'

"He disagreed with me and made an affirmative motion with his head; 'I have heard of it, but a long time ago and never paid any attention to it. I gave it the same credibility as the Key.'

" 'Hear me out before you form any opinions.' Ben Abou Jusef pressed on.

" 'It is said that The Key carries the power of opening the Gates of Heaven, just as the Catholic Church teaches, but in the meantime it also stores all the deeds of each persons' life, good or bad.

" 'In addition it will unlock the 'book or Gate' where the names of all the people ever born or will be born until judgment day are recorded. Further the legend reveals that the Book and Key will be reunited that fateful day and the Gate will be unlocked.

" 'Once the Book is unlocked the information will be transferred from the Key to the Gate. Each name will be matched to the virtues and sins in the Key and the fate of the human race will be sealed. Until that day everyone while they live have an opportunity to make amends or changes to what has been recorded and stored in the key.

" 'It is also said that Christ has said to Peter Simon that it will not be He that would judge the masses, but their own deeds as recorded in the Book. He will be present, but his love for humanity would not allow him to sit in judgment. He said that the Father had given everyone a free will and all will be judged by their own deeds.'

"I figured that Ben Abou Jusef was distorting the Christian teachings to his own end. Only he knew the reason. 'This story is going beyond any religious teachings. It would seem that whoever made it up went to great lengths to add something to the Christian belief, which has no basis in tradition or theology, let alone any historical value. By the way is it a Book or a Gate?'

"The Arab glared at me. 'Can't it be both?'

"I was exasperated. 'I give up.'

"He continued. 'Believe what you want, but that is what I heard. Also it is said that if anyone finds both the Key and the Book, and unlocks the Gate, judgment day will be upon us. Furthermore if anyone can hold the Key long enough in his bare hands and can withstand the burning pain will get to know the secrets locked inside. Can you imagine if you knew the secrets of the powerful and rich of the world? What power you would hold?

" 'There are evil forces today that would give anything to have it in their possession to control the world. They could also end human kind, as we know it anytime they pleased or keep Heaven locked for eternity. It is said that these forces are searching for the Key and the Book presently as we sit here. They don't care what they have to do to get them.'

"I cut in. 'The Christians believe that the Key is only a symbol used by Christ to illustrate the power that He was passing on to Simon Peter and not something tangible that actually fit into a lock, let alone some Book or Gate.' "

After listening to the story for a long time, the Jesuit priest cut the *monk* off, "I never heard of such a Key or anything about any Book or Gate. If there would have been such things I'm sure that the Church would have known about it."

The *monk* ignored the remark and pressed on. He wanted to get the whole thing over with as soon as possible, but could not leave until he concluded his mission. He figured once he finished this business it would be the Jesuit's baggage and the future owner deserved the right to know the whole story.

"Ben, Abou, Jusef continued ignoring my interruption. 'The Key is real and the Book as well. There is enough documentation to prove it.'

"Turning to my companion he said, 'The latest account is the parchment that you, Nachman have discovered.'

"Nachman was surprised. 'How did you know about the parchment?

" 'The writings didn't mention any book. By the way you weren't at the dig when we made the discovery and very little news has filtered out.'

" 'I have my sources. I knew about it even before Mr. Scott mentioned it earlier. I'm an amateur archaeologist remember? I'm also a businessman and have many contacts. I don't think it matters.

" 'What counts is that The Key really exists. You two can think whatever you please.'

"The Arab's eyes were continually searching the dark. He was also fidgeting just as he did in the hotel, which brought back my frustration with him.

"Ben Abou Jusef continued. 'So you can appreciate that an item like that would be priceless. The legend recounts that the sinner can erase the sins as long as they are within the Key through atonement. In addition to some other supernatural powers the Key can also heal or bring back the dead to life. The story goes that Peter used it many times to create miracles. It can also give the holder a glimpse of heaven, hell and eternity just as the Gate can by itself without the other, but if anyone uses this privilege who is not entitled, the consequences are terrible.'

"As Ben Abou Jusef related what seemed to have been a preposterous old myth, his eyes glimmered in the dark like a couple of small flashlights reflecting the tongues of flames dancing in his pupils which were transfixed at the fire. He seemed to be in a trance.

"I thought he was getting carried away. 'It's a pretty good story for the evening campfires, but you can't be serious about your belief in its reality.'

"I turned to my companion. 'What is our plan for tomorrow, Nachman?'

"The Arab did not rebuke my rudeness, but only stared at me. His eyes shone like a couple of daggers in the light of the flame. 'Don't mock me, because of my belief and don't be too sure that you might not end up telling this story to someone else that is just as cynical as you. One day you may wish that you had never heard of this Key just as I do today.'

THE KEY OF DAMASCUS

"Nachman kept mostly silent. He sipped his tea and while deep in thought he stared into the flickering flame. 'Not that I believe what you say is true Ben Abou Jusef, but perhaps you are over dramatizing, as though you carry the whole burden of the Key and or the Book on your shoulders.'

"I wanted to find a hole in Ben Abou Jusef's story. 'Since no one knows where the Key is how can you be sure it exists?'

" 'No one knew where it was until now. I have it. I touched it and can assure you that the description and some parts of the legend are true. I haven't searched for the Book or the Gate to see if that part of the tale is true because I'm afraid."

"Nachman shook his head from sided to side.

"I couldn't believe my ears. 'Now the legend becomes fact around this campfire. Incredible!'

"Ben Abou Jusef continued. 'Brad, you said that anyone having it would sell it to the highest bidder and as I said the object is priceless. On finding it I planned to do exactly as you said.'

" 'Then what's stopping you?' I shot back, because I figured this was some type of ruse by the Arab to separate me from some of my cash.

" 'Once I touched it, my whole life flashed in front of me. I saw myself from birth to where I am today and believe me it's not a pretty sight. I saw my life not from my viewpoint, but from another's. I also realized the immense power that the Key yielded and decided that it must again disappear as it had for centuries. I could not withstand the heat to hold it long enough to see the secrets of others. Later, after some thought I realized that I didn't want to try again.'

"Nachman asked. 'Where and how did you find this Key since no one knew where it was hidden?'

" 'Just like your find of the urn. It was an accident. Since this place is deserted most of the time I came here to look around to see if I could find anything worthwhile and found the object a couple of weeks ago. A man must make a living.'

"I poured myself a cup of tea. 'Just as I said before materialism isn't only a vice of the West.'

" 'It is s.o.o.o.o' the Arab whispered.

"Then Ben Abou Jusef went back to his monologue. 'Since I have had the Key I've been in fear of my life and that is the reason why I wanted to meet you here.'

" 'So you have the Key here with you?' I asked.

" 'No. I would not dare to carry it around. I have it hidden in a safe place.'

"I figured that at least he wouldn't try to sell it to me this night.

"Nachman inquired. 'Who beside us did you tell of your find?'

" 'That's it I've told no one, but I couldn't stand it any longer. I tried to figure out whom I could trust. I have this feeling that eyes are watching me to see if I would lead them to the Key.'

"I cut in. 'Perhaps the two reporters are really following you not us.'

"I noticed a flicker of recognition and terror in his eyes that told me he knew about the two men, but he didn't say anything to acknowledge it.

" 'D.o y.o.u really think so?' Asked the Arab quietly as his head turned from side to side scrutinizing the dark.

"I figured that I had enough of his tale. I was tired so I excused myself and told my companions that I would retire.

" 'Enjoy your rest under the stars while you still can,' said Ben Abou Jusef as he glared at me.

"As I was leaving I waved back at my comrades. I picked up my satchel and headed towards my tent. Unzipping my sleeping bag I settled down for the night. I could hear in the distance the low drone of their voices. Not being able to distinguish in what language they spoke because I was too far and began to doze off.

"I don't know how long it was when all of a sudden I became lucid hearing Nachman's voice in English shouting, 'I don't want any part of it.'

"I sat up and could see that my companion was agitated and was waving his arms as the two men argued.

"Suddenly they became aware of me watching them, and became silent. They both turned towards me, then Nachman waved. 'Sorry,

Brad go to sleep. It won't happen again. Ben Abou Jusef and I had a small disagreement.' They returned to their discussion in low voices.

"I turned over and went into a troubled sleep.

"I guess Ben Abou Jusef's story must have made an impression on me because I began to dream. It didn't make any sense I saw the Arab trying to present Nachman with some object and the latter waving his hand refusing to accept it. Then the Ben Abou Jusef turned to me and handed the object wrapped in some kind of a cloth saying, 'Since Nachman doesn't want to buy it I'll sell it to you.'

"In my delusion I repeated the words that I had said during our conversation that evening. 'Just as I said before materialism isn't only a vice of the West and I don't want to buy it either.'

"Before I could say anything more the package was in my hands and caught by surprise I dropped it because it was heavier than I expected. When I bent down to pick it up I saw other hands grabbing for it and screaming, 'It's not yours. It belongs to us.' I lifted my head to see who it was and I awoke.

"It was still dark, the fire had burned down and I could see the glowing embers. I heard Nachman snoring in his tent by the crumbled wall, but the visitor was nowhere to be seen.

"I figured that they must have stayed up late for the embers to be still glowing. I tried to sleep, but couldn't and began getting a headache from lying there.

"I got up sauntered over to the fire and threw a couple of twigs that were left on it, then shaking the kettle I squeezed out half a tin cup of tea from it. I must have sat there for half an hour sipping the brew. It was still dark so I decided to go back to my sleeping bag. I glanced at my watch, pushing the button to illuminate the face and saw that it was five thirty. I crawled into the bag and this time fell fast asleep.

Chapter X

"Sunday morning during breakfast Nachman was in a jovial mood. I hadn't seen that side of him since I met the man. As we made small talk about our trip and the surrounding countryside he seemed to have a smirk on his face even though there was nothing funny in what we were talking about.

"He was like a cat playing with a mouse. I saw the grin on his face from the corner of my eye, but made it disappear as soon as he saw me looking at him. He would not explain the reason for his excitement. 'You seem to be full of yourself today. You appear to have something amusing on your mind that you're not prepared to share with me. Somehow I have a feeling that your pleasure is at my expense.'

"After I made it known that I knew about his behavior, he did not care whether I saw his grin or not. 'I wanted to save it until tonight. I wanted to celebrate with a cognac and enjoy the surprise, but since you're making an issue of it I'll tell you.'

"He paused as though trying to make sure of what he was going to say to me would be right. He kept his silence until I couldn't stand it any longer and pressed him on. 'It must be something good since you're making me suffer as long as you can.'

"He was excited. 'OK, when you went to bed I couldn't sleep so I made a call on my cell phone to my contact in Jerusalem. He told me that all the findings indicate that the parchment is genuine even though they can't explain its near perfect condition anymore than we could. They are putting their results down in writing. A full report will be ready shortly and I should be able to get my hands on it as soon as I arrive in Jerusalem. If I find that I can't be there within a week I will request to have them send it to Tel Aviv.'

"He paused. 'By the way you won't have to have the urn's test results authenticated by anyone else. I'm releasing you from our bet and you don't have to pay me anything. To know that the document is genuine is enough of a triumph for me.'

" 'You must be sure of its authenticity and be very pleased to forego five hundred bucks; or is there something else that you're not telling me.'

" 'There is nothing else. If I were money hungry I would have gone into business and not archaeology. Besides the university, my colleagues and myself are not yet prepared to release this material to the public or anyone else.'

" 'Oh? Is this one of those academic games that you people play?' I was annoyed at his patronizing attitude as though the information is presently a privilege of only a few academics and I felt like I have intruded into some private domain.

" 'No. Its just that sometimes if the news gets out prematurely, speculation and rumors could destroy or compromise the scientific report when it's released.'

" 'Since you are prepared to forego our bet, I can assume that you are certain of your facts and have won the wager fair and square. I'll pay up. Wagering is a debt of honor.'

"Nachman quietly went on, 'I told you that I'm releasing you from any obligation in this matter.'

" 'That's very sporting of you, but I believe that one should stand by one's word once it's given, especially in a matter of a wager. Therefore I will pay you at the end of this trip as agreed.'

"Nachman shook his head. 'You are an obstinate character. I will not argue the matter any further.'

" 'I didn't succeed in business by faltering on my given word.'

"My companion ignored what I said. 'The mystery thickens. I know that the parchment was packed in dry salt, but how it completely escaped decay is puzzling. The salt should have had some effect on the material. Normally it would have dried it out and the hide would have hardened into a solid scroll.'

" 'What puzzles me Nachman, more than the condition of the parchment is the Key. What kind of Key and what does it open? Perhaps the people hid some kind of treasure from the Romans? I wonder what is the real story about this Key of Damascus? It's incredible, but could Ben Abou Jusef's tale have some truth in it?'

" 'The argument is moot. Sometimes legends have a real basis in fact,' said Nachman.

"I resumed our original discussion. 'The writer seemed to be very anxious that the Key did not fall into the conquerors' hands. Can you imagine what this treasure would be worth today if it's gold and jewels? Not only its intrinsic, but also historical value.'

"I could sense Nachman's quizzical look. 'Why do you always think that treasure must at all times be measured in money?'

" 'Because whether gold or not everything today is measured in money.'

"He didn't comment, he seemed to be preoccupied with some thought. 'I believe that the text on the parchment does refer to the Key in the old Christian legend, but I don't believe in the rest of the myth in spite of Ben Abou Jusef's tale and his supposed possession of the object'

"He was right and I was getting tired of the subject. 'Since I have been on this trip everywhere we go someone's talking about this Key of Damascus and now you more or less admit that you believe that the Key exists'

"Nachman said flatly, 'I just mentioned that I believe the text in the parchment refers to it, but I'm not too sure that the Key itself exists.'

"I thought it was my turn to twist the knife. 'Yeah I know but your words don't seem to have the conviction now as they did before.'

"He didn't reply.

"Now I was hooked. 'I don't know anymore. The only time that a Key is mentioned in the teachings of the New Testament is when Christ said to Simon/Peter, I give you the key that will unlock the gates of heaven, or something like that. Of course we were always thought that he was only speaking figuratively not referring to any real Key and I tend to believe these teachings.'

" 'Some Christian you are. You can't even quote a passage correctly from your new testament.' He quipped.

"I told you that I learned all that stuff when I was a kid and I'm not too sure I believe in any of it today."

"Nachman went back to the find. 'I'm beginning to be convinced that the parchment refers to the Key in the legend. The place where we found it and the reference to the Romans attest that I'm right, but I'm still skeptical.'

" 'I guess you guys really thrive on these intrigues, but regardless which of us is right, it is fascinating.' I told him.

"I helped my companion to clean up our breakfast utensils. 'Are we going to stay here for the day or head out to Hatzor?'

"This is the first time I saw Nachman hesitate. 'I don't know. Perhaps we should spend some time here this morning and have a look around.'

" 'You don't believe that the Key would be around here even if Ben Abou Jusef's story has any validity? When he said that he had it stored in a safe place I'm sure he didn't mean around here.'

" 'No., but the ruins are interesting and I'll try to give you a short tour.'

" 'Ok by me.'

"We walked around the rubble and some of the restored walls with Nachman giving me the lowdown whether an enclosure was a living area or some type of workshop. We had covered most of it and I was beginning to get bored. There was nothing else until we saw a large stone in an open court.

"Nachman pointed to it. 'This was their altar. This is where the inhabitants sacrificed animals as well as grains and fruits to their gods before the arrival of the Israelites.'

"I stopped to take a picture of the stone. Nachman kept on walking and only then did I realize that he was scrutinizing every corner and opening of the walls. Some of them were too high for him to see inside as we walked by, so he stuck his head in the portals to get a clear view.

"I had to run to catch up with him. 'Are you looking for something?'

" 'Not really. I want to see if anyone has been camping here lately.'

"We walked up to the large stone that had peculiar markings on it and some grooves where Nachman said the blood of the animals would run down to receptacles near its bottom and made a cursory inspection.

"I noticed that somehow his enthusiasm had lost its passion since yesterday from being energetic in his descriptions of the digs to an attitude of indifference.

"It bothered me that the fun of our trip was evaporating. As we stood in the shade of a wall near the altar admiring the construction of the ancient people I noted. 'We have been together now for ten days and I have not seen you so depressed. Only this morning you were full of zest.' There was an awkward silence for a moment so I continued. 'I think that we have become friends so I will risk the question, is it something I did and you would rather cut our trip short?'

"Nachman was pensive. 'No, it's nothing that you did. I haven't been completely candid with you. The other night when you saw me talking to someone and I told you that I would be with you in a minute I did not want you to come and overhear us. The other person was Jacob from the dig in Samaria. You remember Jacob?'

" 'Of course, he was eager and quite helpful in the orchestration of the opening of the urn.'

"Nachman went on quietly, 'When we arrived here he was waiting for me with the news from Jerusalem. He was hiding behind one of the walls and when you turned your back on the truck to unload our supplies he signaled for me to come. I was sure that he wanted to talk to me privately so I didn't say anything to you. After we unloaded and sat down to cool off I waited until you fell asleep and slipped over to see him. He told me about the results of the tests, but I didn't lie to you when I said I called on my cell phone, because I wanted to confirm what Jacob had told me, but this is not what has upset me.

"After telling me about the results, Jacob told me that an Arab had approached him and offered to sell us the Key mentioned in the parchment. I have known Jacob from undergraduate days when we were together with Sarah at the university and I have never seen him so obsessed as he is with this find.'

"Nachman seemed crushed so I tried to cheer him up; 'It's an important find, especially with the positive results from Jerusalem. You can't blame him. As far as buying the Key is concerned, I think that it was quite admirable for him to tell you. After all he didn't have to say anything to you about it and could have made a deal with the seller. He could have tried to make a name for himself with the university and the world. Even though you were present at the instant when the urn was found, the dig is not directly under your jurisdiction.'

"Nachman nodded. 'You're right of course, but it's not the fame or the purchasing of the Key per say. He wanted him and I to raise the funds personally to buy the Key. Then he wanted us to sell the artifact to the highest bidder. I have never seen that side of Jacob before.'

"I chuckled. 'I know it's not funny, but its ironic how things seem to go in circles. Even greed.'

" 'Yes and that's why I'm so miserable. My best friend…In addition he told me that he had already been approached by some buyers who said that money is no object in this case.'

"I gasped. 'Wow! I should get into this business. In our dealings money is the only thing that we haggle about and then never get what we originally ask.'

"Nachman took a last look at the altar. 'Let's go unless you want to hang around and take some more pictures.'

" 'No it's enough.'

"As we walked back towards our truck I asked, 'I guess it was Ben Abou Jusef who approached Jacob about the selling of the Key.'

" 'Yes and after you went to bed he began to work on me. Since I already knew that he had talked to my friend I told him to go back to Jacob and not bother me. He told me the only reason he approached Jacob was to get to me. I got angry and that's when we woke you up.'

" 'My, my it seems that everyone carries on business including the non-materialistic Mr. Ben Abou Jusef. The way he talked I thought that he would be happy to give the Key away just to get rid of it.'

"When we reached our camp we packed everything in the truck and took off for Hatzor.

"As we drove I asked. 'Since we know it was Ben Abou Jusef who was trying to sell the Key to Jacob and later to you, do you have any idea who the buyer or buyers might be? It must be a group or someone that wants this Key very badly.'

"Something else bothered me in this scenario. 'I got another question for you. Why doesn't Ben Abou Jusef sell the key himself directly to the buyer? Why is he trying to go through a third party? I'm sure he could get a better price from the buyers without the involvement of someone else.'

" 'I don't know unless he is afraid of the buyers and wants to keep his identity secret,' replied Nachman. 'Perhaps he wants to keep his hands clean in case the authorities get involved.'

"We drove for a while in silence until we saw a small house, some twenty feet from the road. It had a bunch of branches piled up against its fence. We almost passed it when Nachman stepped on the brakes screeching the truck to a halt just pass the house.

" 'What the Hell..,' I gasped.

"Nachman looked in the rear view mirror. 'We almost passed it.'

"I looked all around and couldn't see anything except the house. 'Passed what?'

"Nachman backed up the truck to the driveway. 'Wood. Fuel. Remember we used up our last stick last night.'

"The pile did not seem very big to me. 'It looks like the few pieces piled against the fence are for household use. Do you think that the owner will sell some of it?'

" 'Fuel is scarce and we will have to do some hard bargaining, but I'm sure we'll be able to get what we want. Money talks.'

"I couldn't believe my ears. 'You, know what you just said? Money talks. One minute you tell me that the reason you're an archeologist is that you're not concerned with capitalism and then you say such things like 'money talks.' '

" 'It's a pity but the world does not run according to my principles.'

"Nachman drove the truck close to the fence, then got out and walked towards the house. I got out to stretch my legs. I looked at the wood, which was dry and would make good fuel, but I figured that we were out of luck, since the pile looked smaller close up.

"As I was contemplating how much we would need and more importantly how much the owner would sell if any when I heard voices from the direction of the house. I turned and saw an elderly man talking to Nachman. At first the voices were muffled, but they got louder. After a few seconds they seem to be shouting at each other and I was getting concerned that they were going to come to blows.

"Then all of a sudden there was silence. I looked and saw Nachman shaking hands with the owner. Then my friend reached in his pocket took out his wallet and handed the old man some bills. The owner pocketed the cash and both came towards me.

"When they reached our truck the elderly man went over to the pile of wood. He untangled some branches from the pile and began handing them to Nachman and me.

"When we finished loading and had tied the wood down I saw that the little pile was less than half of what we had originally seen.

"We thanked him and as we drove out of his lane he waved goodbye and then walked back to his house.

" 'Well I told you that we would get our wood,' said Nachman his smile widening as he turned to me. He was his old self-full of confidence.

"I saluted him. 'I got to hand it to you, but for a moment I thought that you guys would come to a blow, and I would have to become the referee.'

" 'You just don't understand. Bargaining is an art and one of the elements is the pitch of your voice. If you don't establish the pecking order in the early stages of negotiations you are lost. Finally there comes a time when both parties know that there is no sense in continuing because they have reached their limits. Then you either close the deal or leave without the merchandise.'

" 'I know that sometimes one could get emotional during the bargaining, but I never thought that it could be tuned to such a fine art.' I quipped."

"For us westerners the people and their customs here are strange, but if you would have lived here as long as I have it becomes quite normal," commented the old priest.

The *monk* continued. 'We arrived at the tel (mound) dig of the ancient city of Hatzor located in the upper Galilee fourteen kilometers north of the Sea of Galilee. The sun was still above the horizon. As we had done at the other digs we immediately searched for a spot to set up our camp.

"Nachman explained to me. 'There are two distinct parts. There is a lower tel to the north and the acropolis or upper tel to the south. Many large areas of both mounds have been excavated, first in the fifties, and then in the sixties. Now there are only excavations on the upper tel.'

" 'Since there is not much going on now in the north tel where the city stood lets make our camp there. We will have more peace and quiet, but we will visit both tells and meet some of my acquaintances in the active digs,' said Nachman looking around for a good spot for our tents.

"He continued with some pride. 'Normally it's not allowed to camp here, but since I'm an accredited archeologist I have the privilege of putting up a tent anywhere I go as long as I don't interfere with a dig.'

" 'There is nothing better than having contacts or privileges.

That's the reason I thought I should be with someone who not only knows history of the places that I wanted to visit, but also have some pull where ordinary people can't go.'

"Nachman looked at me not knowing whether I was being sarcastic or complimenting him. I didn't elaborate and thought I'll leave it alone unless he questions it.

"He drove to a spot in the western part of the lower city where a small fourteenth century BCE temple had been uncovered. At the back of the building stood a row of basalt steles (upright pillars of stone). He drove around them and we found the spot we wanted.

"We went through our ritual of setting up the camp. Placed our tents near the steles and got our teapot to boil some water. Since we had both coffee and tea we interchanged our beverages to whatever we felt like having that day. After we agreed to coffee for this day Nachman added the grounds to the boiling water and we waited for it to boil.

"As my guide broke some of the branches for additional fuel he commented. 'Lucky we ran across that place with the wood, otherwise we would have had to spend time searching around to find someone who had some to sell. Of course we could have used our burner, but I like a bonfire at night. It not only provides heat, but also light. The burner with its blue flame is good during the day, but at night...' He pretended to shiver.

"To show my gratitude I praised him. 'Yes and thanks to your astute business acumen we were able to buy some of it.'

"Again he looked at me, but this time I was sincere. 'I mean it. I'm not being sarcastic.'

" 'Then I thank you for your compliment.'

"By this time the coffee was ready and we poured ourselves a cup and sipped it slowly in silence for a few minutes.

" 'When I finish my coffee I'll take a run over to the south tel and see if I can find anyone that would guard our things while we wander around the area. These digs are far enough apart that we would loose our gear if its not guarded.

" 'That's a good idea.' I agreed. 'I'll organize our things so if you find someone perhaps we'll be able to take a little tour tonight. It seems like there is much to see here.'

" 'Ok. I'll try to get back as soon as possible.' He got in and drove off in the truck.

" In a short time I got our tote bags separated and left them by our tents. The others with food and general necessities I placed near the campfire. Then I poured myself a cup of coffee and sat down on a square building boulder savoring the black highly sweetened liquid. I sat there thinking about the history and the people that had lived there for millennia wondering what type they were, when suddenly a feminine voice came out of nowhere and interrupted my reverie. 'Good evening! Are you with any of the groups digging here?'

"I turned suddenly, to see a beautiful young woman in her late twenties behind me. I didn't hear her approach. Yet it was quiet in the late afternoon and I had heard my own footsteps earlier crunching on the stone chips or clacking on the bare stones as I moved around.

"The young woman was slender wearing tight slacks and a blouse tied around her waist that accentuated her figure. When she moved, her feet were silent like a cat's.

" 'Good evening. You startled me. I didn't hear you coming, and the answer is no I'm not with any of the teams digging in these excavations.'

" 'I'm sorry I didn't mean to frighten you. I guess I walk very lightly. I have been told by many that they never hear me coming…,' Her voice trailed off.

" 'What about you, are you with one of the teams here?' I asked.

" 'No just passing through. I'm traveling trough the country on my own.'

" 'Are you interested in archeology?'

" 'No. I'm looking for historical excavations. I'm interested in all aspects of life. Social, cultural and historical.'

"I was curious what a beautiful young woman alone was doing traveling on her own in this country. After all there are places where civilization is some distance away and anything could happen. 'Are you a historian, or sociologist?'

" 'You could say I'm an amateur in many things. I like to spend time with people and see what makes them behave or act the way they do.'

" 'Would you like a cup of coffee?' I offered.

" 'I would love one.'

"As I poured her a cup I noticed her standing there staring at me. I felt uncomfortable. I should have been flattered that a gorgeous woman was paying attention to me, but somehow she seemed cold and aloof.

"I filled the cup and handed it to her. 'Would y…o…u…l…i…k…e…some sugar or creamer?'

" 'Neither thanks. I like my coffee strong and black without spoiling it's taste.' She purred.

"I felt strange. After all I was a man of the world not a kid in high school. I got over any inhibitions I had with women many years ago. I did not know why she made me nervous and a bit afraid. 'I. I..'m sorry you did say that you take it black and no sugar. How absent minded of me.'

"There were a few seconds of uncomfortable silence. To keep the conversation going I asked, 'So are you working towards a degree or are you trying to get credits for post graduate work?'

" 'Neither, I'm what one would call a financially independent person. I travel and learn for its own sake and pleasure.'

" 'That's commendable. Many people with wealth waste their time on drugs, and booze until they destroy themselves.'

"I looked at her eyes that seemed to gleam with pleasure. She was lithe and reminded me of a large feline as she moved over some boulders to sit on a round stone. 'Yes, I know many people like that.' As she moved she never took her eyes off me.

"I didn't know what else to say. My mind seemed to have blanked out. I had to work to keep reality in perspective. She seemed to penetrate and occupy every part of my brain. All of a sudden she surprised me. 'Have you heard of a certain Key that seems to have surfaced and is being offered on the market?'

"I was swallowing some coffee and chocked. I was stunned. Who was she really? How did she hear of the Key and what was her interest in it?

"I felt like my thoughts were an open book to her, because as soon as something came to my mind she would pop a question about it before I had a chance to put it into words. 'I heard at some of the digs that a parchment was found with reference to an ancient Key. I also heard that this Key is available on the market, shall we say through certain exclusive channels.'

" 'Are you a collector?' I asked.

" 'It depends. I do not collect everything, but I'm fascinated by certain objects and things of interest.'

" 'What kind of objects or things?'

" 'It's difficult to explain. Not everything I collect is ancient, but I do find relics and certain religious finds interesting.'

"I took a sip of my coffee. 'Getting back to your original question, I don't know anything about any Key. I'm sorry I wish I had it, I would be happy to negotiate with you.'

"She smiled at me and tipped her cup to her lips. 'I'm sure that we could reach an arrangement that would bring immense rewards to both of us. I have a feeling that we'll meet again.'

" 'Are you leaving now? I have a friend that should be right back. He is very well-informed and perhaps he could help you with the whereabouts of this Key you seek.' I lied to keep her there.

" 'Thank you, but I'm pressed for time. *Auviedersehn* Mr. Scott or may I call you Brad?'

"She turned around and walked off briskly towards the front of the temple before I could ask her name. As she disappeared around a crumbled wall it hit me that she knew who I was and also said goodbye in German. Yet I had not told her my name nor did she have a German accent.

"I called to her, but she was already out of sight so I ran to catch up, because I wanted to get her name and find out where she was staying. As I turned the corner there was no one there. I looked around, but it was futile she was gone. I could have kicked myself for being so infantile.

"Once she was gone my mind became clear and all the usual lines that I had for picking up women came back to me."

"In your profession and travels you must run into many opportunities to pick up women as you say," commented the long-limbed priest.

The *monk* ignored the remark and went on as time was of the essence to him and he didn't want to waste it sparring with his old teacher.

"I went back and poured myself another cup of coffee looked around and listened to see if I could glimpse or hear the truck coming back, but everything was silent. I figured that Nachman must have run into some of his buddies and got tied up. When it came to archeology and artifacts one could keep Nachman talking for hours.

"Another good half an hour passed and by this time the western sky had turned purplish red as the sun slid just below the horizon. Suddenly I saw headlights appear in the distance.

"I checked the coffee pot, which was three quarters empty so I replenished the water and grounds so that we would have enough for the evening and the next morning. It's always easier to warm it up in the morning than to make a new batch. Some people think that if you leave it overnight it gets too bitter to drink, but I like it that way.

"Nachman jumped out of the cab and rushed over to me. His face looked drawn. 'You won't believe what I heard at the dig.'

" 'What? Don't tell me that someone found the Key or knows where it is. We were already told that by Ben Abou Jusef.' I teased.

"Nachman was so distraught that he either ignored my taunt or it went right over his head.

" 'No. Nothing about the Key or maybe it did have something to do with it. I heard that Jacob was dead.'

" 'Impossible you said that you just talked to him the other night at Munhata. How can that be?' It was my turn to be shocked. I couldn't believe it. 'What happened?'

" 'Apparently he was murdered.'

" 'Murdered? What do you mean?'

"Nachman went over to pour himself a cup of coffee. I warned him. 'Check it first. I had to make a second pot. There was little left of the first one after I gave her some.' I was waiting to tell him about my visitor, but it was trivial in view of this new development. 'So tell me all about it.'

"Nachman sat down on the same round boulder that the woman sat on earlier. 'They told me that one of the diggers found the body when they came to the sight this morning. It was lying in the Canaanite palace on the acropolis by a couple of stones that stand in the center of the courtyard. The current opinion is that these stones were used for cultic functions.

" 'The body was positioned in such a way and mutilated as though he had been sacrificed to some ancient god. The woman that found it is sedated and not too coherent. She keeps mumbling about the way he looked and the manner in which he died.

" 'They said he was tied up, stripped naked and with some strange signs carved into his skin, but the most appalling part was his facial expression as though he had seen something too horrible to bear. The witness said there were two gaping holes where his eyes were. The eyeballs were splattered allover his face and the stone as though they had exploded.'

" I urged him on. 'What was the cause of death?'

" 'They don't know yet. The police were called. They made a preliminary investigation, and questioned the witness as much as they could the poor wretch. She was so distraught that they figured they should let her rest before they questioned her again.'

" 'I guess we won't know until they get the autopsy results.'

"We sat there drinking our coffee in silence pondering all the events of the last week until Nachman said. 'This week has turned into the worst week of my life. Don't get me wrong I enjoyed our trip Brad, but when I think of those two creatures pretending to be reporters following us around, Ben Abou Jusef telling me that he had the Key to sell, then Jacob trying to convince me to join him in some crooked scheme and now this, I feel like throwing in the towel and going home.'

" 'I'm sorry that your pal ended up this way. I hope that the autopsy will clarify matters.'

"He was depressed again so I changed the subject. 'Perhaps I have some pleasant news that will change your mood.'

"I told him about the young woman and made sure that I spent time describing her attributes so that his mind would get off the grizzly thoughts about his friend. I embellished some of the descriptions and told him that she as much as promised to see us again.

"His frame of mind became lighter. He went over to his satchel by his tent and brought the bottle of cognac back. 'I think that tonight we are entitled to a neat drink unless you still want yours in some coffee.'

"By this time my cup was empty. I extended my arm holding my cup towards him. 'When anyone offers me cognac neat I would never be so vulgar as to suggest putting it in coffee, not that there is anything wrong with that.'

"He dumped the contents of his cup on the ground and poured us a generous measure of the elixir.

"We sipped away at the liquid that danced like quick silver in our cups whenever the light reached it from the flickering flames.

" 'So what's the plan for tomorrow?' I asked.

" 'This is a large area. I would suggest we stay here for a day or even two depending on how things go. I would like to hear the results of the autopsy and perhaps talk to the police. After all he was my friend and I'm interested to know what would have caused his horrible death. It's unlikely that they will have many answers, but anything they have to say might help me come to terms with what has happened.'

" 'If you want to leave of course I'll bow to your wish.'

" 'No. We can stay here for a while and a day or two won't interfere with my plans, but if it's any longer then I would have some concerns as I would like to see the Dan dig before I leave.'

"We finished our drinks and made our way to our tents.

"The cognac, the fresh air and the exertions of the day took over my consciousness as soon as I laid down, causing me to fall fast asleep.

"Even though I was tired the sleep was fitful. I began to dream about the girl, that gave me some pleasure, but somehow intermittently I could see Jacob tied up lying on a slab of stone naked with his eyes bulging from their sockets. On one side stood the two journalists and the girl, all three of them were staring at him and chanting some bizarre words. I stood on the other side yelling at them to stop and let Jacob go, but there was no sound coming from my throat.

"It was strange that the trio ignored me as though I was not present. Regardless of how much I tried to yell it was hopeless as though I was a ghost and was unable to interfere with their macabre ritual.

"At the end of the chant the trio bent down towards Jacob's contorted face, his mouth open seem to be screaming, but no sound came from it. His eyes swelled with terror, until they exploded throwing a black gooey substance all around the area, and the trio. All through this gruesome ceremony I was stiff as a statue bolted to the ground and could not move. My heart was ready to explode when I woke up all bathed in sweat. I sat up in my tent and thinking that I was caught in some ghastly casket began to flay my arms and scream.

"Nachman ran over with a gun in his hand yelling, 'What's going on!'

"He opened the flap of the tent with a flashlight and rifle pointing at me.

" 'My God man what's happened to you? You're all wet. Looks like you had quite a nightmare.'

" 'I'm..m.. sorry I did, but now I'm Ok.'

" 'Glad to hear it.' He glanced around the inside of my tent and then went back.

"I stayed awake for sometime with those horrible scenes of my dream flashing before my eyes. Finally they began to fade and I fell asleep. Even though the nightmare did not reoccur I had a very restless night.

Chapter XI

"Monday morning we got up around seven o'clock. This time Nachman didn't need to call me. I was wide-awake when I heard the clinking of some pans around the fire. I got up used my electric razor that I had recharged in the truck during our trip the day before and had a quick wash.

"When I arrived at the fire the coffee was on. Nachman handed me a cup after sloshing it with some water and dumping it out. 'You had quite a night last night. I thought that you were attacked by some wild animal or something, although there aren't any man eating tigers around here.' He teased.

"I went over to the fire and poured myself some coffee. 'I don't know about man eating tigers, but I've never had such horrible nightmares as the ones I've experienced this past week.'

" 'Do you think it's the company?' He quipped.

" 'Clever, but I keep dreaming about those two guys and now the girl.'

" 'What girl?'

" 'I mentioned it to you yesterday. When you went off to visit your friends I had a visitor.'

" 'I guess I was preoccupied with Jacob's death and did not hear much of what you had to say.'

" 'Let me tell you she was some looker. I have seen women, but this one was something else.'

"Nachman poured some coffee in his tin cup and sat down. 'Tell me about your visitor.'

" 'I don't know how and where she came from. She just seemed to appear.'

" 'Don't tell me you also see apparitions. Perhaps our sun is getting to you. Strange things happen to people when they suffer from sunstroke.'

" 'Don't patronize me. If you're going to make fun of me let's forget the whole thing.'

"Nachman's voice became calm and serious. 'I'm sorry. This whole business is bizarre.'

" 'As I was saying she came out of nowhere and after some preliminaries she asked me about the Key. She had heard that the Key is on the market to the highest bidder. While she was beautiful there was something sinister about her. I can't put my finger on it, but while I was fascinated with her she also gave me the creeps.'

" 'She had a coffee with me and then just walked off saying that we would meet again.

" 'She also called me by name. By the time I realized that I hadn't told her who I was and decided to ask her about it, she had rounded that corner over there, which as you can see is no more than a dozen steps away. I called after her and ran to ask her how she found out my name, but as I turned the corner there was no one around.'

" 'I checked every angle, but no luck. You can see that there is no place where she could have disappeared so quickly.'

"Nachman looked around and took a sip out of his cup. 'I'm not trying to be funny, or insult you, but these ancient places sometimes have a weird effect on people.'

" 'So what are you saying? I have become delusional and have hallucinations? What about the coffee she drank how do you explain it? I had to make another pot when you came back.'

" 'Of course not. Sometimes the mind plays tricks on you. We've all had it happen to us.' Then he tried to reassure me. 'As far as the creepy feeling; I know how it feels because I felt the same thing when we saw those two journalists.'

"There was a long silence then he asked, 'Are you all right after that terrible nightmare you had?'

" 'I'm not going to talk about it. If I do you'll only find another reason to say I'm sick in the head.'

" 'I already told you that I was sorry, but if you choose not to tell me so be it.'

"Nachman got up went over and brought the satchel with the food to the fire. He opened it and unwrapped some pieta bread and cheese. He handed me the flat pancake like bread and some cheese that he had cut from the slab. We ate in silence for a while and as the atmosphere cooled off I told him of my dream.

" 'How could you have known where and how Jacob died? Or did I tell you? If so then the rest is history, considering what has been happening. I mean the girl, the two reporters and the sun did the rest.'

"He poked the fire. 'Let's leave it all behind us. We have a good day ahead and there is a lot to see here.'

"After breakfast I helped him clean up our utensils and he packed them into one of the satchels. 'I hired a young fellow who should be along anytime. He will look after our things and the truck while we wander around.'

" 'Where did you find him and can you trust him?'

" 'He's reliable. He's a local teenager hired for some menial tasks by the professor heading up the dig. They told me that they could do without him so I offered the lad some money and he was glad to spend the day relaxing, and getting paid for it.'

" 'I don't know whether you know it, but normally the workers on a dig come from all over the world to gain credits towards their degrees or to obtain post-graduate experience. They don't get paid to gain this experience. In addition there are always a few locals that are hired for menial tasks and get a subsistence wage. The grants usually received from the sponsors barely cover the essentials, but there is always a little left over for miscellaneous expenses.

" 'Usually the head of the dig hires someone to run errands. This person recommends local merchants where supplies can be bought at the best prices. I'm sure that the agent also gets something from the merchant, but he still has to find the best value for the money, because he has to keep his reputation unblemished. If he doesn't then word gets around and no one will hire him again.'

" 'Wouldn't a person like that have tendencies to steal?' I asked.

" 'Not the experienced hands. As I mentioned before the ones that work on the digs regularly have a reputation to uphold, because if they are caught stealing the game is also over for them. The word spreads quickly in this business as you have found out during the last couple of days.'

"I looked around. 'While we wait I'll wander around the temple a bit for exercise.'

"Nachman didn't make any move to come with me. 'Go ahead, I'll finish off here and will be with you as soon as the kid arrives.'

"I wandered around looking at the strewn rubble in some places and inspecting a number of the restored walls by past diggers when I heard someone call, 'Brad!'

"Turning around I saw Nachman beckoning me.

"Before I even reached him, he started his recital about the old city. 'There are thoughts that Hatzor was built by Solomon during the nineteenth and thirteenth centuries BCE. The architecture and especially the city gates have a distinct character that is similar to the gates in Megiddo, and some excavations in Jerusalem. Yet no concrete evidence has been found to confirm that Solomon even existed except in the Bible. You will understand as we walk through these ruins that this city was a very rich one during the Bronze Age.

" 'As I mentioned before the digs and the city is divided into two parts. The upper tel here or the acropolis, and there the lower tel where the city stood. Along the western and northern sides a huge earthen rampart was constructed. A wall protected the Eastern side above a steep slope. This is where the two city gates were located.

" 'You can understand the interest in the lower tel because this site contained public buildings where the administration was located.'

"We went through a large portion of the lower tel. As the morning passed the sun got hotter and beat down on us mercilessly. I checked my watch noticing that it was eleven thirty. I took another swig from my water flask. The liquid was protected from direct rays by a canvas material so it kept it drinkable, otherwise it would probably have been hot enough to steep tea. I came up to Nachman who was pouring some water on his head to cool himself. 'By the weight of my hip flask I think I'm getting to the end of my water supply.'

"He wiped his brow with a bandanna. 'It's getting close to noon. By the way I forgot to tell you that the director of the dig invited us for lunch. He wants to meet you and probably give you a lesson in archaeology 101. Remember these guys are essentially teachers and never pass a chance to show off. I think it would be faster and give our feet a break if we took the truck,' suggested Nachman.

"I climbed into the truck. 'I'm looking forward in meeting the gentleman. With all the lessons I'm getting at the different locations do you think that one of them would give me a credit towards a degree in archaeology if I decided to change my profession?' I quipped.

" 'I doubt it. They'd want you to get your hands dirty and earn it, but they're always ready to give a lecture on their digs except when its something very important and they want to keep it secret until a formal announcement is made.'

" 'It' a break for us that we won't have to cook anything in this blasted heat.'

"Nachman gave me a preamble before we got to meet the professor. 'The dig is supervised by a German, but the project is a joint venture between the US, Germany and Israel. The man in charge is professor Shulehausen. He's an expert in his field and a great gentleman. He wanted to meet with you when I told him that you have traveled extensively in Germany and spoke his language.'

"As we approached the dig we could see the workers file towards a tent that was set up to serve as a mess hall. Someone must have warned the professor, because as soon as we parked the truck the old fellow was outside the tent heading towards us with his outstretched hand.

" '*Willkommen*! Welcome!'

"Nachman reached out greeting the host. 'Shalom again Professor Shulehausen. I brought my friend that I told you about last night. Meet Brad Scott.'

"He came towards me. '*Willkommen* Mr. Scott Nachman told me that you speak excellent German."

" '*Danke Herr Professor*. I was also looking forward in meeting you. Nachman told me that you are a great expert in your field, and call me Brad. My father is called Mr. I'm just Brad.'

"For a moment the professor was lost. 'Your father?...But of course. Ha! Ha!'

"He stretched out his hand to me. 'It's a pleasure meeting you Brad.' The professor had a firm grip and shook it a few times too many for my liking, but it's a common European practice when the person wants to demonstrate his sincerity of being happy to meet you.

" 'Thank you professor.'

" 'Nachman! Brad! Come inside and have some lunch. It's nothing much, but in this heat its enough. We usually have a heavier meal at night.'

"The inside of the tent was organized in a cafeteria style. On one side there were a number of tables set up end-to-end where stood some Thermos' marked coffee, tea, milk, and water. Then further were pans with bread and plates containing cheese and a bowl with preserves. There were other baskets with fresh fruits.

"We stopped for a moment at the entrance. The professor pointed towards the long table. 'Brad, Nachman don't be shy. Help yourselves. The dishes, cups and utensils are here at this end.'

" 'Thank you.' Beamed Nachman 'You lead the way and we'll follow.'

" 'Very well.' He brushed past both of us towards the utensils.

"As we filled our trays with the food and the drinks the old man said, 'For Brad's benefit I must tell you that the milk comes from a goat. Europeans enjoy it, but I know that not all Americans like the distinct flavor and the sharp taste.'

" 'Thank you for your warning. I'm not a milk lover regardless where it comes from except in coffee. There I like it.'

"We found a little table at one corner of the tent. As we sat down and began our meal the professor extended his sympathy to Nachman. 'I'm sorry again about your friend Jacob. That was a dreadful business. At my age I know that death stares us all in the face, but that's no way for anyone to die.'

" 'Thanks. Have you heard anymore about the autopsy or any other news?'

"As I ate I listened to the conversation between the two at the table with apprehension.

" 'No, but the police said that they would be back today. I don't know whether to bring us news of the autopsy or more questions.'

"Nachman put some preserves on his bread. 'What I don't' understand is this thing with his eyes. How can anyone's eyes just explode? Regardless of fear or anything else.'

"The professor took a sip from his cup. 'There are many things we still don't understand in spite of our advances in science or the psyche. Who knows what reaction you or I would have if we were confronted by something that our brain could not tolerate. Who knows what would be the final outcome?'

"As they spoke I thought of my last night's dream, but didn't have the courage to tell it to a stranger for fear of being ridiculed.

"Through my reverie I heard the professor ask. 'What do you think Brad?'

" 'I..I.. don't know. All I can say is that this trip turned out to be a greater adventure than I had anticipated.'

" 'I guess we'll know more when the police come. That is if they come.' Concluded our host.

" 'Brad how would you like to view some of the artifacts that we have uncovered? Nachman do you want to come along?'

" 'No. I want to wander around the dig if you don't mind. I want to talk to some of the diggers.'

" 'If it's about Jacob there is only one person that saw anything. That is if there was anything to see, and she has taken some medicine to help her relax. She is off for the day and is resting in her sleeping quarters. If you intend to talk to her be careful she is very vulnerable right now. Try not to upset her.'

" 'I do want to talk to her and I'll try my best.' Nachman left us and went off in the direction of a group of tents.

"When we finished our tea the professor stood up and pointed toward to a table where the soiled cups and dishes were piled. After we disposed of our utensils he motioned to me. 'Brad let's go and I'll show you some of our finds. They are very interesting. This place was rebuilt many times on the ashes of the previous destructions.'

" 'The majority of the digs that I have visited with Nachman seem to have been built and rebuilt on the ashes of a previous settlement.'

" 'That's man's legacy,' replied the professor.

"We entered another tent where a number of artifacts were scattered on a table with some notebooks beside them.

"Professor Shulehausen picked up an ivory carving of an ugly figure that looked like half beast half human. 'Isn't this beautiful. Look at the work of the ancient carvers. The skill of the artisan.'

" 'Amazing.' I breathed. There was nothing else I could say because if I really told the professor what I thought of the statuette he would have thrown me off the dig as an ignoramus. That part would have been true, but no one could have told me that the horrible thing he was displaying was an object of beauty.

"We went through a number of bronze figurines, pieces of jewelry and statuettes made of clay.

"We spent a couple of hours browsing though the relics with the professor giving me the run down of each piece and their history.

"I got immersed in the old man's explanations and completely forgot about the heat. Time flew by quickly, but it was beginning to get tiresome. We were inspecting a clay bowl when a young girl entered the tent. 'Everyone is waiting for your lecture professor. The other two are finished.'

"The professor glanced at his watch. '*Mine Gott*! I got so wrapped up that I completely forgot. It's my turn today to lecture on yesterday's finds.'

" 'Brad, are you interested in sitting in?'

" 'I wouldn't mind, but I should find Nachman to see what our plans are since he's the leader of our little expedition.' I lied because even though the last hour was interesting I had enough.

"I wandered outside until I saw my guide standing talking to a girl near the east side of the palace being excavated.

"As I approached them he beckoned me. 'Come here I want you to meet someone.'

"Since originally I didn't know whether he wanted me in on his conversation I took my time, but now that the invitation was granted I quickened my pace.

"As I came up Nachman gestured to a young woman in her late twenties beside him. 'I want you to meet Dorothy. She would rather we call her Dot. She's from the University of Nebraska. She was the unfortunate person who found Jacob yesterday.'

"I shook her hand. 'My name is Brad Scott. I'm happy to meet you Dot. It must have been a terrible shock. Are you all right? I wish it was under different circumstances.'

" 'I'm beginning to come around, but the vision…It's like a bad dream.'

"Nachman reassured her. 'We'll not ask you to repeat what you have already told the police and the professor, but can you think of anything else that might have skipped your mind? No matter how trivial it might seem to you.'

" 'Nothing…Wait a minute…when I arrived even though I could not see anyone I heard this strange sound. I didn't say anything to anyone about it because I thought that it might have been the wind blowing through the ruins.'

"I became very interested when she mentioned the strange sound, because of the dream. 'I know that it's too much to ask, but could you make out the sound or sounds?'

" 'What do you mean?'

" 'Think. What kind of a sound was it? I know that you said it may have been the wind, but was there anything else that you can remember about it?'

"She frowned for a moment. 'Yes I remember now. It was more like a chant.'

" 'Was the chant of one pitch? I mean did it sound like it came from one person or several?'

"Nachman stood there motionless looking at us as though we were performing for his benefit.

" 'Now that you mentioned it there was something about it that sounded like a mixture of baritone and one of higher pitch voice, but as I said there was no one present when I arrived. The police said that the preliminary examination revealed that he had been dead for several hours.'

"Nachman looked puzzled. 'What's your fascination with the sounds Brad?'

" 'Oh nothing. I was interested in what she had heard. I wanted to know whether she could have overheard any talking or part of the words of the ceremony, if there was one.'

"Nachman's voice was gentler as he turned to her. 'Could you show us the spot where you found him Dot?'

"She pointed towards the partially excavated Canaanite palace on the acropolis. 'It was in the courtyard on that raised platform. I'm sure that you'll find it without me. I..I.. really.. don't want to go there again.'

"Nachman thanked the woman. 'You helped us more than you know. Go and rest. We'll take a walk over there by ourselves.'

"As we walked in, there was a large raised stone in the center of the courtyard. To me it looked like some type of altar. It had grooves in the corners. It was similar to other altars that we had seen at some of the other digs. Nachman again pointed out to me the channels that were made to let the blood flow down into holding vessels from the offerings. In some cases the priests drank this blood after making a gesture to the gods. There were two enormous stone bases, one supporting the massive columns at the entrance of the hall.

"It was still light when we walked into the courtyard and as we approached the lateral stone we could see some stains on it. It was quiet and eerie. Both of us shivered as though we had entered a freezer.

"Nachman walked over towards it. 'Let's have a closer look.'

"Approaching I could see some postings. 'I see some kind of signs.' As we got closer I saw a cordoned off area. The notices were in several languages, but we were too far to make out what they said.

"When we got close enough to read them I recognized some words in English. It was a police poster warning people to stay out of the area.

"Nachman looked around and not seeing anyone stepped over the rope. I followed him. 'Aren't we going to get in trouble with the police by disobeying them?' I asked.

" 'There is no one around and I just want to take a quick look. As long as we don't touch anything what harm can we do?'

"Nachman walked around the flat stone looking at the grooves. I stood there for a minute and all of a sudden I had a flashback of my dream, but instead of Jacob lying on the slab it was I and could see through his eyes. The three human figures that I saw in my dream had turned into some hideous creatures. They were getting closer and closer to my face and were so horrible that my heart started pounding as though it would jump right out of my chest.

"All of a sudden I felt someone shaking me and heard someone shouting. 'My God man! What's the matter with you? Brad what's the matter?'

"I awoke from my trance and I swear that if Nachman hadn't been there to shock me back to reality I don't know what would have happened.

" 'Your face…Your eyes…If you hadn't come around you might have ended up like Jacob. What happened?'

" 'N..o..t..h..i..n..g I saw myself on the stone looking up to some unholy trio. They were hideous and scared the hell out of me or should I say could have scared me right into hell.'

" 'Are you sure you're all right now?'

" 'Y..e..s..'

"Nachman stooped down and pointed to the bottom of one of the groves. 'Strange. See how the groves show traces of blood, but when they get to the bottom there is nothing. It's almost as though it was caught in receptacles.'

"There was still enough light so that I could see the streaks in the grooves. 'Didn't some of the ancient religions practice human sacrifices?'

"Nachman kneeled down at the groove and inspected it closely. 'Yes. They did.' Then pointing to the channel he whispered. 'By the flow of the blood it looks as if it was a sacrifice rather than just a random killing. Brad, I don't know whether you are aware, but the Israelites considered some of the pagan gods as the incarnations of evil, which we now call devils. Have you read the Bible?' Asked Nachman.

"When I didn't answer he continued. 'The Bible states that God told Joshua and other Israeli kings to destroy these pagans not only because they worshipped other gods, but that they worshipped and practiced evil rites.'

"A shiver ran down my spine. 'I don't know about you, but this place gives me the creeps. Let's get out of here.'

" 'I've seen all I want to see. Let's go.'

"We went back over the rope, then once outside of the forbidden area, we continued back out of the palace in silence. Then Nachman cocked his head. 'Brad, listen.'

"I had to stop for a moment to silence my steps. 'Listen to what? I don't hear anything.'

"Again we began our trek. It was amazing a how quickly the afternoon had passed and dusk arrived. We looked towards the fire that the diggers had lit in the distance. Nachman gawked around. 'The weird part is that there is absolutely no sound. No birds, crickets, other sounds not even a breeze around this place.'

"I had to stop again. I turned around several times on my heels to make sure that I wasn't missing anything. 'You're right nothing. An absolute stillness.'

"As soon as we stepped outside the portals of the palace everything became normal. It was uncanny, but neither one of us wanted to admit that something weird had occurred. It was Nachman that broke the silence. 'Amazing how the senses play tricks on you when you find yourself in an unusual situation. First you with your vision and then that eerie silence.'

"My companion lit a cigarette. 'Let's go to the camp and see what we can pick up there.'

"Since it was dusk I was concerned about our gear. 'What about the guy watching our goods? How long is he going to stay?'

" 'He's Ok. He'll stay there all night if necessary as long as we pay him. It's more money in his pocket.'

" 'Do you think that the professor got any more news? He did say that the police was suppose to come again today.'

"Nachman took a drag from his cigarette. 'Perhaps the police have already been there. We have been wandering around all afternoon so who knows. Lucky that some of the walls offered protection from the sun, otherwise we would have had to wait until the heat was bearable to make our rounds.'

"As we got closer to the fire we could see that there was a van parked beside our truck. It was dark in color and had no markings.

"When we got closer to the fire the crowd turned to look at us. Two men stood up and came towards us. I could not distinguish who they were until they came closer.

"One of the men was the professor who greeted us warmly. 'I told you that the police promised to come back, but the inspector didn't show up until late this afternoon.'

"Beside him walked a middle-aged man, short and stocky. He came towards us extending his hand to Nachman. 'Shalom.'

"My guide grasped the man's hand. 'Shalom inspector. I didn't know that the military police traveled this far from Tel Aviv to investigate a simple murder case.'

" 'This case may be a lot of things, but one thing it isn't, and that's a simple murder case.'

" 'Come, sit by the fire and have a cup of coffee,' invited professor Shulehausen.

" 'Thank you for the coffee, but I want to talk to Nachman privately,' replied the inspector before either one of us could answer.

"The inspector turned to me. 'Nachman you didn't introduce your friend.'

" 'I beg your pardon how rude of me. This is Brad Scott he's from America. We are traveling together visiting some digs in Israel.'

"The inspector extended his hand. 'Welcome to Israel.' He didn't waste any time. 'I understand that you met the deceased at the Samaria dig.' It was a statement and not a question.

" 'Yes for the short time that we were there.'

" 'Then perhaps you would be interested in joining Nachman and me.' Again it was not an invitation but rather more like an order.

" 'I would be happy if I could assist you in any way I can inspector.'

"The policeman looked around and pointed to a couple of large stone slabs about twenty feet away from the fire. 'That looks like an ideal spot. The dusk and the fire are bright enough to give us some light if I have to make some notes. In any case I brought a lantern.'

"This time he turned to the professor and still talking to us. 'Now let's accept the professor's invitation and fill our cups.'

"One would think that the host was the inspector rather than the old gentleman the way he took control of the situation.

"We didn't move for a minute, until the professor cut in. 'By all means gentlemen help yourselves, and when the inspector is finished, please join us for some conversation.'

"Professor Shulehausen fell in beside me as I walked. 'Brad I would like to hear your opinion of Germany and the places you had a chance to visit.'

"The policeman was already on his way to the fire.

"By the time we got there the inspector had his cup full and headed towards the area he had designated. As one of the diggers was filling my cup another said, 'Nachman, come and sit over here, we would like to talk to you about your find in Samaria.'

" 'I can't now, but my friend and I will join you shortly after we are done with the officer.'

"Another turned to Nachman. 'I guess it's your turn. We already had ours.'

"I waited and then both of us walked over to meet the inspector.

"He was sitting on a slab of stone and pointing to one facing him said, 'Please, sit down. It's a dreadful business.'

"Unceremoniously he went into his spiel. 'We have received the results of the autopsy and it's most peculiar. The pathologist says that it's difficult to determine the cause of death.'

"Nachman looked at the inspector. 'I don't understand.'

" 'There were two major traumas that could have caused his death, but so far it has not been determined which one. One assumption is that he died of fright as his heart and his aorta had virtually exploded. Of course this could have also been due to high blood pressure, but there was no evidence, such as hardening of the arteries or other indications that he had this condition.

" 'The second is of course that he died from the wounds that were inflicted on his body. Whoever did this must have had a terrible grudge against him. Beside the carvings of ancient symbols, his gut was slit open from the top to the bottom. In this case he might have still been alive and experienced terrible pain before his heart gave out.'

" 'Could this have been a political act by some terrorists?' I asked.

" 'One never knows, but up to now we never had a case such as this one. It almost looked as though he was sacrificed during some barbaric ritual.'

"The inspector went into his pocket and brought out a small notepad. 'I told you fellows everything we have. Now you tell me what you know. Who wants to go first?'

" 'I might as well since I know nothing about Jacob.' I wanted to get this over with as soon as possible. 'My only contact with him was in Samaria when he was very helpful volunteering information on an artifact that was discovered that day. Otherwise I don't know nor have I ever met him before.'

" 'Ok. What about you Nachman? I understand you knew him from your undergraduate days. What can you tell me?'

" 'Not much either I knew him and we were friends, but not close so I don't know what I can add to all of this business.'

" 'Can you tell me about any of his close friends? Were there any clashes with anybody about a girlfriend?'

" 'Not that I know. As far as his friends are concerned I really can't tell you anything about them as I don't know any of them.'

" 'What about business or his financial affairs?' The inspector's voice told me that he knew something and was fishing, but I didn't get involved. This was Nachman's show.

" 'I don't know anything about his finances.'

"The inspector was making some notes in his book and didn't raise his head from his writing. 'We checked into his finances and found that he was deeply in debt. He was quite a ladies man and when he traveled it was always first class all the way. Of course on his modest income he was getting into trouble.

" 'Nachman I'm sure that you know education is not cheap so it would be virtually impossible for anyone to carry on a lavish lifestyle and pay for one's studies unless one is well off, and Jacob was not that lucky.'

"I was sure that the inspector was baiting Nachman to see whether he would volunteer any additional information.

"My travel companion took the opportunity to think of his next move by taking a deep drink from his cup. Then he told the inspector about Jacobs proposition of buying and selling the Key.

" 'I told him that I wasn't interested in any illegal transactions and since the Key seems to be a figment of peoples imagination rather than a real artifact I didn't bother reporting our conversation as the law requires. After all the legend has been around for a long time and no one has taken it seriously.'

"The inspector lifted his eyes from his notebook. 'What Key are we talking about here and is anyone taking it seriously now?'

"Nachman sipped his coffee and said in a barely audible voice as though he was ashamed to say it out loud. 'It's an old Christian legend about a Key that Christ gave to his apostles. It has been widely circulating as long as I can remember. I'm sure you've heard it and probably know other such myths.'

"While making note in his book the inspector commented, 'So after all these centuries this Key seemed to have surfaced or at least certain people think it has, and perhaps it even had something to do with Jacob's death. He must have taken it seriously since he wanted to make you a partner in a business venture involving this Key.'

"The inspector turned to me. 'What about you Mr. Scott you are a Christian am I right? What do you think about this Key business? I must be truthful with you we have done some checking and find you very interesting. You are a successful businessman who decides to take a tour of Israel with a private guide so that there are no others to witness what you may really be doing here. We also uncovered that you are a collector of ancient locks. Are you looking for a Key to one of those locks?'

"I couldn't believe my ears. 'I'm a collector of old locks. That's no secret. Everybody has a hobby and collects something. Am I under some kind of suspicion in this case?'

"The inspector pressed on. 'Of course not, but it's odd that the whole affair about this Key started at the same time as you began your tour with Nachman.'

" 'I don't know what you mean. I hadn't heard of the legend until I started this trip. Up to now no one has made any connection between Jacob's death and the Key.

" 'Besides I was traveling with Nachman and we were miles away from here yesterday when this horrible nightmare took place. The first I heard about Jacob's death was from Nachman when he returned last night after visiting the diggers here in Hatzor.'

"The inspector was becoming a bore. He seemed to have one thing on his mind, which was to close the case as soon as possible. He didn't care around whose neck he was going to tie the noose. 'Forgive me, but I must consider all possibilities and avenues.'

"I was getting impatient. '>From everything I heard it would appear that Jacob was killed either by some madmen or got himself involved with some fanatical religious cult and paid the price. No one will ever know the reason unless you catch the perpetrators.'

"The inspector raised his eyebrows. 'That's quite some theories you have Mr. Scott. Why do you say perpetrators in plural? Why couldn't he have been killed by one person?'

" 'It doesn't seem possible after all the man was young and in good physical shape. It would have been pretty difficult for one person to overcome him.'

" There was a moment of silence, then the inspector said, 'Perhaps, but if he was drugged...?'

" 'Was there anything in his autopsy showing any traces of drugs?'

"At this point Nachman interjected, 'As I said before I wasn't very close to Jacob, but if he had used drugs he would have been exposed by now. The life he would have led would have betrayed him.'

"The officer quit writing and looked at both of us. 'Maybe, but no one knew that he had debts or spent money like water either.'

"Nachman squirmed in his seat. The officer continued. 'The truth is that the autopsy did reveal some sedative in his blood, but we don't know whether he was addicted, or if he had taken it this one time. There were no needle marks on his body so that the drug would have had to be administered orally by force or of his own free will.'

" 'The other scenario is that someone could have administered it to him without him being aware of it.'

"He closed his notebook. 'That's all for now. Where are you going from here?'

"Nachman stood up. 'We have one more place to visit before we return to Tel Aviv. I want to show Brad the digs in Dan. There are many interesting excavations going on there presently.'

" 'Good luck to both of you, but be careful because it's my belief that whoever murdered Jacob is after this imaginary Key. If he or they would decide that one of you know anything about it, you could be next and they don't care how they get the information they want. You know what happened to Jacob.'

"Nachman asked. 'Do you think that he was tortured to obtain the location of the Key?'

" 'I don't know, but I have this uneasy feeling in the bottom of my gut that this is why he died in such a horrible way.'

"The policeman looked at his watch. 'Well I must return to Tel Aviv. Again be careful and we may be talking again when you return to the city.' He looked at Nachman. 'I know where to reach you.'

"Then he turned to me. 'Where are you staying Mr. Scott?'

" 'I have a reservation at the Dan Tel Aviv Hotel.'

"The inspector stared at me with his piercing eyes. 'Curious.'

" 'What do you mean?'

" 'The last site that you plan to visit and your hotel in Tel Aviv have the word Dan in them.'

" 'I never tied the two together, but you're right. Quite a coincidence.'

" 'I must be on my way.' He extended his hand to Nachman. 'Shalom and have a good trip.'

"Then he turned to me and said, *Auviedersehn* as they say in German Mr. Scott I hope we will have a chance to meet again before you leave Israel.'

"He walked off towards his van while we made our way to the bonfire.

"As we walked towards the fire it hit me that the inspector was using German to say good-by just like the young woman did. When we arrived Nachman asked, 'Is there any coffee left?'

" 'Sure, plenty we already made several pots. We thought that you fellows would be going off with the inspector. He took long enough before he let you two loose.'

" 'I think the inspector is grabbing at whatever straws he can. I think this thing has him completely baffled.' Nachman said as he held out his cup.

"Someone else added. 'I think that this terrible incident has everyone baffled.'

"We sat down and the conversation for the rest of the evening revolved around the discovery of the urn in Samaria, some speculations about the existence of the Key and the death of Jacob.

"I was getting tired so I glanced at my watch and saw that it was ten to eleven. I walked over to where Nachman was sitting talking to Dot who had decided to come to join the group. 'I'm beat. I'm going back to our camp and hit the sack. Can you drive me?'

"One of the diggers overheard us and volunteered. 'I can drive him back Nachman if you let me take the truck.'

"Surprised Nachman looked at him, then reached in his pocket and threw him the keys. 'Thanks.'

" 'What do you want me to tell the boy that's watching our stuff?' I asked.

" 'Tell him that I'll be along soon, probably no longer than a half an hour. Also tell him that I'll settle the account when I get back.'

"As I turned to walk away he shouted after me. 'Good night!'

"I never did get a chance to talk to the professor. He had retired before we came back from our bout with the inspector."

Chapter XII

Suddenly there was a terrible 'clang'. It came from a side alley as they passed. The *monk* jumped as though he had stepped on a nail barefooted. At the same time recoiled away from the direction of the noise.

The priest also jerked, but not as violently. "Some dog must have overturned a garbage can." He said.

The man in brown was not easily convinced. "Are you sure?" His eyes were open wide with terror.

The priest tried to calm him down. "Relax. You're wound up like a clock. If you want we can go over and take a look."

"No. Let's keep going."

The *monk* kept glancing from left to right. Then he began his account again of the events that led him to the edge of collapse from some unknown menace. "Tuesday morning I woke up tired as though I hadn't slept a wink. I was restless with intermittent dreams of the horrific scenes of Jacob's death, the inspector arresting me for murder, and being chased by unseen phantoms, who wanted to kill me. I didn't know who they were, but I knew that if they caught me I would die. I woke up many times and fell back to sleep only to slip into another nightmare.

"Nachman beat me again to the morning fire that he started from the previous night's embers. He had the tea boiling and began to pour me a cup as soon as he saw me coming out of the tent.

"When I got closer he looked at me. 'My God man you look like the next morning after a party. What happened to you? It looks like the last couple of nights you have been brawling instead of resting.'

" 'I don't know, but sleep has not come easy. Last night again I had some disturbing dreams and to make it worse I dreamt that I was arrested for Jacob's murder by the inspector.'

" 'I guess that third degree he put us through yesterday left an impression on you.'

" 'Lucky that we're nearing the end of our journey and on schedule so that perhaps we can take it easy and I can catch forty winks sometime through the day to catch up.'

"Nachman brought out some dried sausages that he originally bought in Tel Aviv and the last of the fresh bread. 'Tomorrow night should be our last day camping. We have no more fresh bread so we'll have to be satisfied with the pieta bread.'

" 'Ok by me. We can celebrate with a good meal when we return to Tel Aviv.'

" 'We have seen as much as there is here. Anything more will be a repetition of what we already know. Your interests differ from that of an archeological scholar.'

" 'You're right it will become repetitious and boring.'

"After a moment's silence Nachman caught himself. He explained, 'I didn't intend to insult you, by insinuating that you are not a scholar. I meant it from a formal perspective where details are scrupulously sought and studied by members of the fraternity and whereas others get weary.'

"He got some pieta bread from the satchel that resembled a thin crust of a pizza because it also had dried out from the heat. He pulled the sausage from a paper bag and threw them to me. 'Are you prepared to hit the road as soon as we finish breakfast or is there something that you still want to see?'

" 'No I think I've seen quite enough of this place. Too bad, that the arrival of the inspector cut into our time. We could have spent it more profitably. I could have spent talking with the professor about Germany. Interesting place that country.'

"Nachman glanced around. 'This dig has also a long history with many stories, but we must push on.'

" 'Yeah, now it can add another one. Jacob's story.' I mumbled.

" 'I agree it's been a sad time for me. I guess I didn't know Jacob as well as I thought I did even though we went through school together. Yet I knew him better than I wanted to admit to the inspector.'

" 'Should we go over and say goodbye to the diggers and the professor?' I asked.

" 'I think we better leave without goodbyes. Since the professor didn't have a chance to quiz us last night, he will want to know what transpired with the inspector and we won't get away until this afternoon.'

"After we finished eating we packed our gear into the pick up and made our way out of the dig to the road and our final destination.

"As we arrived at the road Nachman pointed to our right. 'Dan is about twenty-four miles or thirty- two kilometers in that direction. If we take our time we will arrive there before lunch. That will give us time to set up our camp and visit some of the ruins before it gets dark.'

" 'What about fuel?' I asked.

" 'That's right I forgot we only have a few pieces left for the fire, and that won't keep it going for long. When we arrive we'll unload our gear and while you set up camp I'll take a run around the area and see what I can find. I don't think that we'll be lucky to find anything on our own. I will probably have to buy it again.'

" 'Ok.' I agreed. 'I'll put the tea on the burner, we have plenty of coal oil so that when you come back we'll have time to take a walk around the area.'

"We arrived before noon and found a likely spot for our camp. Someone else must have stayed there before us because the ring of stones was still in place where the fire had been. As soon as we had dumped our gear out of the truck Nachman took off.

"First I got the burner going and put the pot on to boil some water and then I set up my tent in a likely spot near a crumbling wall. I piled up my companion's gear a few feet away so he could pick out his spot when he got back without dragging his things from the truck, which would have to be parked some thirty feet away. An hour must have passed and there was still no Nachman.

"I waited for a while and when he didn't show up I added tea to the boiling water. I let it steep for a few minutes then I poured myself a cup to test it. It was perfect so I sat down to wait for my friend.

"It was warm and very bright. I moved into the shade of the wall a few feet away. I found my blanket and spread it under me, then laid down gazing at the sky. The breeze was blowing and there were a few low white puffy clouds in the sky. I closed my eyes for a second, when suddenly I sensed that someone was standing at my feet. I sat up and saw that the sun was half way down to the horizon. I guess the few seconds had turned into a few hours. The person stood just aside of the sun's rays that hit me directly in the eyes, so that I couldn't distinguish whether it was a man or a woman. The silhouette was just a large black figure. Assuming that it was Nachman I sat up. 'You must have traveled quite a distance to get the wood. The sun is half way down to the horizon. What time is it?'

" 'Salem Alekum Mr. Scott. It's close to five o'clock.'

"I recognized the voice. It was Ben Abou Jusef.

"I got up. 'S..a..l..e..m Alekum. What brings you to this part of the country?'

" 'I was on business in the area and knew that you two were planning to be here sometime this week so I took a chance. So Nachman is out hunting for fire wood.'

" 'Yes, he should be back soon. I must apologize I fell asleep and feel groggy. Can I offer you a cup of tea?' I felt the pot. The tea had cooled off. I turned on the burner again and in a few minutes the tea was gurgling.

" 'Yes, thank you. It's most gracious of you Mr. Scott.'

"I poured him some tea. 'I don't know how long he's going to be, but you're welcome to wait for him.'

" 'To tell you the truth Mr. Scott I'm glad that we have a chance to talk alone.'

"There was silence for a moment as I waited for him to continue. I figured he would propose to sell the Key to me assuming a rich foreigner wouldn't know the difference between a real artifact and one made for the naive pilgrims that buy anything because it comes from the holy land.

" 'I mentioned in Munhata that I knew of the existence of the Key and now I have it in my possession'

"I thought that I would catch him off guard. 'Are you going to try and sell it to me? I already know that you offered it to Jacob. Do you know what happened to him?'

" 'Yes I do, but I don't think that it was because of the Key.' Something was strange about him. He was calm and serene like he didn't seem to have a care in the world. He wasn't fidgeting like he did during our previous encounters and the awful question didn't upset him. I wondered why?

" 'Nachman told me that Jacob had some real hot buyers and tried to get him interested in a partnership. Why don't you offer it to Nachman?' I didn't tell Ben Abou Jusef that I already knew of his offer to my guide.

" 'Nachman is what we call a righteous person. He would never enter into a business deal unless everything was legal and honorable.'

" 'So, are you trying to put a price on my righteousness or honor?'

" 'O..f c..o..u..r..s..e not Mr. Scott, but this Christian relic must arouse your curiosity shall we say from a different perspective.'

"I took a sip of my tea. 'If it really exists can you imagine the impact on Christians worldwide? Regardless, I'm not interested.'

"It was getting dark. 'I understand you're a collector in your own right,' whispered Ben Abou Jusef as though someone might be listening. He kept glancing around, but this time without the usual fear in his eyes. He was rather making sure that no one else was out there in the semi darkness.

" 'I'm surprised! You're very resourceful to be able to obtain such personal information.'

" 'To be frank with you Mr. Scott I have had second thoughts and realized that this relic is beyond a poor businessman like me. It should be in the hands of someone who understands its value and I don't mean monetary.'

"I gasped. 'Mr. Ben Abou Jusef you mean that you would be willing to part with such a valuable object without making a profit?'

" 'You will find Mr. Scott that sometimes you will come across forces that are beyond your control and as the Christian writings say, what have you profited if you have gained the whole world and lost your soul.'

" 'Don't tell me that God is trying to punish you for attempting to sell His Key?' I teased.

" 'There is nothing amusing about what I said. The person that sold me the Key died a horrible death and he was a Christian. It was similar to what I heard happened to Jacob.'

" 'Perhaps you will admit to yourself now that Jacob's death was tied to the Key.' I squeezed him.

"'Ignoring my remark he sat there staring at his cup. 'God is angry and does not care to what faith one belongs when it comes to mocking his relics or trying to make a profit by selling them.'

"He looked distant and I felt sorry for him. 'I don't mock anyone's belief, but I guess you have a problem whether the Key that you have is really this Key of Damascus. Regardless why don't you take it to some church or priest? I'm sure that after you tell the cleric your story he would be glad to take it off your hands and relieve you of this tremendous burden. The church is always interested in pursuing old legends that might lead it to a real relic from the days of Christ.'

" 'What about you Mr. Scott? Suppose I put the object in your trust, would you take it to someone that would protect it and keep it safe until it is needed?'

" 'Thanks, but no thanks. I live a simple life. I work, enjoy life as much as I can and do not want it muddied by relics or legends. I admit I collect all sorts of antique locks, for fun and some of them even have keys, but it's just a hobby with me. I don't invest great amounts of money and don't have to worry about their safety.'

" 'Maybe you're right. Perhaps I should take it to a Christian church for safekeeping.' Again his eyes shifted into the darkness. I don't know why, but I had a feeling that the façade of calm was breaking down and I began feeling sorry for him.

" 'Why don't you wait until Nachman comes back and perhaps he can help you with your dilemma? He has a great deal of experience in this field.'

" 'I thank you for your suggestion, but I've made up my mind that I would leave the Key with you or take it to Jerusalem myself. I know a Jesuit at the Pontifical Biblical Institute there. His name is Father Boniface.' "

The lanky priest stopped again. "But my name is Boniface. Is that the reason why you came to see me? I know Ben Abou Jusef, because he always came to me soliciting information about some Christian relic. I have a degree in ancient civilizations and God forgive me for my vanity, but some consider me an expert in that field. Whatever happened to Ben Abou Jusef? I haven't seen him for almost a year."

The *monk* ignored the question and continued. "I told Ben Abou Jusef that he had made the right decision. The defense of the world against evil is in the hands of religion, so clerics are the people who have the time and can authenticate relics. They will also be less tempted to sell it.

"I still didn't believe that the Key really existed and thought that it was the best way to stop him from trying to unload whatever he had on me. I figured if I showed any curiosity in this Key Ben Abou Jusef would take it as a sign that I'm interested in owning it. The next thing on the agenda would be the price.

"I couldn't get over his behavior. He didn't seem to be the same man I talked to the last couple of times. He didn't press the matter any further. I couldn't put my finger on it, but he was different. He thanked me for the tea. 'I must go now. Time is of the essence. Salem Alekum.'

"He promptly turned around and walked away before I had a chance to say goodbye.

"I stood up and went around the wall to see if I could see Nachman coming, but no such luck. I also realized that Ben Abou Jusef was gone just like the two reporters and the young woman that had visited me. They all had disappeared as though in thin air. I considered the idea of telling Nachman when he came back that we cut this visit short. I was beginning to wonder about my sanity. Lately people seem to disappear all around me. There was still some daylight so I should have seen him go.

"About half an hour later Nachman showed up with some wood in the truck. 'I had a hard time getting these pieces. Everywhere I went the people sent me to someone else. For a moment I thought that we would have to go without a fire tonight. I should have made sure that you saved the few pieces that we had left until this evening. At least we would have had some heat to keep us warm when we ate our supper.'

"I threw a few pieces that we had on the small pile that he brought. 'Lucky you found some because now we'll even have a fire in the morning.'

" 'I picked up the teapot and sloshed it around to find out how much was left. 'Ben Abou Jusef came by so I gave him some tea. There isn't much left in the pot. I'll make some more. I asked Ben Abou Jusef to wait until you came back, but he said that he was in a hurry to get to Jerusalem.'

"Nachman reached out. 'Give the pot to me. I'll make the tea.'

" 'Ok. I'll get the wood and set up for the fire.'

" 'What did Ben Abou Jusef want?'

" 'I really don't know. He's obsessed with this Key of his. I don't know whether the one supposedly in his possession is the genuine article or if he's just trying to run a scam. This time he started working on me and before it got out of hand I told him I wasn't interested. I suggested he give or sell this Key to people who are in the business of saving the world. Finally he said he was going to visit a Father Boniface in Jerusalem and left.'

"Nachman shook his head. 'I guess he just can't take no for an answer. Of course he's also trying to make some money.'

" 'That's just it. Near the end of our conversation I got the impression that he was willing to give it away, but I thought I better not go down that road, because he might be fishing to see if I was interested and we would be back to square root one. He was somehow different than when we talked the last time."

Nachman lit the bonfire. 'What do you mean?'

" 'I can't quite figure it out, but while he was still passionate about the Key he said that God does not want anyone to make a profit on this transaction, and he really seem to believe that the culprit would be punished dearly. He said it with such conviction that it almost sounded like he had seen God's anger himself.'

"The water was boiling so Nachman threw some tea into it and took it off the burner to let it steep. 'Something must have frightened Ben Abou Jusef. I have never known him to pass up a chance to make some money. It's too late to try and visit any part of the ruins now, but if you want, we can call on some friends of mine at their bonfire.'

"I went over and brought some of our provisions. 'Let's have a bite before we go, I'm hungry.' I dropped the satchel beside Nachman who opened it and took out our bread and cheese as well as some of the sausage again. 'What about our things? Are they safe here if we go sightseeing?' I asked.

" 'You stay here for a moment while I go over and see if there is anyone there that I can hire to guard them.'

" 'To save time I'll clean up so that if you find someone we'll be ready as soon as he shows up.'

"I had everything done and no Nachman again. I was getting annoyed because I could see the bonfire in the distance and he should have been back a long time ago.

"I glanced at my watch and it was getting past nine o'clock in the evening. I had decided that I wasn't going anywhere tonight and if Nachman found someone to tell him he wasn't needed. I poured myself a cup of tea, laid back and stared at the clear starry sky.

"All of a sudden I herd footsteps in the dark, I called out. 'Nachman? Is that you?'

"There was no answer. Again I called out this time putting my hand around a heavy piece of dried wood. 'Nachman?'

"Again there was no answer, but I could see in the darkness two figures coming towards me. I was scared. I thought that they could be a couple of bandits who wouldn't think twice about slitting my throat and making off with our gear. I tightened my grip around my club.

"As they approached I recognized the two journalists. Seeing them didn't relieve my anxiety.

"It was the one named Lucis that spoke in a soft polite tone. 'Good evening Mr. Scott. It's a pleasure to see you again.'

"I stood up still holding the club in my hand. Nohmed his associate with the unblinking eyes that seemed to glow in the dark stood beside him.

" 'Y..o..u.. surprised me. What brings you here?'

"It was Lucis that did all the talking. Nohmed stood still, frozen like a statue. He looked as if he couldn't move or act without permission from his companion. In the light of the fire he looked like a zombie without a trace of emotion on his face.

"Lucis looked around. 'I don't see Nachman. Is he around?'

"His voice was not convincing. He seemed to know for sure that my guide wasn't there, which made me that much more nervous. 'He went to see his friends at the bonfire and will be back soon.' I lied.

" 'It doesn't matter.' continued Lucis. 'It is you I wanted to see. You understand business and are a man of the world.'

"I figured he was softening me up for whatever scheme he had in mind. I made a gesture of hospitality with the stick in my hand. 'Would either of you like a cup of tea?'

"I looked a Nohmed who didn't acknowledge my question, but Lucis volunteered. 'Let Nohmed pour while we talk.'

"Lucis came closer to the bonfire staring intensely at the flames. He sat down on the ground and still gazing at the red coals motioned to me. 'Please sit down Mr. Scott. What I have to say could be very rewarding for you.'

"It was more like an order than an invitation.

"Nohmed brought Lucis his tea and made a gesture with the teapot towards me. I extended my arm. After refilling it and returning the pot to its place, he went off to one side behind his colleague and stood there.

" 'Doesn't Nohmed drink tea?' I asked.

" 'He's not much for socializing.'

"For an instant I felt the hulk's loneliness and felt sorry for him, but immediately pity was replaced by a feeling of fear and revulsion.

"Lucis interrupted my thoughts. 'I understand that the Key mentioned in the scroll in the Sebasti dig might have surfaced. I'm prepared to pay a handsome price for it.'

"I played dumb. 'I don't know anything about any Key. The only time I heard about this particular object was in that scroll.'

"Lucis looked intently at me as though trying to read my mind. 'Perhaps you don't know where it is right now, but if you discover its location I would be prepared to pay several million US dollars or the equivalent in gold.'

" 'That does sound interesting, but how would I ever get my hands on such an item. There are many people involved in the antiquities trade that probably could serve you better.'

"Lucis looked back at the flames. 'Isn't fire beautiful? The way it dances to its own rhythm. It doesn't need anyone or anything to direct it.'

"I couldn't resist. 'That may be so, but even fire without fuel burns out and dies. To keep it going there is always a need for more fuel.'

"For a moment he looked as though he longed for something, but it was short lived and he became his cold self again. 'Rightly so everything in the universe needs to be replenished to be reborn. What do you say Mr. Scott? Do we have a deal?'

" 'I already told you that I have no idea where the Key is so how could we have a deal?'

"Lucis pressed on. 'I would be prepared to give you a retainer. Say a fee of good faith. If you make contact with the Key in any way you would get in touch with me.'

" 'It's a tempting offer, but I wouldn't know where to reach you and I don't take payments for things that I might not be able to deliver.'

" 'It's a win, win proposition for you. If you find the Key or know where I could find it and let me know you keep the fee. If on the other hand you have the Key, and sell it to me then I'm prepared to pay you the full amount in addition to the deposit.'

"I didn't want his money, but the moment of hesitation made him think that I was interested. He leaned towards me as though revealing a secret, and whispered, 'The retainer is one hundred thousand US dollars or equivalent in gold.' I could see the flames in his pupils. They looked like a myriad of belly dancers enticing me to accept his offer.

"He was hypnotic in a way and only the crack of a log in the fire as it burned brought me back to reality. 'Thanks, but no thanks. If I ever have this Key, then you can get in touch with me and I'll let you know whether we can make a deal.'

"Suddenly his face contorted and he turned to Nohmed who made a menacing gesture to move towards me, but Lucis extended his hand and hissed. 'I don't understand him Nohmed I offered more than anyone else would have in this case and he turned me down. I can't understand it. He turned me down.'

"All of sudden I lost all fear and grabbed the club. 'Who do you think you are? I'm all for making a few bucks, but this is ridiculous. Find yourself another patsy now get out of here and I don't want to see you again.'

"Instead of ordering Nohmed to hit me he just sneered at me. 'We'll meet again and the next time it will be different. You will be mine to do with what I wish.'

"With these last words he motioned to Nohmed to follow him and they disappeared in the darkness.

"I sat down again and as time passed I was getting angrier by the minute for Nachman not being there.

"A few minutes later I heard uneven footsteps in the dark. I figured my two visitors had changed their minds and were coming back to teach me some manners so I grabbed the club and prepared myself for the worst.

"As the figure came into the faint light of the fire I could see that the person was staggering as if he was drunk. I walked up towards him and saw Nachman coming into view holding his head. 'What happened to you? I didn't think that you would be back tonight. It's almost midnight.'

" 'Y..o..u'..r..e almost right. I nearly didn't make it back tonight.'

" 'Why what happened?' I moved his hand and saw a wet spot on his scalp. As his hand came into full view I could see blood on it.

"He staggered towards the fire and collapsed on his knees in front of the flickering flames.

"I ran to the satchel with the water and brought him a bottle from which he drank deeply.

" 'Brad, get the first aid kit for me. It's in the truck behind the seat.'

"I ran over and got the box; opening it I took out some hydrogen peroxide and bandages. 'Let me clean the wound. You can't do it yourself.' I took some sterile cloths from a sealed envelope, poured some water in a bowl and washed the gash in the back of his scalp. Then applied some hydrogen peroxide and bandaged his head.

"I poured him a cup of tea. 'What happened? You could have been killed.'

" 'I don't know I was on the way to the bonfire across this excavated courtyard when suddenly I was struck from behind. That's all I can remember.'

" 'Do you still have your wallet?'

"Nachman reached in his pocket and pulled it out. He opened it and looked inside, he then pulled out a wad of bills and counted them. 'Nothing seems to be missing. If it was robbery then they made a mess of things. Perhaps someone scared the muggers off.'

"We sat there in silence for a moment.

" 'Do you think that there was another reason for this attack than robbery?' I asked.

" 'What other reason could there be? Keep me from reaching my colleagues at the dig? Why?'

" 'I don't know, but it was odd that the two journalists showed up here.'

Having forgotten about his wound Nachman abruptly turned his head to me. 'What!' He gasped, 'Where in the hell did they come from?' The pain hit him instantly. He grabbed his head between his hands to ease it.

" 'I don't know, but this time the visit deteriorated quickly from a cool and polite one to an instant when at one point I thought Nohmed was going to bash my brains in. Lucis got angry when I wouldn't accept his offer to take a retainer and become his agent. He wanted to be kept informed about the whereabouts of the Key. He said he would pay several million US dollars to anyone who would bring him the Key, but did not actually quote a figure. He sweetened the pot by telling me that I could keep a retainer he offered of one hundred thousand US dollar if I got my hands on the Key and sold it to him. This was in addition to the price he would pay for the Key.

" 'When I refused he turned really ugly. I could have used your help, because I wasn't sure I could have handled Nohmed let alone the two of them.'

"Nachman rubbed gently the back of his head; 'I always thought that there was something strange about those two. Now we know for sure that they're not journalists.'

"I stood up and headed towards my tent. 'It's past midnight I think I'll hit the sack. In view of what happened tonight I would suggest that you keep your rifle close to you.'

" 'What about you.'

"I lifted my arm showing him the heavy club that I had picked up. 'This should do me until I can get your attention. Good night.'

"By this time I got used to having restless nights and they always seemed to involve a trio, whose faces I couldn't identify. This nightmare differed from the others. I dreamt about Ben Abou Jusef coming towards me covered in blood and carrying a Key in his extended hands offering it to me. I stood there transfixed and then stretched out my arms to receive the object when all my senses told me to turn and run. Once the Key was in my hands Ben Abou Jusef was gone. Clutching the object I looked up to see the trio reaching grabbing and groping for it. Terror came over me. I turned and ran. When I looked back I could see that there were two men and one woman but I couldn't make out their faces. Just when they were about to catch up with me I woke up.

Chapter XIII

"Wednesday was the last day of the excursion. My program was at an end. We had to cut the sightseeing of the Dan dig short, because I wanted to get to Tel Aviv that day. It was still dark, but I couldn't sleep so I got up and made myself a cup of tea. The eastern sky began to lighten and I could see shadows forming by the jagged walls and trees that were close to our camp.

"The night was short and I was tired, but it was too late to think about any more sleep. I looked at my watch and saw that it was seven o'clock. I heard Nachman stirring in his tent so I added more water to the pot and then steeped some more tea. A few minutes later he showed up. I guess neither one of us looked too well. When I saw him I couldn't help myself and I broke into laughter. I guess our minds were on the same wavelength, because he also began laughing.

" 'How's the head?' I asked.

"He reached and rubbed it. 'The sharp pain is gone. Now it's just a dull pounding. It feels something like a hangover.'

"He looked around. 'Where is the first aid kit? It has some pain pills in it.'

"While he was looking for it, I poured him some tea and we sat down sipping it slowly without a word between us.

"After some time Nachman said. 'Immediately after breakfast let's begin the tour. We're a bit behind schedule maximizing our time as much as we can.'

" 'Are you sure you're up to it?'

" 'It would take more than a headache to put me out of commission.'

"My guide got up. 'We should load up our truck and always keep it in view so that our gear will be safe. I'll pack the food in a handy spot so that we can have a piece of cheese and bread on the run. Should try to make Tel Aviv early enough to grab a shower and have a decent meal in a restaurant. We have a ways to travel.'

" 'Ok. Here I'll give you a hand.'

"We finished our meal and after packing our truck we started our tour.

"Nachman stood up pointing around us made a circle with his finger. 'As you can see the Biblical city of Dan was located at the foot of Mount Hermon. The site covers about fifty acres. The city's name derives from the tribe of Dan who conquered it during the twelfth century BCE. The Dan River, which is one of the sources of the Jordan River, emerges here at the foot of the mound.

" 'Its location was very important because it was situated on the main trade route from Galilee to Damascus.

" 'During the Canaanite period the city was known as Leshem.'

"We reached a small courtyard. In its center stood a large stone. 'This was a cultic center where the Israelites set up statues of graven images for themselves. Its mentioned in the Bible Judges 18:30.

" 'The object of their worship was a golden calf. The sanctuary covered about forty five by sixty square meters.'

" As we walked about it we found a reddish brown substance on the ground. Nachman looked at it and rubbed his head. 'I don't know exactly where it happened, but I think this is the place where I got clobbered last night.'

"I turned my head and surveyed the surroundings. 'Strange. The violence and all the weird occurrences that we have experienced during this trip has always been near some cultic stones.

" 'First Jacob, then the young woman I met in Hatzor the other day and last night you. I..I..I.. never did get her name. She also promised to see me again like the two reporters. I wonder will I..I..I'l ever meet her again?'

"There was no reply from Nachman. He was in his own world. I guess he was trying to reconstruct the previous night to see if he could remember anything pertinent.

"We visited some of the active excavation sites where Nachman always knew someone.

"By noon we were done.

"It was hot and once we got into the truck Nachman turned on the air conditioner. 'I'm glad you decided to turn on the air. I don't care whether I catch a cold or not I don't think I can stand this heat any longer.'

"It felt good. We drove for a few miles. He turned to me. 'Brad do you have an international drivers license?'

" 'Yes.'

" 'Would you like to drive? The traffic here is sometimes a little different than in America or Europe, but you should be able to handle it.'

" 'Yeah, sure. I'll give it a shot.'

"We stopped by the side of the road while we changed places.

"Nachman brought the satchel with the food from the box of the truck and placed it in the cab. 'While you drive I'll get the food ready and the water so we can snack on the go.'

"The drive back was without incident except for the odd car that we met who was going at break neck speed. My patience was wearing thin so I started to swear at the passing vehicles. It always seemed that the driver decided to pass us in the most dangerous places on a curve or going up a hill. 'That S.O.B.'

"Nachman saw my anger mounting. 'Do you think you've had enough? At least you'll have something to tell your buddies back in Brussels about the drive of your life in Israel.'

" 'Literally this is the drive of my life. I figured our goose was cooked several times. If there was any traffic on the road coming towards us we would have been minced meat.' I pulled over to let Nachman drive.

"The rest of the trip was routine. I surveyed the countryside and dozed off a couple of times. Nachman seemed to be in his own world rubbing his injury once in a while.

"We arrived in Tel Aviv late in the afternoon. When we entered the city my guide asked. 'What do you want me to do with the gear? Since you paid for it, do you want to take it home with you?'

" 'No. I would like to keep one of the satchels, but I don't have any use for the rest. Can you sell it to someone?'

"Nachman thought for a while. 'I can use some of it. I have to visit digs and write up reports for my thesis.'

" 'Take what you need and see if you can get enough out of the rest for us to pay for a good meal tonight.'

"Nachman glanced around to get his bearings. 'I'll drop you off at your hotel so you can freshen up. Then I'll pop round the place where we bought the stuff and see what I can do. I'm sure that they can always sell the equipment to people who want to go hiking across the country. When I'm done I'll go home, take a shower and later return the truck to its Eli Wulf.'

"During the last ten days I learned to trust Nachman like a brother. 'If you're going to return the truck, can I give you a travelers check for him to cover the balance of the rental cost?'

" 'Sure I'll be glad to take it to him.'

" 'I want to keep some dollars in cash for my own use. If he quibbles, then bring him around and I'll pay him in cash.'

"When we arrived back at the hotel, I got the bellboy to unload my personal belongings. Then I wrote and signed the traveler check to the owner of the truck for the balance of the rental fee.

"I looked at my watch. 'It's five o'clock. What time do you want to eat? I'm a bit tired so if you don't mind I'd rather eat at the hotel instead of going out.'

" 'Fine with me. I'll be back at around eight thirty. That should give me enough time to handle everything.'

"Nachman got into the truck and took off. I went to the front desk and registered. I handed the bellboy my claim chits for my things that I had left in storage and asked him to deliver everything to my room.

"After he brought up my luggage I got some clean clothes and took a bath. Normally I shower, but it felt good to sit in the warm soothing water. After some time I got out of the tub, had a quick rinse under the shower and then I set my alarm clock. In addition to the alarm I phoned the front desk for a wake up call at eight o'clock that evening, which would give me enough time to get ready before Nachman showed up.

"I slept soundly for a change and woke up when I heard my phone ring. It was the wake up call form the desk. A minute or two afterwards my alarm went off. I got up dressed and went downstairs to wait for Nachman. I was early so I bought the Herald Tribune and sat down in the lobby to read it.

"In the Middle Eastern section they had a heading in capital and bold letters 'FIVE CAR PILEUP.' It was on the road that we had driven up from Dan. It had happened three days ago, but I didn't remember seeing any trace of it along the way. Of course I dozed off for a while so I may have missed the tell tale signs of the accident. Reading the details I saw that only one person died in the mishap. His name was Ben Abou Jusef a local entrepreneur. You can imagine my surprise because I had seen him only two nights ago. According to the newspaper he was already dead. Then I remember that there was something different about him that evening. He was more serious and serene even though he was still fidgety as ever. I couldn't believe my eyes and figured that there was either another Ben Abou Jusef or the paper had gotten their dates mixed up.

"As I sat there trying to untangle the puzzle I heard, 'Shalom.'

"I looked up and saw Nachman standing in front of me. I didn't see him arrive. 'Shalom.'

"We went into 'La Regence' grill and were directed to a table. We ordered our drinks and told the waiter that we would want our food later.

" 'Have you seen the news?' I asked.

" 'What news?'

"I handed the paper to Nachman. 'Read the paragraph on the second page about the accident on the same road that we took to Tel Aviv.'

"He let out a low whistle; 'I saw some black spots on the road as though something had spilled on it while you were asleep, but never imagined that it was from such a bad crash.'

" 'Keep on reading it gets better.'

" 'Ben Abou Jusef! I can't believe it. Didn't you say you saw him a couple nights ago?'

" 'Yes. Now I'm beginning to question my sanity.'

" 'There must be some type of a mix up with the dates, because you couldn't have seen a dead man. Isn't it amazing the way fate works?'

"The waiter arrived with our drinks, and we ordered our meals.

" 'Yes. When I think about him trying to sell me the Key that he said he acquired and then deciding to take it to a priest in Jerusalem…

" 'I can't get over how strange he looked and acted.'

"We drank our cocktails in silence for a while; each absorbed in our thoughts. Then I heard Nachman. 'Here comes our food. It's going to be good to have something prepared by a cook for a change rather than the rations that we have been on the last ten days.'

"While we ate our meals we rehashed the trip and the unusual experiences that we had at several of the digs.

"After dinner we each had a cognac. 'Tomorrow I leave for Europe. The Lufthansa flight goes to Frankfurt where I will change to Sabina and fly to Brussels. Since it doesn't leave until eleven o'clock at night I will have a chance to wander around the shops and pick up something for a memento of this trip. The real souvenir will be my memory of all that's happened to us and your friendship.'

"I raised my glass. 'Cheers and good luck to you in the pursuit of your doctorate.'

" 'Thanks.' We clinked our glasses and finished the cognac.

"The waiter brought our bill. When I reached in my pocket to pay Nachman raised his hand. 'Just a minute I forgot to give you the money from the sale of the gear.'

"He handed me a wad of bills. When I got done there were still a few Shekels left. I counted them. 'As a tourist I think I got enough here for a *genuine antique* memento from the holy land'

"Nachman laughed. We got up, and said our goodbyes in the lobby. He took my hand. 'If you ever decide to come back and I can be of help don't hesitate to call me.'

" 'Thanks,' and we parted.

"Even though I had slept that afternoon I felt tired. I found my elevator and returned to my room.

Chapter XIV

"Thursday morning I felt good. It was the first night in the last ten days that I can remember getting a good night's rest. As I was getting ready to go for breakfast the phone rang. I thought that it was probably Nachman with some information or something he had forgotten to tell me before we said our goodbyes. Lucky that there was a phone in the bathroom otherwise I wouldn't have heard it with the noise of the water drowning out all other sounds. I scrambled out of the shower almost falling on the slippery floor. 'Hello.'

"The voice on the other end sounded happy that I answered. 'Mr. Scott. This is inspector Reichman. Remember me? We met at Hatzor. I need to talk to you. Could we meet now? I'll buy you breakfast.'

" 'You don't have to buy me breakfast. I'll be happy to talk to you.'

" 'I insist. That's the least I can do to pay you for your inconvenience.'

" 'Ok. I'll be down in a minute.'

" 'Why don't I go into the Patio Café and grab us a table? If you want I can even order your meal so that it will be ready when you get there, which will save you time if you're in a hurry.'

" 'Thanks, perhaps some cold cuts, rolls and a carafe of coffee would be nice. I'll be down directly.'

"I found the inspector in a remote corner of the Patio Café. The tables around him were empty providing us with some privacy. 'Shalom inspector.'

"He stood up. 'Shalom Mr. Scott.'

"The table had a dish of cold cuts and a carafe of coffee on it. We sat down and I poured myself a cup. There was an awkward silence for a few seconds. I felt that the inspector was sizing me up or being polite before he revealed what was on his mind. He let me start my breakfast. The silence weighed heavy and I could feel the pressure building up, so to release the uncomfortable tension, I prompted. 'Yes? What can I do for you inspector?'

" 'I wanted to meet with you to find out if there was anything else you could add to that dreadful incident with Jacob. I also understand that you knew an unfortunate merchant named Ben Abou Jusef.'

" 'I wouldn't say I knew him. I talked to him a couple of times, but like Jacob I didn't really know him'"

" 'What did you talk about? We're trying to find out as much as we can about the people involved in the accident in which he died.' He studied my reaction. 'You don't seem to be surprised that he's dead.'

" 'I was surprised when I read it in the Herald Tribune after we had arrived in Tel Aviv. I showed the article to Nachman. The last time I saw Ben Abou Jusef he told me of his plans to go to Jerusalem to visit some Jesuit named Fr. Boniface.'

" 'He was not a Christian so did he say what his business was with this priest?'

" 'Something to do with the Key that everyone I meet is talking about.'

"The inspector let my reference to the Key slip by without raising an eyebrow. I didn't think much about it then, but later I found it strange that he didn't even ask what this Key was all about. He did not deviate from his course. 'The time of the accident was unfortunate. I planned to talk to him about Jacob, because my investigation leads me to believe that Ben Abou Jusef was the last person who saw Jacob alive.'

" 'I'm sorry I can't help you with anything further inspector. This trip turned out to be a greater adventure than I had expected or wanted. I was told that this land was one of mystery. Now I'm beginning to believe it.'

" 'So what are your plans now Mr. Scott?'

" 'I'm catching a flight tonight for Frankfurt where I change planes for Brussels.'

" 'Could you leave me your address in Brussels in case I wanted to get in touch with you? I wanted to make sure that we met so I could have it for my records.' It was more of a directive than a question.

" 'Why? I don't mind giving you my address, but I thought that you wouldn't need me anymore.'

"The inspector took out his notebook and handed it to me. I wrote down my address and put it on the table in front of him. Chaussee de Tervuren 1462 Apt. 12, Brussels, Belgium.

"He picked it up. 'I'm sorry if I detained you, but one never knows where one finds the answers to riddles in this world.'

"I thought to myself. 'What other worlds could he mean?' But I had decided not to irritate him with my humor. His eyes told me that he was convinced that I knew more about the whole affair than I was telling him, but he didn't press

"He motioned for the waiter. 'I have investigated many cases in my life. Some under very unusual circumstances, but this one has an eerie aspect to it. The circumstances seem to revolve around this Key and you Mr. Scott. . .'

"He mentioned the Key, but only as a passing remark as though he was aware of its existence and that there was nothing unusual about it. Again I noticed him staring at me waiting for some comment. I was stunned. 'How could it involve me? I never heard anything about it until these last ten days. Nor do I know anything about it's whereabouts.'

" 'Nevertheless Mr. Scott, be careful.' He settled the bill. 'Now, I must go Shalom and good luck.'

"As he walked out of the café I pondered his words. The whole idea made me angry, because this obsession with the Key by others messed up what could have been a perfect holiday.

"I decided not to dwell on it. My watch told me that it was ten o'clock and that I had the whole day before I was due at the airport at ten that night.

"I decided to take a walk around the shops and see what I could pick up as a worthy memento of this trip from Israel. The thought of an antique padlock crossed my mind, and I didn't care whether it was a real antique or made to order for tourists.

"A rest before going to the airport would be a treat so I checked at the front desk and asked them if I could stay in the room until my departure for the airport that evening. The hotel agreed for half the daily rate.

"I called a cab and went to the Carmel and Jaffa Markets on Allenby Street. I made my way through the tortuous alleys avoiding collisions with customers standing around the closely placed stalls by pushing them aside. The stands were full of fruits, vegetables, and spices. Some piled up like pyramids and others in neat lines.

"I must have walked for a good hour until I found myself in a quarter with small shops selling brass, cloth, plus many other strange and useless things. It was nerve-racking. The owners were hawking their wares and trying to pull me inside their stores.

"I decided that there was nothing I wanted and began to head towards the outskirts of the market so I could catch a cab. As I was pushing my way through a narrow street that was more like an alley I noticed a small shop with trunks, locks, and other such bits and pieces displayed in front. It was located between a brass retailer on one side and a jewelry establishment on the other. I stopped for a moment to look at the wares. I wanted to see if there was anything of interest. I didn't want to get into a shouting match with the proprietor before I was really interested in buying something.

"It felt weird. There was no one in front of it trying to entice me inside. As I stood there studying the merchandise on display I saw people walking by and staring at me. Even when they passed they would turn around to look back. Some would even stop; bewildered they would look at the shop, then at me and carry on. I felt like something on display so I looked at myself and then twisted my back to see if my pants were ripped. I could not find the reason why everyone acted so bizarre.

"Peeking inside the shop through the door I saw a large iron padlock with a Key in it on the floor propped up against a chest. It looked like the perfect gift for myself.

"I walked in. No one was around so I made my way to the lock. I picked up the padlock to examine it when I heard a voice so faint that I thought it was my imagination. 'May I help you?'

"Even though the old man spoke softly he shocked the hell out of me. I guess it was because I was so absorbed with my prize and he snuck up on me.

" 'Perhaps. I'm interested in this lock. Does the Key go with it and does it still work?'

" 'The Key goes with it, but alas it does not belong to this lock. I thought it would make a good combination, and together they would sell better. They would make for good conversation with friends. Especially when the Key does not work. I'm sure sir, that you could have an amusing tale back home about how you purchased a lock with a Key that doesn't open it.'

" I would have liked a lock with a key that worked. I don't know why, but the longer I looked at objects the more they fascinated me. 'How much?'

" 'What is it worth to you my friend?'

"I prepared myself for the haggling, but first of all I had to establish a starting point. When he asked me for the value I knew that he was trying to see how badly I wanted them.

" 'Both the lock and the key are old and I have only a slight interest in the padlock and as you say the key doesn't work so I'm not too sure I even want to buy it.'

"Suddenly his approach changed. 'Will you pay in Shekels or some other currency? Francs? Perhaps Deutchmarks? Pounds?'

" 'US dollars if necessary although I still have some Shekels.'

"He picked up the items in his hands as though he was handling crystal. Gazing at them at length he said, 'Eighty US dollars.'

"I laughed. 'You sure start high enough. That's too high for me. I think I'll pass.'

"I began to move towards the door. I don't know how, but as I turned the aisle there was the old man in front of me. 'You don't understand sir. These objects may look like nothing, but they are worth much more than all the treasures of the world.'

" 'I'm sure they are to you, but to me its an old rusted padlock with a Key, which I might repeat doesn't work. I'm prepared to give you ten dollars.'

" 'But sir that would be stealing! I can't let them go for ten dollars.'

"I took the lock in my hands with the key sticking out of it. I tried to turn it, but as the old man had told me it didn't budge. The lock did look ancient and was very interesting. I handed the items back to him and took out thirty dollars from my wallet. 'Ok. I haven't got time to haggle. I'll give you thirty dollars take it or leave it. I'm leaving Israel and must go make arrangements for my flight.'

"The old man fixed his eyes on the objects for a few seconds as though he knew that he would be parting with something very dear to him. 'I will agree on one condition.'

" 'And what is that.'

" 'I want your oath that you will never sell them to anyone even if the money offered is more than you ever saw or may ever see in your lifetime. Think carefully for the break of such an oath would damn you for all eternity.'

"I was getting annoyed. 'Let's not get melodramatic. Its only an old rusty padlock and a key, but to make you happy Ok. I promise never to sell them.'

"He took my thirty dollars and went to a table to wrap them while I was browsing around the shop. He had many unusual items. All of them looked old. Some were in terrible condition. Many of them probably would need expensive repairs in order to restore them. I figured much of it was just plain junk.

"While I stood there looking at a rusted sword I heard the old man approach. 'Here is your prize sir.'

"Again he reminded me. 'Remember your oath and don't take it lightly for the price to break it would be terrible.'

"I figured that now that I owned the objects I could tell him. 'I'm a collector and the creed of a collector is never to sell anything he buys. It's not the money that matters, but the possession of the object. The pleasure comes from being able to handle and admire the piece and not to treasure it because of it's price.' This statement gave me a great satisfaction. I had outwitted one of the most experienced traders in the market. After all he was an old man and had been there many years dealing with people from the whole world and all walks of life. I'm sure that he had his share or victories over many a sappy tourist.

"As I approached the door he followed me to the entrance. 'I know who and what you are Mr. Scott. Salem Alekum.'

"When I left I was so elated that it didn't dawn on me that he called me by my name. I must have passed four other shops before I realized what he had said. I quickly turned around and went back to ask him where he got my name. I figured it was a set up.

"When I got to the spot I found an alley. I looked around and even stepped into the alley, but there was nothing there.

"I looked at the adjacent shops to check and make sure that I was in the right place. No question the same brass shop on one side and jewelry store on the other. I went into the jewelry shop. The owner was all over me trying to entice me into buying something. I pretended to be interested in some of his rings. 'What happened to the old souvenir shop next door to you?'

" 'What souvenir shop?'

" 'The one that has all the old trunks, locks and other second-hand things.'

" 'There never was a store there as long as I have been here sir, and my family has been at this location for a hundred years.'

"I was inspecting a gold ring that had caught my eye. I showed him the package under my arm. 'It's not possible. I bought these objects here just a few minutes ago.'

" 'I'm sorry sir, but it's not possible.' Then he thought for a few seconds. 'There was shop of antiquities in that spot just as my family was planning to move in here, but it burned down. I remember my grandfather talking about it.'

"I decided to buy the ring. 'Do you want me to wrap it for you or are you going to wear it?'

" 'I'll wear it.'

"I left the shop and found my way out of the market where some cabs stood. Returning to my room I opened the crumpled paper that held my treasures and examined them to make sure the old boy didn't wrap something else.

"Both the lock and the Key were there. He had removed the Key from the padlock and laid it on top. Wrapped around it was a folded piece of parchment. I laid the objects on a table, poured myself a cognac and sat down beside them.

"As I reached for the rawhide I thought that it was a nice touch to make the lock and the key appear authentic and old. I pulled on it so that it unwrapped itself leaving the Key on top of the padlock on the table. I unfolded the hide. On one side it was written. 'I'm a collector and the creed of a collector is never to sell anything he buys. It's not the money that matters, but the possession of the object. The pleasure comes from being able to handle and admire the piece and not to treasure it because of it's price.'

"How was it possible for him to write it before I had even said it? I told him of my creed only when he gave me the package. So I mused, he got his oath in writing after all. I inspected the skin on either side, but there was nothing else unusual about it and laid the shammy back down on the table.

"As I sipped my drink I stared at them. The Key attracted my attention. It was strange looking. When I looked intently at it, the ancient metal object seemed to change from dull dark to a glowing golden color. I had to blink several times to clear my eyes. I didn't know whether it was the drink or my eyes playing tricks because of the length of time I had stared at the table without blinking. I rubbed my eyes and everything was back to normal.

"I sat there trying to make some sense out of it all. If the shop wasn't there, then I understand why the people walking by were staring at me. I would have looked foolish standing there, staring into an alley. Also how did the old man know my name? Then I realized that he looked familiar, but why, I hadn't seen him before that day?

"I poured myself another drink and the warm liquid seemed to brush a few webs out of my head. I could see the man's face again. All of a sudden I realized where I had seen him before. It was Ben Abou Jusef, but at a very advanced age. If the shop was there and somehow I got mixed up when I went back to find it, then the old man was a relative to the Arab and that's how he knew my name. I felt a lot better thinking that I had solved the mystery.

"I finally gave up trying to make sense of the whole thing and dropped down on the bed to get some sleep. I figured by the time I get on the plane and the crew gets done serving me I won't be able to get any sleep until the wee hours of the morning.

"I fell asleep, but I sensed as though I was awake in a twilight state. My mind was preoccupied with Ben Abou Jusef trying to sell me the Key. All of a sudden I sat up in bed fully awake. It became crystal clear that somehow the Arab found a way to sell me that damned Key. At this point I still refused to believe all the hocus pocus about it. Even if the object was an antique it brought nothing, but misfortune to all who came in contact with it. Suddenly I felt uneasy as I looked at the Key again.

"I got out of bed and picked it up. The room was air conditioned, but the Key felt warm. I figured it was due to the sunlight hitting the objects on the table through the window. I picked up the parchment, it felt soft pliable without any difference in temperature than normal. I held the Key for only a few seconds in my hand and then wrapped it up in the hide again and laid it on the table.

"I picked up the lock. It felt cool to the touch. I packed the souvenirs into a suitcase and started preparations to leave for the airport. It was seven o'clock in the evening.

"I thought that the old man was right I'd have quite a tale for my buddies back in Brussels.

"I settled my bill, had the hotel call me a cab and went to the airport.

"After a trying three hours I finally found myself in my seat on the plane. My place was by the alleyway, but since there was no one by the window I moved over. I was happy as it gave me some extra space to stretch out.

"After we took off I ordered a couple of cognacs to settle my nerves. Once the meal was over I ordered another cognac with my coffee and then settled down for the night.

"The drink helped me sleep. I awoke to the sound of the intercom announcing the distribution of warm towels. As I regained some of my consciousness I realized to my surprise that I was in my own seat and the empty one next to the window was now occupied. Awkwardly I rubbed my eyes. Sitting next to me was a beautiful young woman. Half asleep I bumped her arm. 'I..I..'m sorry. I wasn't aware that the seat was occupied.'

'That's Ok. I was in the wrong seat when I boarded and you know the efficiency of the German airline, eventually they made me take my assigned place. We had to make you move to your seat, but you must have done it in your sleep since you don't remember it.'

"The flight attendant brought us the hot wet towels to wipe our faces, which was refreshing. 'Is Frankfurt your final destination?' I asked.

" 'No actually I'm going to Brussels.'

" 'What a coincidence? So am I. My name is Brad.'

" 'I'm called Angela.'

" 'A beautiful name for a beautiful woman.' I turned on my best charm. I thought what a stroke of luck. Perhaps I can arrange to meet her and get to know her better. Yet somehow as we spoke and I flattered her I felt uncomfortable as though she already knew my lines in advance.

" 'What do you do if you don't mind me asking?'

"She turned to me with a puzzled look on her face. 'What do you mean?'

" 'What type of work do you do or are you a lady of leisure and don't have to work?'

" 'Oh! I'm in the security business and I have an assignment in Brussels.'

" 'If you don't want to talk about it I'll understand, but let me ask you. Are you in the private sector or with some government?'

"She thought for a while. 'It's difficult to answer that question.'

" 'I understand. Confidentiality must be the principal creed in your business.'

" 'Oh! It's nothing like that, but I'm trying to rationalize the organization to myself. I have never been asked this question before.'

"She turned to me with long flowing blond hair and when I looked in her face it was almost glowing. She had a smile that would turn a man into mush. 'And what do you do Mr. Scott?'

" 'I'm just an ordinary businessman trying to carve a living out of this world.'

" 'That's a strange way of putting it. Are you successful?'

" 'I have done well. I make enough money so I can enjoy life to its fullest. I travel for my employers so I can get to see the world at their expense.'

" 'Does that fulfill you? I mean as a person. Are you completely happy?'

"I felt a little uncomfortable under her scrutiny. 'I don't think that anyone is completely happy, but I'm grateful that I have this chance. I know many that would give their eyeteeth to be in my shoes.'

"She looked at me through her wide eye. 'Indeed.'

"The attendant brought us our breakfast and while she ate she took out a book and began reading. I glanced at the cover before she opened it and it looked like it had some kind of occult or supernatural design on it.

"After we finished she read for another twenty minutes or so and then put the book away. 'Do you like reading Mr. Scott?'

" 'Sometimes, but I do so much reading in my business that I lost interest in reading as entertainment. I saw the cover of your book. Are you interested in the occult or the supernatural?'

" 'Yes. The majority of it is so much gibberish, but there are some writings that are most interesting. Do you believe in good and evil Mr....?'

" It was weird that she answered with one 'Yes' to a multiple query, but it didn't really matter so I didn't push. 'Sure doesn't everyone? All you have to do is look around you and you can't miss it, and by the way call me Brad.'

"She giggled. 'I know what you mean, but my question relates to whether you believe in the existence of a good force or being and an evil one.'

" 'That realm I leave to the philosophers and theologians.'

" 'Aren't we all philosophers and theologians?'

" 'I suppose so, but I spend as little time as possible in that field although once in awhile I don't mind pondering the question and attend seminars or symposiums on my own time. It's a good change from my daily routine, but at the end of these discussions I leave with more questions than answers. Nothing can be proven, but it's good exercise for one's brain.'

"She changed the subject. 'Were you in Israel on business?'

" 'No. I took some vacation and wanted to see the country on my own terms so I hired a guide who turned out to be an excellent companion. We visited a number of archeological digs and I learned much more than I understood previously. I'm glad I did although a number of interruptions and certain people spoiled a perfect trip.'

" 'Did you have problems with the Palestinians or other Arabs?'

" 'No. In fact I never saw any conflict between the Israelis and the Arabs. At many of the digs the groups were composed of internationals including both Israelis and Arabs.'

" 'Do you know any Arabs personally?'

" 'Not really, but I had met a fellow named Ben Abou Jusef who got killed in a car accident. Poor fellow. He was a merchant and because I was a tourist he wanted to unload what he said was an ancient artifact on me.'

" 'Did he? What happened?'

" 'I didn't bite so he gave up. I told him I wasn't interested. Not having any success with me, he decided to drive to Tel Aviv and got killed in a car pileup on the way. There was a man with whom you could have discussed good and evil all night long. He always appeared to be afraid that some evil was waiting for him around the next corner to pounce on him.'

"You are very cynical. 'Let's suppose that evil exist as an entity…'

"I waved at the flight attendant. 'Would you like a drink? I can't enter in such deep discussions unless I'm relaxed. I'll be honest, completely sober it seems silly to me, but after a couple of cognacs it almost makes sense.'

"The flight attendant came up and stood beside us expectantly. I looked at Angela. She slightly shook her head. So I ordered one for myself. 'Please bring one cognac.'

" 'Anything else? Nuts or coffee?'

"Again I looked at Angela and not seeing a response. 'Just a cognac, thank you.'

"Angela asked curtly, 'Do you need a drink to talk about good and evil? Are you hiding something in your life that you're trying to drown with alcohol?' I was startled. Her soft gentle voice suddenly turned hard almost menacing.

" 'I..I..I..'m sorry I didn't mean to offend you, but that's the way I feel. I can't think of anything at this moment that I have to hide or that needs to be drowned by a drink, but I enjoy it. I have traveled widely in the world and if anything I try to forget is probably the poverty, and cruelness that human beings exercise over each other. I cannot understand how people can be so cruel to strangers and then go home and be loving within their own families or circle of friends.'

"She softened a little, but was assertive. 'I know for sure that evil exists as an entity and it causes much suffering and many hardships in the world, but it has no power unless it's invited in. It does not have the power to enter or take over where it's not wanted.'

"I thought I would play along. 'Let's suppose you're right that evil does exist as an entity. Then how come one sees so many poor people suffering in the world? I'm sure that they don't go around inviting the devil into their lives. What about the stories of possession of innocent children? I can see adults inviting the devil, but not children.'

"She continued, 'Strange.'

" 'What do you mean?'

" 'You. A non-believer in the existence of evil as an entity, yet you are debating the subject.'

" 'I got carried away. The cognac makes one see things from a different perspective.'

"She pushed on. 'This evil is called the devil. You must bear in mind that he is known by many names and is the supreme magician as well as the greatest deceiver. Why do children follow some pedophile or other person who has an evil intent? It's because they trust him. Evil in any form can mask itself as good and attract the youngster. This is how Lucis disguises and befriends the child until he gains the youth's trust and is invited to join in the play. Even though the evil one hadn't been invited for his reasons; the invitation is legitimate enough for Lucis or any of his demons to gain the trust until he fully takes over the child's spirit.'

"I choked and began coughing violently.

" 'What's the matter?' She slapped me a couple of times across my back.

" 'N...n...n...o...t...h...i...n...g the cognac went down the wrong pipe.'

"After wiping the tears from my eyes I continued. 'I presumed that you meant the devil Lucifer when you said Lucis?'

"Of course both names are synonymous. It means light in Latin. In your religion Lucis is known by several names including Satan or The Beast. 'I like to study ancient languages and sometimes a name describes a person or thing much better in that language than in any modern tongue.

" 'You see in ancient times God and the devil were real entities and their names had a different connotation. Today they are only referred in abstract, which is the plan of the deceiver. Have you heard the name Lucis before?'

" 'Yes I did. There were a couple of characters that seemed to always appear wherever we traveled in Israel. They told us that they were journalist, then one night they told us their names. One was

Lucis and the other Nohmed. Lucis acted like he was the boss and told me he was a collector. He offered a large amount of money for some Key that floated around in a legend from antiquity. It sounded like the same Key that Ben Abou Jusef was trying to peddle. When I refused to enter into any kind of an arrangement with him, he got furious. I thought he was going to have Nohmed bash in my brains.'

"By this time I had a few more cognacs and had no inhibitions to spilling everything I knew, maybe to get the load off my chest.

"She went on. 'Yes Lucis was God's first and favorite until he rebelled and was cast down. The reason being of course that he refused to bend his knee to a human. He felt that it was humiliating since he was created from light and fire. On the other hand humans were created from water and mud.'

"By this time the cognac made me very smart. 'I guess it must have been a drag. One minute you're on top and the next minute you're being bumped a couple of notches down the hierarchy. He wouldn't like working for a corporation today, because this type of thing goes on all the time. Ha! Ha!'

" She looked at me. 'I'm glad that you find it so amusing. In my business we take it very seriously.'

" 'I'm glad that someone looks after us, because we sure can't take care of ourselves. You know something just dawned on me. Your name is Angela and you work for a security firm doesn't that make you a Guardian Angel?' I joked.

"She turned to me and said quietly yet firmly. 'Yes it does. Doesn't it?'

"I looked at her serene face and even in my drunken stupor felt sorry for making fun of something that apparently was a very serious topic to her. 'Listen I'm sorry I don't mean to belittle the things you say, and sometimes I make fun of things that I don't understand. Will you forgive me?'

" 'Of course don't worry.'

"The cognac made me sleepy. I had closed my eyes for a minute. In my stupor I heard the announcement. 'Fasten your seat belts.' We were getting ready to land in Frankfurt. I glanced at the seat next to me and it was empty again. I figured that I angered Angela or she just got fed up with my stupid remarks and moved somewhere else. I could have kicked myself for acting like a jerk. I figured that's the last I'll see of her.

"We landed in Frankfurt, I cleared my baggage and took them over to the Sabena airline desk and checked them in for Brussels. When I cleared customs, immigration and security I headed for the gate. I felt I had made a perfect ass of myself on the plane from Jerusalem, which was enough for one day.

"As I entered the waiting area by the gate I saw the back of a slender woman sitting alone. I thought that I might still salvage the day. At least perhaps I found a traveling companion that I could talk to on the plane to Brussels if she had a seat close to me.

"When I drew closer to her imagine my surprise. There was Angela. She was reading her book. She lifted her eyes above her rimless glasses. 'Hello again Brad.'

"I sat down beside her. 'Hi. Listen if I'm bothering you let me know and I'll move on. I shouldn't have drunk so much especially since I was tired and a bit stressed out by the last couple of weeks.'

" 'It's Ok. I already forgave you on the plane.'

" 'When I woke up and you were gone I thought that you moved to get away from me.'

" 'I had to move to the other seat because my carry on luggage was stored there.'

" 'That makes me feel a lot better and I can assure you that I'm a decent fellow when you get to know me.'

" 'Did you have any problems clearing customs?'

" 'No. I didn't bring anything back except an old padlock and a Key that doesn't fit it. I bought them as souvenirs. When the customs agents looked at them curiously, I explained that I collect old locks and that the Key didn't really fit this lock. They tried it and when they got nowhere they put the items back inside, then grinned at each other and let me through.'

" 'Does anyone else know that you bought this lock and Key?'

" 'No one else except the guy that sold me, the two customs officials and now you.'

"She glanced around. 'Perhaps they are valuable. I wouldn't advertise that I have them.'

" 'Right it's our secret.' I couldn't resist it since I paid thirty bucks and the vendor wanted only eighty dollars.

"Our flight was announced so we boarded the Sabina 737 to Brussels without any delay. Again as luck would have it she got the seat next to me. 'It's lucky we're sitting together again.'

"She smiled. 'Yes I'm glad to have company it's been a long trip. I think I'll get some sleep.'

" 'Since I didn't bring a book, can I borrow yours?'

" 'Sure, but I thought that you didn't read outside your business correspondence.'

" 'I was intrigued by our conversation and want to see what type of literature interests you.'

"My real intentions were to get to know her better through her interests. While she slept I read the book, which was about satanic worship, and witchcraft in the modern world. I thought that it was some fictional tale about the occult, but the author claimed that it was a collection of real events and practices.

"I must have read about a third of the book when she woke up. 'So what do you think? Do you believe that the author is right about such things?'

" 'I can't say from personal experience, but I can believe almost anything about people these days.'

" 'You are a cynic.'

" 'I guess so. How long are you going to stay in Brussels?'

" 'Until I complete my assignment.'

" 'Would you have time to go out to dinner or a movie?'

" 'I'm not sure I'll be busy, but give me your address, telephone number and I'll get in touch with you.'

"I didn't say anything, but I figured that I had just been given the proverbial brush off. So be it you can't win them all. Just in case, I gave her my address.

"When we landed in Zaventem airport and since we had come from another EU country we had no formalities to worry about. The immigration and customs agents stood idly by surveying the passengers, but didn't bother anyone. We went outside looking for taxis and found the row along one side. Angela was ahead of me and grabbed the first one. While I was inching my way towards the next one through the crowd I heard her yell something at me.

"I turned around. 'What did you say?

" 'Remember I'm a guardian angel so when you need me just call and I'll be there!' She shouted back.

" 'How can I? I don't know your address or telephone number.'

"I told my driver to hang on for moment and was about to run over to ask her again at least for her phone number or company name, but her cab roared off into the traffic.

Chapter XV

"I went back to my cab and gave him my home address in Brussels. It was a normal Friday morning in Brussels. The sky was overcast. The drizzle felt like a heavy fog. It didn't look like it was going to clear. The sky was covered with a gray blanket as far as one could see.

"As I figured she never called me and as the days passed she began to fade from my mind. Once in a while when I sat down with a cognac after my evening meal my mind would wander and I would reflect on my flights from Tel Aviv and Frankfurt wondering what happened to Angela.

"I would go over and handle my souvenirs that I had bought in Israel, which were mounted on one part of a wall where I kept other similar objects collected over the years. I had picked up a number of old locks and some keys during my travels. My recent purchases fit well in my collection.

"It was strange, that every time I touched the Key it would make my fingers tingle as though it was electrically charged. Several times I tried to hold it to examine it, but I would feel a painful sensation as time passed until I had to drop it or risk burning my hands. Yet the burning felt peculiar and not like anything I felt before. It was hot, yet cold.

THE KEY OF DAMASCUS

"It was impossible to touch it for more than a few seconds. Of course it was just an illusion, because once I brought a wet cloth and picked up the Key with it. Nothing happened. There was no steam or anything else visible.

"A week or so later one Saturday I decided to have lunch at a small restaurant in the Grand-Place, because it was a beautiful sunny day near the end of August. In Brussels when the sun comes out one makes the most of it, because it rains nearly all of the time. I sat down on the sidewalk patio to enjoy the fresh warm air and ordered a glass of wine. I was reading the menu when I heard a seductive woman's voice. 'Well isn't this a surprise?'

"I looked up and noticed a slender young woman with dark flowing hair standing before me. 'I..I..m afraid you got the advantage of me.'

" 'I'm disappointed. Remember we met for a short time in Israel one evening and you gave me a cup of coffee.'

" 'Yes, of course.'

"I stood up extended my hand. We weren't introduced. 'I'm Brad Scott.' For a moment there was an awkward silence. She hadn't told me her name that night and wasn't volunteering it now.

" 'Aren't you going to invite me to sit down?'

" 'S..o..r..r..y. Please join me.' I waved to the waiter for another glass for wine. 'I'm just about to have something to eat. Please let me make up for my rudeness and buy you lunch.'

"The waiter brought another glass and filled it from the bottle on my table.

"I raised my glass. 'Here's to a most delightful occasion. Our meeting again.'

"We each took a sip. She kept her glass to her lips just a little too long. I noticed that she was staring at me over the rim with her eyes that looked like pools of some dark liquid. I could feel the electricity of the moment and the passion radiating from them.

"She still hadn't given me her name. I figured I had better get it before she disappears again. 'Our meeting in Israel was so short that I didn't get your name.'

" 'Lilith.'

" 'Lilith? Is it the same as in Lilly Marlene?' I teased.

" 'Could be, if you want it. I can be anyone you want.' She laughed in a deep throaty voice, but did not volunteer a last name.

" 'So what brings you to Brussels?'

" 'I told you that I was a person of independent means and travel on my own, but I 'm also under obligation to find certain special antiques and 'other things' for my benefactor.'

" 'Presently I'm acting as a buyer hunting for antiques. Brussels is a good place for such things. If I'm lucky I find some valuable items in Europe as well as the Middle East. The searching is tedious, but the results of the assignments bring great rewards.'

" 'I would think it would be exciting. Are you staying here long?'

" 'I really don't know. I'm here to find a specific object and if I'm successful, then I'm out of here.'

" 'I don't want to wish you bad luck, but I hope that it will take you some time to find this object.'

" 'What about you Mr. Scott? How is your collection? Do you have anything that you may want to dispose of?'

"I didn't remember telling her about my collection, but I assumed that she found out during some contacts with antique dealers. 'I have a few old locks of no consequence. They give me the pleasure of being part of me, but have no great intrinsic value.'

"She leaned closer to me and gazed directly into my eyes, then whispered, 'Perhaps you're wrong. Would you like for me to come by and give you my appraisal?'

"As I stared at her hypnotic eyes and before I could reply I heard a nervous cough. I looked up and there stood the waiter. '*Monsieur et Mademoiselle* are ready?'

"He broke the spell. I looked at Lilith. 'I think I'll have the *beeftek*,' she said.

" 'And I'll have the *porc provenciale*.'

"The waiter made some notes. '*Merci*,' and disappeared.

"The magic was broken and we could not recapture it again.

"While we ate I asked, 'Where are you staying?'

" 'At the Hilton downtown.'

"This time I wasn't going to mess up my chance. 'Would you really like giving me an appraisal of my collection?'

" 'Of course I'd love to any night you say. I'm free in the evenings.'

"Since I didn't know her last name and she didn't volunteer I didn't push. I learned that a long time ago in my travels to know when to stop asking for one's identity. 'It would be interesting to get the opinion of a professional to find out whether I have so much junk or if any part of my collection is worthy of being called antiques. I'll give you a call. What is your room number?'

" '666 near the elevators.'

"As we ate we made small talk about Israel and Brussels. After finishing the meal I pulled out a cigar. "Excuse me do you mind if I light one of these?'

" 'No, I love the smell of a cigar. Actually the smell of smoke excites me.'

" 'Some people think it's a filthy habit, but I enjoy it once in a while.'

"The waiter came by and stood beside us expectantly. I turned to Lilith. 'How about an aperitif?'

" 'Something sweet would be nice.' She cooed.

"I ordered the aperitifs and while we were waiting I was in the middle of taking another puff when she suddenly blurted out. '"Did you ever find the Key?'

"The Key was the furthest thing from my mind. 'What Key? Oh! The one that had been referred to in that parchment?'

" 'Yes.'

" 'I never got involved any further, because I thought it was a smoke job. I don't think it ever existed. The Arab Ben Abou Jusef said that he had it and tried to sell it to me, but I figured it was a ruse to stiff a tourist and refused. Shortly afterwards he got killed in a five car pile up. His death ended the whole affair.'

" 'Are you sure that you don't have it? It's worth a great deal of money. More than you would ever see in your lifetime.'

"All of a sudden the words of the oath on the parchment that was wrapped around the old lock and key that I bought flashed in my brain.

" 'I assure you that I haven't got it. When you come to see me you can make a thorough inspection of my collection and see for yourself.'

"She looked disappointed, but quickly regained her zeal and said, 'I look forward to your invitation.'

"We finished our meal, which took us several hours. I almost asked her to come over that night, but something held me back.

"She lingered expectantly then stood up. 'I must run now, but don't forget our date.' Knowing that I was watching her she turned around and gave me a last inviting glance before disappearing into the crowd.

"I settled my account and took a long walk back home hating my stupidity. This was another sample of my hesitation and lost opportunity, but I knew her name and place where she was staying. This time she would not slip through my fingers.

"I figured I would call her on Monday and make the arrangements as soon as I knew my schedule for the following week.

"On the way home I thought about taking a weekend trip sometime soon to Germany to get a change of scenery so I picked up some information from one of the travel bureaus.

"Since I was well versed in German I figured it would be nice to travel to a country where the language wouldn't be a difficulty. I thought that fall season would be nice. Its not too hot yet I wouldn't have to deal with the slush and snow of winter. My first opportunity would be late September, as I had to clear up some backlog at work and could get an extra day to make it a long weekend. I had heard of a small place called Assmannshausen near Rudesheim on the Rhine River. It was across from Bingen where the best of German white wines are grown. I figured I'd make further plans the next day.

"Normally I wasn't a church going person, but once in a while I would attend a mass when it suited me. That Sunday morning I had an urge to go to church."

"You must be a devoted catholic." Quipped the priest. "Now I know why you didn't want to have this confession heard in a church. Are you afraid that you might become a devoted believer? The tale that you are telling borders on the spiritual and supernatural rather than the world you live in."

The *monk* didn't answer but pressed on with his story.

"As I left the church out of the blue only a block away staring in a store window was Angela. 'Fancy meeting you here.'

"She smiled at me. 'I noticed that you came out of the church. I'm surprised. From your conversation I didn't think that you were a church going person.'

" 'I feel one must have insurance just in case there is something to this God business.'

" 'Are you jesting because you don't understand again?'

"I let the sarcasm go. 'I thought that you had finished your assignment and left since you didn't call me.'

" 'I was busy and then I decided to call you yesterday, but I saw you in the Grand-Place with Lilith so I made up my mind not to bother you.'

"I was stunned. 'You know Lilith?'

" 'Our paths have crossed.'

" 'I was getting angry. I figured she was using Lilith as an excuse to get herself out of a jam because I caught her in a lie.

"She kept looking around as she talked to me. I was getting upset. 'You remind me of Ben Abou Jusef. You seem to have developed the same annoying habit that he had of not paying attention.' I didn't care whether I hurt her feelings or not. She lied to me once too often.

"She ignored my remark. 'You are in great danger Brad. We must talk, but this isn't the time or place.'

" 'What is it that we need to talk about? What possible danger could I be in Brussels? I'm just a businessman. There are many more important people here with the EU and NATO. Why would anyone be interested in me?'

" 'I can't tell you now. You're planning a trip to Germany aren't you? Why don't we meet there?'

" 'I don't know where you get your information, but I just picked up some pamphlets only last night and was musing about a trip there. I haven't made any plans yet. How could you have known it?'

"Again she didn't answer my question. 'That's not important, but I'm going there next week and we could meet somewhere. We could spend some time together and I would explain everything to you.'

"I figured it was just another promise that she didn't intend to keep. 'Is this like your promise call me in Brussels?'

"She looked hurt. 'I really did intend to call you, but I couldn't until yesterday and that's the truth. You only gave me your address at the airport and I had difficulty in finding you since you have an unlisted phone number.'

"Some years ago I decided to get an unlisted number so I wouldn't get calls from some of my lady friends that I didn't want to see again. I kept my number scrupulously to myself and in this case I forgot to give it to her.

"She continued. 'I don't blame you for not believing me.

" 'I guess I could advance my plans, but I promised to call Lilith this coming week and I don't want to break my word to her.' I thought I'd show her that she's not the only game in town.

" 'It's of the utmost importance that you don't call her. She mustn't know anything about our conversation.'

" 'Why? Is she a competitor of yours or are you jealous?' I quipped.

" 'The truth is yes, she is a competitor and no I'm not jealous.'

" 'These intrigues just confuse me. I don't understand what in the hell is going on.'

" 'Exactly. However you will if you meet me as I ask.'

" 'I'll agree on one condition.'

" 'Yes?'

" 'That you spend the weekend with me.'

"She hesitated. 'Ok, I promise. Why don't we meet in Trier. It's not far and we can travel to the Rhineland together.' Again it hit me. How does she know that I intended to travel to the Rhineland? I was so happy that she accepted my invitation and thought it better not to antagonize her with questions lest she cancels the whole deal.

" 'It's a deal. When do you want to leave?'

" 'Tomorrow.'

" 'I can't until Tuesday, but why don't we leave together from Brussels?'

" 'Because I must be in Trier tomorrow.'

" 'Ok. I'll meet you there. You want to pick out the spot?'

" 'Why don't we meet at the entrance of the amphitheatre on Tuesday afternoon?'

" 'Ok. Do you want to have some lunch or dinner with me tonight?'

"She looked sheepish. 'I really want to, but I have a surveillance job until late and probably will leave for Trier when it's over.'

" 'I'm glad I don't work for your boss. Won't he even let you get a night's sleep?'

" 'He's a good boss and sleep isn't as important to me as it is to you,' she replied curtly.

"We said our goodbyes and I headed home.

"She fascinated me. The next day I got the most important tasks completed and since I still had some vacation coming I told the boss that I wanted a couple of days off to go to Germany. He agreed as long as I would keep in contact with the office once a day in case something important came up that needed my attention.

"I was like a kid in high school with my first romance. I didn't sleep too well and couldn't get Angela out of my mind. On Tuesday early in the morning I took off for Trier, which is about 250 kilometers or 156 miles from Brussels. It took me three hours with pit stops to get there. Arriving around noon I thought about finding a hotel, but decided to meet with Angela first in case she had made reservations for us already. There was no hurry. There were many smaller pensions if the hotels were filled. We planned to stay in the city only one night, so if we had to find something outside the city it wouldn't be a calamity.

"I met her at the entrance of the coliseum as agreed. We visited the old ruins and subterranean cells where animals, condemned criminals and gladiators were kept in between the games. We talked about the conditions that must have existed in this place two thousand years before. Angela seemed to be very sad and from time to time would stop at a spot in the grottos, which served as cells and putting her hand on the wall. She would become silent for a while as though seeing or remembering something.

"While we walked around the city she was very nervous and continually turned her head from side to side as though expecting to see someone jump out at any second.

"Somehow I got drawn into the paranoia and began to act like her.

"We decided to eat in an outside courtyard cafe near the Porta Negra. It has been so named because the original light yellow sandstone has turned black from smoke and pollution over the centuries.

"After lunch we went inside and visited the gate itself. Later we went to see the ruins of the Roman Baths. Some of the walls are still standing from antiquity and others have been restored for tourists. We also had a chance to enter some of the Roman quarters that have been half buried over the centuries. Small windows placed high in the walls allow a little light inside. The semi darkness in most of the halls and rooms gives it an eerie feeling. One can almost feel the presence of the men that once enjoyed these luxuries close to two thousand years ago.

"I felt strange. Every time we turned a corner in the gloomy hallways, I had a sensation that there were others ahead of us. 'I thought that we were alone?'

"Angela cocked her head listening. 'I don't hear anything, but if there are others they could be wearing rubber soles.'

"I felt a chill up and down my spine. 'Somehow I feel uncomfortable in here.'

"Angela studied the hallway ahead and behind us. 'Perhaps you're right. Its dusk outside and it's getting harder and harder to see in here. Rather than visit the whole complex let's leave as soon as we find a way out.'

"I was sure that she was aware of other presences and was beginning to get nervous. She put her arm through mine. 'Let's move faster, because if it gets dark we could get lost in the labyrinth.'

"She was pulling on me so much that we almost began to run. 'I wouldn't worry too much, this place has many exits and we're bound to come across one around the next bend,' I told her.

"She was like a woman possessed and did not hear what I said, but continued to exert her pressure on my arm to find a way to get out of there as soon as possible.

"Finally we found one of the exits and hurried outside. 'Whew!' She sighed.

" 'You were really scared in there. For a person in the security business you sure got spooked.'

" 'In my business we only confront our enemies when we pick our time and place. You know the old axiom that goes something about run while you can so that you can fight another day.'

" 'I heard it, but I don't think that your quote is exact.'

" 'It's not important to quote accurately, but it's important to know what it means and apply it when the need arises.'

"When we left the baths, there was still some light outside, but the sun itself had already disappeared behind the city buildings and hills. I thought that we should start making plans for the night and also the next day. 'I didn't get a chance to ask you. Did you drive down here from Brussels yesterday? Do you have a car somewhere in the city?'

"She turned to me. 'No. What about you? Did you drive or take the train?'

" 'I drove. My car is parked in a little courtyard not too far from here. What about your baggage? Do you have a room already and have you booked accommodations for me?'

" 'No. I thought that we should do it together. My bag is checked in at the railroad station and if you don't mind maybe we could drive over and get it.'

" 'Fine with me.'

"We found my car, drove to the railroad station. I hadn't paid attention that she kept referring to 'bag' and not 'bags' and thought that as a woman she would have several suitcases, but as long as I could get them into my Mercedes all our problems would be solved. However to my surprise all she had was a small single traveling bag.

"As I put the key into the ignition she put her hand on top of mine before I had a chance to start it. 'Would you mind terribly if we didn't stay here tonight?'

" 'Oh! Is there any reason? It's getting dark.'

" 'I must confess I don't have as much time as I previously thought and I would like to spend as much time on the Rhineland with you as possible.'

" 'Ok. Let's drive until we run across something that looks interesting, but we'll have to quit before nine o'clock because many of the *Gasthouses* lock their doors after that hour.'

"I could see the tension dissipate from her face. She squeezed my hand. 'I'm so glad that you agree with me. It makes things so much easier.'

"I didn't question her. We found our way out of the city and headed towards Koblenz. About 50 km out of the city we turned right and headed towards Oberstein. The drive from Bussels and the sightseeing began to take its toll on me. 'We have been driving for half an hour, but I've had a long day, what do you say that we quit in the next thirty minutes.'

"After some time we found ourselves near a place called Thalfang where found a small *Gasthouse*. It still had a couple of vacancies, which we were happy to take.

"The next day we drove all the way to Bingen, then a small place called Kempten where we grabbed a ferry across the Rhine. Once across we drove for another fifteen minutes to Assmannshausen.

"On the way I noticed the ruins of an ancient castle on my right side. There were others, but most of them had been turned into museums or some other tourist attractions. I planned to visit the crumbling old citadel and once we get to the hotel I'd find out how to get to it.

"We arrived in mid afternoon and registered at a quaint place called Bauernschanke and after dropping our luggage off in our rooms we came downstairs to the patio and ordered some of the area's famous white wine.

"While we sipped our grape nectar, I casually asked the waiter about the ruins that I had seen and was told that the castle was called Ehrenfels located between Rudesheim and Assmannshausen. It was the Bishop of Mainz that built the castle in the early thirteenth century. The ecclesiastic Elector of Mainz used it as a residence after 1386. The castle had a rich history, but in 1689 the French conquered and destroyed it. Since then the place has stood as a reminder of the folly of man to think that a fortification can keep him safe from his enemies. As we sipped our third glass Angela left for a few minutes and when she came back I could see that she was distressed. I didn't push and at last she confessed. 'I must go to Rudesheim for a few hours, which I'm afraid will take care of this evening. Let's get together in the morning and we'll plan the day.'

" 'I thought that you were done with business and that we would enjoy this trip. That's the reason I took off earlier than planned from my office.' I said tersely.

" 'I know, but I got some news that need my immediate attention. The circumstances are such that a life depends on it. I must go.'

" 'I wouldn't want to be responsible for anyone's life.' I grumbled angrily. I was getting tired of her act. 'I think that you're here on your own agenda and only came with me on some pretense of your for your end.'

"She looked at me with tears in her eyes. I felt bad for being so harsh. As she was about to walk away I pulled the keys out of my pocket. 'The place is about eight kilometers from here so you'll need some type of transportation.'

"She took the keys and disappeared towards the parking lot.

"I finished the bottle and since there was a lot of daylight left I decided to take a walk through the vineyards towards the ruins. I figured that Angela would in all probability not be interested in a hike through the steep slopes. It most likely wouldn't hold the same appeal for her that it did for me.

"I settled my bill and started up the narrow winding road until I reached the junction of a gravel path and followed it further up the mountain. After a half an hour's trek I realized that I was too high and cut across some bushes and vineyards to a path that I felt would either take me to the castle or very close to it. After another twenty minutes I reached the ruins. By this time the sun was over the mountains and the broken stonewalls cast a foreboding shadow.

"There was a steel gate to keep out unwanted visitors, or perhaps for safety reasons. The place was a shambles of fallen stones from the crumbling walls that could either injure or kill a person if any got dislodged from the top of a wall.

"I walked around and found a hole in the wall where I could crawl inside. The ramparts in the courtyard cast long wide shadows that made the light even dimmer than it had been outside.

"All of a sudden the inner yard got cold. It was unusual because it was early September and the normal temperature for this time of the year is still balmy. The sky took on a gray foggy texture and it got darker much quicker than I thought it would. I decided to get out. I didn't bring a flashlight and didn't want to crawl around the ruins in darkness.

"As I made my way towards the hole in the wall, which was in a little alcove I heard a voice behind me. 'Well Mr. Scott we meet again.'

"I turned to see Lucis standing to one side. 'Y..o..u surprised me. I never thought that we would meet again. What brings you here all the way from Israel? Surely there are no relics or antiques in this place?'

" 'You bring us here.'

" 'Us?'

"Looking around I saw two other figures in the shadows. As they stepped out I recognized them. It was Nohmed and Lilith.

"The three looked menacing. Their faces looked cold and I thought I could hear wheezing sounds coming from them.

"Lucis took a step forward. 'We're not going to play your game any longer Mr. Scott.' He hissed.

"I turned trying to get by him, but he shifted so quickly that he ended up in front blocking my path. I didn't see him moving his legs. It was as though he disappeared in one place and appeared in the other.

" 'You're not leaving here until you tell us where you keep the Key.'

" 'You people must be crazy. I don't have any Key that would interest you.'

"I turned to Lilith whose eyes shone in the semi darkness. 'So you work for the same guy as he does?' I looked at the Nohmed who stood beside them frozen like a statue. 'What's the matter you're angry because I didn't invite you to my place?'

"She didn't answer, but just let out a menacing hiss.

"I looked back at Lucis whose face was contorted with rage.

" 'Enough. Nohmed help Mr. Scott remember what he did with the Key.'

"Nohmed stepped forward and raised his hand. He never touched me, but the force threw me across the courtyard. I landed hard on some rubble. Lucis screamed, 'Where's the Key?'

"Then I heard Lilith. 'Let me at him Lord I will make him talk.'

"He waved her away. 'You'll get your chance.'

" 'Now Mr. Scott this is a very small and painless demonstration of my powers. We can still do business if you are interested or we can continue with our little amusement until you talk. You will talk one way or another.'

"I was dazed.' I still don't know what you're talking about.

" 'Mr. Scott we know you have it and we have all night because no one is going to come here in the darkness.'

"I was about to deny again when Nohmed raised his hand and this time all my clothes ripped off my body except for my jockey shorts. Lucis turned to Lilith. 'Now my dear it's your turn, but mind you I don't want him dead.'

"She raised her arms with her fingers extended that looked like claws with needle sharp points. I saw what I thought were beams of blue light extending from them towards me. When they reached me the rays cut into my flesh diagonally like butchers knives. They were so quick that at first I didn't even feel the pain until the wounds began to bleed. I screamed. The sound seemed to resonate within the walls.

" 'You can scream all you want Mr. Scott. No one will hear you.

The acoustics are such that all the noise is being contained within these walls. Are you ready to tell us where you keep the Key?'

"He glanced towards Lilith who raised her hands again and the same rays cut my chest diagonally in the opposite direction. The pain was excruciating.

"As I lay there moaning Lucis looked at Nohmed who raised his hand and again sending me flying across the yard into a wall. I crumpled at the base barely conscious.

"I heard Lucis. 'Let me have a little fun.'

"Through my tears I could see him raising his hands. The force picked me up off the ground and pulled me up the wall. At the same time I felt my arms being stretched away from my body. I was dragged helplessly up the wall. I looked down and I could see the trio standing about ten feet blow me. They had their faces lifted towards me. 'Maybe we should pay homage to him like we did to that Jew in Jerusalem.'

"Then Lucis lifted his hands and I felt excruciating pain in my wrists and feet. 'Is this worth it Mr. Scott?'

"He turned to his followers and screeched, 'He looks good. He is suspended in the same place where the old fool from Mainz used to hang his cross.'

"Then he looked at me. 'You're a fool. I can't begin to tell you the pleasures and power that you could have if you cooperated.'

"The pain was so bad that I didn't know how long I could endure it, and only hate for the trio kept me alive. I could see the glee in Lucis' eyes. 'I love the way you hate Mr. Scott. When I see this passion it makes everything worthwhile.'

"Finally my brain was coming to my rescue and I began to loose consciousness. The pain was far away and I didn't care any longer. Suddenly I felt cold water all over my body, and with it came a stinging pain and I regained my senses.

"Lucis shouted. 'How do you like some cool ocean water? The salt is very stimulating or would you rather tell us where you keep the Key.' To this day I don't know how he got this water being so far away from any sea.

"This time Lucis raised his right arm as though to throw something at me and I felt the sting of whips tearing at my flesh. I had seen others near death and I figured this was the end so I began to pray. 'Have mercy on me Lord. I have been proud and arrogant in my life, but if you can find it within you stop this pain...' I figured that when I passed out this time I wouldn't recover.

"As I began to drift into oblivion, again I saw Angela and remembered what she had told me. 'If you will ever need me just call and I'll be there.'

"So in my stupor I called to her. 'Angela! Angela! Where are you?' I closed my eyes and thought I was dying because I could see a bright light seeping through my eyelids. I opened my eyes and saw Angela standing between the trio and me. She didn't have any clothes on, but rather a thick cloud of light. She stood there with her arms and hands extended from her side. She turned towards me and I saw that the soft round lines of her face had turned into straight and hard features, but even through them I could feel the compassion for me. She turned towards the trio.

"Surprised Lucis and his cohorts shrunk back from her.

"Then Lucis took a step forward. 'Ha!..Ha! So they sent you to save this wretched creature? Why don't you join me?'

"She stood there motionless. 'We meet again Lucis.' She was unafraid. 'Every once in a while you must be taught your place within the order of things. Leave here now and return whence you came.'

" 'You forget Angela that my powers are far greater than yours. You must remember that I was His Light and still retain all the powers that I had."

"She warned. 'Go. We have fought before and you lost so shall it be this time.'

"I looked and saw the same type of light beams extending from her fingers towards Lucis as I had seen from Lilith's, but these were pure white.'

"Lucis raised his hands and they radiated even more intense light and stopped her rays before they reached him. They stood there before each other for a while without making any headway one-way or the other. Suddenly her form began to quiver and her beams wavered. I heard Nohmed and Lilith cackle with pleasure.

"Then I heard her voice. 'Lord Jesus help me for without you I'm lost.'

"All of a sudden her beams increased to such intensity that the light began to hurt my eyes. This time it was Lucis' turn to bend under the new force.

"He fell back on the ground.

"Angela made a circle on the ground before the trio, which opened a dark bottomless hole. The trio crouched began whining and pleading with Angela. It was to no avail. Her light beams extended into wings that gathered the trio and began herding them into the pit. All of a sudden the human forms of the trio changed to hideous creatures and began to whimper like some hurt animals. 'Lucis remember what you said. It's better to rule in hell than to serve in heaven. Go back to your kingdom over which you rule.' With a quick sweep she pushed the trio into the hole and made the phenomena disappear.

"Then she turned to me and with the same extended white wings lifted me from the wall.

"I laid there covered with blood weak and ready to meet my maker. 'So you were an angel after all. Are you really a guardian angel? Whose guardian are you?'

" 'Yours. My mission was to keep you safe and prevent the Key from falling into Lucis' hands.'

"I looked at her face. It had turned soft and compassionate again. 'I guess I won't be able to help.' I could barely breath. 'My time has come.'

" 'No. It hasn't.' She put her hand on my forehead. 'Behold the mercy and the love of God.'

"As I lay there I could feel my strength return and felt the pain disappear from my body. I sat up and looking at myself I saw the scars of my encounter with those hellish creatures, but the wounds had healed.

"I looked around for my clothes. Angela stood up took me by the hand and raising the other made a motion and my clothes came flying to me from in between the rubble. In an instant I was standing there completely dressed as though nothing had happened to me. I couldn't believe it. I thought the whole thing was a hallucination. At that moment I noticed that my wrists had scars left from the spikes that had held me to the wall.

"Angela beckoned me to sit down on a stone. 'Now you must know everything.'

" 'You were chosen to protect the Key and move it to a safe place. Ben Abou Jusef tried to sell it to Jacob who had made a deal with Lucis. I told you that evil couldn't harm you unless you invite it or make a contract with it. However Jacob couldn't find the funds or means to buy the Key from Ben Jusef. Therefore reneging on his deal with Lucis, he had to pay the price with his life.'

" 'What about me? As far as I know I hadn't made any contract with him and look what happened to me?'

" 'You flirted with them. Unknowingly you invited Lilith into your apartment. If she had entered your residence then even I couldn't have saved you. Your fate might have been the same as Jacob's.'

" 'What about Ben Abou Jusef?'

" 'That was a quirk of fate and a freak accident. By the time the trio had figured out his role in the scheme of things he was dead. Since Nachman didn't play their game and chased them away they didn't have any power over him. They were not finished with him and would have tried until they found his Achilles' heel, but somehow they figured out that you had the Key. Your weakness is money and women. That's the reason why Lucis sent Lilith. She has seduced the best, the bravest and some that thought that they were the most holy. In your case it was luck and some of my interference with your plans.'

"I felt sheepish. 'I guess I'm lucky.'

" 'When you decided to go to Israel for a vacation events began to unfold that could have spelled disaster for the world. I was ordered to help you in case Lucis and his group used supernatural powers that you couldn't fight. I did not interfere until they did and if you wouldn't have asked for help I still wouldn't have been able to help you. You see, good must also be invited and cannot just walk into your soul.

" 'The times when I left you I spent checking out how close Lucis was getting to you. Sometimes I found him searching for you and other times he was watching you with his demons from a distance even though you were not aware. He did not know that I was guarding you and I couldn't afford for him to see us together because he is cunning and has greater powers than I. So I had to outwit him. Even at the end I had to ask for help to defeat him. He knows it and keeps hoping that one-day help will not come in time and that he would win. Remember Brad what I have told you. These lessons must serve you until the end of your journey.

" 'Now go back and get the Key that you bought with the lock and take it to a safe place. Few people over millennia have been privileged to hold it without the parchment, feel and see its powers, but again it comes with a price. It can only be handled wrapped in the hide that you found in the package. Without it you wouldn't be able to lift it, because it is so heavy with sin. Also contrary to normal beliefs, evil is cold and not hot. That is why in certain places where evil exists as an entity in this world one always finds the cold spots and can see one's breath. When you touch the Key you feel your fingers burning, but it's from extreme cold and not heat. If you are one of the chosen ones you will not be harmed, but if you're not then by the time you find out it's too late. Your hands would suffer from extreme frost bite and may even need to be amputated.'

" 'I didn't care about handling this Key except to get rid of it. I'll hide it so no one will know where it is.'

" 'Yes, but now that Lucis knows that you have it he would find a way to trick you into inviting him into your soul without you being aware and all would be lost. The Key must be protected and placed in a secure place on hallowed ground.

" 'I don't know how long he will stay in his kingdom of darkness, because he has so many confederates working in this world that he can travel at will.

" 'So, you must share the knowledge of the Key with someone else who can help to protect it. In case one of you dies, you must develop a system that would allow each of you to find this out as soon as possible.

" 'This message must be conveyed to that person on hallowed ground. Remember that Lucis cannot enter anywhere unless he is invited. An ordinary church is not good enough, because people who go there could bring evil into the sanctuary with them.

" 'You must find a place where the attendance remains constant by the same people who can be trusted. This will minimize Lucis' ability to corrupt someone and gain access to the premises.'

"I thought for a minute. 'I think I know.'

" 'Hurry. If Lucis gets his hands on the Key not only can he dispense the power that the Key contains to whomever he pleases, but also could keep the Gates of Heaven locked forever, since the sins would not be transferred to the Gate at the appointed time.

" 'Go now Brad with God's blessings and hurry. We don't have much time.'

"I looked around for the hole in the wall that had led me into the courtyard and when I turned around again Angela was gone. Only then did I realize how light it was inside the courtyard because of the full moon. The bluish gray light reminded me of the beams that Lilith had used. A shiver ran down my back and all of sudden I started feeling cold so I ran to the wall and plunged through the hole. Once outside I ran all the way, back to the hotel as though all of hell was after me.

Chapter XVI

"Awakening the next morning I felt like the whole episode at the castle was just a horrible dream. I removed the top of my pajamas to check my chest. The scars from Lilith's cuts were visible, but the incisions had healed completely and I felt no pain.

"I took a hot shower, which felt good. I shaved and got dressed.

"I remembered that Angela had borrowed my car the day before, so I slipped out to the parking lot and saw that it was parked in the same spot where I had left it. My anxiety dissolved.

"I had a second set of keys so I didn't worry about starting it, but went over to check and see if she had left the set that I had given her in the Mercedes.

"To my surprise the car was locked. Unlocking it I thought that I would have been in a pickle if I hadn't had my second set with me. I locked the car and returned to the hotel.

"I went into Angela's room, but didn't find any luggage there. She was gone.

"I had breakfast and then went to check out. The clerk handed me an envelope. 'I wasn't on duty last night, but I found this envelope addressed to you when I came in this morning.'

"I opened it and inside was a short note and my other set of keys.

'Remember Brad that speed to dispose of the Key is of the utmost importance. Your life depends on it.

" 'I hope I didn't inconvenience you too much by returning your keys in this way.' I looked inside the envelope and there was my other set of keys.'

" 'Anything wrong?' Asked the clerk.

" 'No. The young lady had to leave early so I'll settle for both rooms.'

"After paying I went back to the room used the facilities, packed my bag and left."

The priest gazed intensely ahead to a point where the street ended. "My son your story is getting more absurd by the moment. Perhaps you need professional help. I know..."

"I'm near the end of my tale. Be patient; give me another half an hour and I'll get out of your hair. Shortly I'll provide you with proof of what I told you."

"I'll give you the time you ask, and won't interrupt you, but no longer. You must promise me that if I'm not satisfied you'll agree to get some professional help."

The *monk* was furious, but could not afford the luxury of delaying his mission. He had to finish the story. "Agreed."

"Getting back to the car I threw my bag on the back seat and took off for Brussels.

"The events of the last few days whirled around in my mind, and seemed unreal; like a dream. I thought that perhaps I have had some kind of a breakdown. I was sure that a hot shower at home would fix all solve all my troubles.

"I had thought about Angela's request and the promise I made her the night before.

"Arriving home I went over to where the Key was hanging and decided that I would inspect it after my shower.

"When I took off my shirt I took a good look at my chest and even though I had seen it before in Assmannshausen I was horrified. It had not registered that morning in the hotel how badly I was scarred. There were marks on my chest and when I turned around to look at my back in a mirror, it was criss-crossed with lines where Lucis used his whip. I looked at my wrists as well as my feet and saw the scars left by the spikes when Lucis hung me on the wall. Yet all were healed as though it had happened a long time ago and I felt no pain.

"After the shower I went and picked up the Key in my bare hands. Slowly it warmed up and got so hot that I could hold it not longer. I realized that the 'heat' as Angela had said, was extreme cold. I opened my hands and shook them to drop it, but the Key was stuck to my palms just as metal does in the winter to ones skin in extreme cold.

"I don't know whether it was the pain or some figment of the imagination, but all of a sudden the hands did not hurt anymore and my head began to swim in a mist until it cleared and I could see through it. I went back in time to creation, saw the sin of Adam and Eve. I saw many important and not so important people passing me by, but not noticing me as though I was a ghost right up to our present time. I saw their good and evil deeds. This vision zipped through eons of time as though it was a movie sped up a million times. Yet to me it seemed like it was in slow motion. There was time to understand and remember everything. Can you imagine what secrets I carry about the people of this world both the poor and the powerful? Imagine the power that I could exercise over them if I wanted? The burden is unbearable."

The priest rolled his eyes in disbelief, but did not interrupt as he promised. The *monk* noticed the contempt in the face of his companion, but did not stop.

"When we began this walk I told you that I didn't want to go to any church, but I've changed my mind. I would like to finish my 'confession' in a church, but it must be a place where few outsiders visit."

The priest was stunned and hadn't been listening close enough to remember what Angela had said. "There are many churches here. What changed your mind?"

"You will know it in a few minutes. It will also be safer for both of us."

"Safer for both of us? What does it have to do with me?"

The *monk* ignored him, "Where do you suggest we go?"

The priest thought for a moment. "Since we are on Freres St. Francis, let's go to the Latin Patriarchate Street and find the Seminary. I have the privilege of going inside whenever I please, but it's not open to the public."

The two men walked in silence for some time until they turned several corners and found themselves before a large building. The priest walked up to the door and pulled an iron rod that was connected to a bell. They could hear the clang faintly somewhere inside the building. It took a few minutes before an old hunched over man in black appeared at the large doors. "Y..e..s? What can I do for you?"

He was short and wore an old-fashioned pair of glasses through which he squinted. His eyeglasses like he seemed ancient. It was obvious that they no longer served his vision as well as they had in the past.

He lifted his head and stared at the Jesuit. "Oh! Father Boniface. Welcome, welcome."

"Thank you Father Ambrozio. I came to visit your chapel and brought an acquaintance."

"Please come in, come in."

The old man shuffled his way through a long corridor. He stopped at a set of steps. "You know your way Father Boniface. Do you need me?"

"No, thank you. We can find our way."

Without another word the Jesuit headed up the stairs and down a long corridor. Arriving at a set of ornate wooden doors he went inside blessed himself with holy water and headed towards a confessional booth.

The *monk* touched the priests arm. The cleric stopped. The *Franciscan* looked around and saw a large candelabra standing by the door. It looked as though it had not seen a candle for a very long time. The *monk* shoved the object that he was carrying deeper into one of his long sleeves so that it rested there. He picked up the candelabra and shoved it through the two heavy brass rings that hung from the door. The Heavy round metal object would keep anyone from entering.

The priest was aghast. He looked at the *monk* in disbelief. "What! What! Are you doing?" He headed towards the door, but the other stopped him.

"We can't afford to be disturbed by anyone. This is very crucial. Trust me for only a few minutes more and then I'll help you to lift the barrier off the door."

Then the *monk* looked around and seeing a side alter in the chapel pointed towards it.

The priest was bewildered, but did as directed. The *Franciscan* checked to make sure the chapel was empty as they walked towards the stone structure.

The altar was covered with linen and in the middle stood a statue of Christ with his hands holding a heart.

Inscription underneath in Latin said, 'Sacred Heart of Jesus have mercy on us'.

The Jesuit didn't know what to make of all this so he stood there like a spectator expecting the show to start.

The *monk* took a parchment from his pocket and stretched it out on the altar, and then he took out a large Key from his sleeve. He laid the object on top of the hide. Then the *Franciscan* bent down picked up the skirt of his robe, pulled it off and threw it on a bench. He unbuttoned his shirt and took it off.

The Jesuit winced. The upper torso of the man was covered with scars. The priest was no stranger to scarring or maiming. He had spent time as a chaplain in the army, but he had never seen anything like this.

"If all these wounds were inflicted simultaneously, you wouldn't have survived."

"They were and if it wasn't for Angela I wouldn't be here telling you about it. Look at my wrists and you will see that what I have been telling you is the truth." The man walked over to the Jesuit and brought up his hands face up so that the priest could see his wrists and scarred palms. "I won't bother you by showing my feet."

THE KEY OF DAMASCUS

The priest stood immobile facing his companion with disbelief. The man turned and went to the bench he picked up his shirt and put it on again. Then he lifted the Key, but kept the parchment between himself and the large object. The Key alternated between shining like the sun and turning black as coal.

The man brought The Key close to the priest. He held it out in front of him his hand flat underneath it. "Touch the Key, but be careful it gets very 'hot' and you could burn your fingers. You have seen the palms of my hands."

The priest still in a daze moved his right hand and slowly extended his fingers towards the Key. He finally touched it, "I..I.. don't know what you are talking about. The Key feels cool even if it emits this strange light sporadically."

"You are a priest and constantly deal with sin and evil which this Key stores inside until the fateful day, but be careful perhaps you have only been given a reprieve from its 'heat'. Since it feels normal to you, then pick it up and hold it in your hand."

The priest wrapped his fingers around the object and tried to take it from his companion. At first with little effort, but the Key would not budge. Then he tried with a greater effort and when he wasn't successful he wrapped both of his hands around it, but the object seemed to be stuck to the parchment. Then he tried to pick it up with the parchment, to no avail. The Jesuit let go of it and checked the man's hands in case he was holding it somehow so that it would be impossible to take it away from him. Looking underneath he saw them flat so that the Parchment and the Key lay level on them. The priest tried again to lift the object, but this time he let out a scream that surprised the man who took a couple of steps backwards and pulled the Key away from the Jesuit.

The priest turned his palms upwards blowing on them to relieve the pain. Both hands were red and the expression on his face attested to the excruciating pain he felt.

He turned to Brad. "My God what is this thing?"

"You heard my story and know how I came to possess this Key. Now you realize that I had to go into every detail of my saga regardless how unimportant it seemed at the time. The Key must be hidden from this world and the underworld so that it will not appear until its time has come to unlock the Gate. The fewer people who know about its location the safer it will be."

The Jesuit was still in shock. "But where could we hide it?"

Brad looked around. He stared at the altar for a moment. "In this chapel somewhere. I'm sure that I have been guided here. Let's put it in the altar. There is a small niche at the bottom of the left hand corner. I will remove the stone and you bring the Key."

Brad seeing the priest's hesitation reassured him. "Don't worry. Even though you will feel some heat, the parchment will protect you. Also it will enable you to lift it. The parchment and the Key are inseparable except to certain chosen few."

"But I couldn't take it away from you even with the parchment."

"Yes, but this time its on the altar."

Brad climbed the two steps of the side altar.

The priest turned and picked up the Key cautiously making sure that it was well wrapped in the animal skin. He was surprised. He had no trouble carrying it and he felt nothing out of the ordinary except the feel of the tanned hide.

As father Boniface approached the altar he could see Brad prying a bottom corner stone loose.

"How did you know that a cavity existed in this altar? I have never heard anyone talking about it. I'm sure that no one knows about it or if anyone did is long time dead."

Brad reached for the Key, "I didn't. I had a feeling that we would end up here and that I would have to find this corner where the Key could be safely hidden."

Brad slid the Key into the cavity and restored the corner stone in its place. When they looked at the spot, it looked as though the corner had never been disturbed. The altar appeared to be in the same state as before.

Brad stood up, "Now the secret lies with you and I. Even the evil ones cannot find it unless we willingly divulge this location. If we are approached by anyone we should tell him or her that we no longer have it. Besides the trail ends with me. No one knows that I have contacted you and passed its safekeeping to you."

"But we can't lie and commit a sin even if it's for a righteous and just cause. We know where the Key is hidden."

"Since we don't physically possess it we should emphasize that we don't have it. We won't be lying; because once we leave here we won't know for sure whether the Key is still here or not. It's like the light inside the fridge. You don't know whether it's on or off once you close the door."

The priest looked at the altar, "I don't know, you're drawing a pretty thin line."

"That's the only line we have. We will also have to provide for a mechanism by which, when the time comes for one of us to depart from this world that the secret be entrusted to a third party. Until the time comes when the Key will have to surface."

They walked back to the door removed the candelabra from the rings and made their way to the front door of the seminary through the deserted hallways. The Jesuit looked at the man beside him. "What happens if death arrives unexpectedly for either of us?"

"I propose that a sealed letter be entrusted to someone for safekeeping to be opened only in the presence of the one that survives about his demise. This letter should be in code so that it will be meaningless to anyone else."

The priest thought for a while, "I'll leave it with a friend of mine in Rome that I can trust. He will make sure to carry out my final wishes. I will supply you with his name and you can from time to time send him your change of address so that he could act as quickly as possible in case something happens to me."

Brad stopped just inside the door and handed the robe he carried from the church to his companion. "I won't need this any longer. I'll leave my copy of the letter with my lawyer and advise him to keep in touch with the person you designate. Third party involvements will distance us from meeting each other in case we are being followed."

The priest took the robe from his companion, "What should we put in this letter?"

"I believe the shorter the better, perhaps something like this. 'I'm leaving for a long journey from which I don't expect to be back for a long time. Give my regards to your friend.' If one of us dies the letter of the departed one should be immediately supplied to the agent of the other one who would contact his client."

The younger man who now looked older than his years with some grayish tinge around his ears extended his hand to the Jesuit. "It's been a long time since I felt at ease. Its as though a great burden has been lifted from my shoulders."

The priest took Brad's hand. The other one looked strange out of his habit. The Jesuit thought that his companion might have made a worthy monk had he tried, but alas his character would have betrayed him. The cleric squeezed gently the extended fingers of the other's hand. He did not dare to touch it with his whole palm, as it was still stinging from the burns.

Brad turned the priest's hand and looked at the palm. Then putting one of his beside it and looking at the scars on both said in jest. "Now we truly are brothers."

"Yes I now understand, because I feel like I've just been harnessed to a heavy yoke, but remember half of it still belongs to you."

"I guess you're right, but at least I'm not alone carrying this burden now. I feel a lot lighter even though I didn't find a way to pass the whole thing on to you the way I planned."

As the *monk* now in civilian garb opened the heavy door a blast of hot air hit him blowing his hair over his face. He brushed it away from his eyes and walked out into the street looking like any other tourist in jeans and a long sleeve shirt.

The priest turned on his heels and walked to a bench in the long corridor where he found the hunched over monk that had welcomed them into the building praying. "Here is a perfectly good robe that could be used by one of the Franciscans."

The little man had learned many years ago not to ask any questions. He took the robe and laid it down beside him. "I'm sure that whoever gets this garment will wear it with a grateful heart." He touched the robe with the tips of his fingers and caressed it gently. "This is cloth has been touched by the hand of God."

The Jesuit opened his mouth as though to reply, but had second thoughts. Instead he turned and walked away.

The monk gazed at the robe for a time and then at the back of the white figure making its way down the long corridor.

The Jesuit had a feeling that the old man knew what had just taken place.

The priest heard the monk's voice behind him, "I'm sure it will be a great blessing to the one who wears this cloth." The priest turned around and saw the old man bowing before the brown pile on the bench paying it homage.

By the time the priest left the building the man that he disliked so much when this whole affair started was nowhere to be seen. As he walked he reflected at the strange story and even stranger ending.

He thought how right he was at the beginning when he told the *monk* that this 'confession' might not need or require absolution.

Now that he was going home he couldn't believe the events, which had just passed had really happened.

He knew that he would never be able to forget the man in the robe even though he would never see him again and the impact that he had on the Jesuit's life and possibly the whole world.

As priest walked he began to pray to God to give him the strength to carry the burden until he could pass it on to someone else.

Printed in the United States
65203LVS00002B